M. Laszlo is the pseudonym of a Bath, Ohio, whose global travels and ...., ... inspired a lifelong habit of journaling and idea collecting. This practice began in childhood during summers spent in Robert Lowell's family home in Castine, Maine, and continued through his time in cities like London, East Jerusalem, and New York.

His notebooks have served as the foundation for several works, including *The Phantom Glare of Day* (Spark Press, 2022), *On the Threshold*, and *Anastasia's Midnight Song* (Alkira, 2025), with *The Nameless Land* as its sequel. Laszlo holds a B.A. in English from Hiram College and an M.F.A. in poetry from Sarah Lawrence College. He has also worked for Harvard University's Semitic Museum during his time in the Middle East.

THE NAMELESS LAND

M. LASZLO

ALKIRA
PUBLISHING

The Nameless Land
M. Laszlo
Copyright © 2025
Published by Alkira Publishing
ABN: 32736122056
http://www.alkirapublishing.com

ISBN: 978-1-922329-93-6

So, it is I that writhe with the twitch
Of the faery blood, and the wizard itch
To attain a matter one may not utter
Rather than sink in the greasy splutter
Of Britons munching their bread and butter;
Ailing boys and coarse-grained girls
Grown to sloppy women and brutal churls.
So, I am off with staff in hand
To the endless light of the nameless land.

Aleister Crowley
'The Wizard Way'

I.

Cairo. 27 August 1919.

Early that evening, Rupert Lux strolled into the heart of the crowded Egyptian *souq* and paused before the door to an abandoned hookah lounge. *Have the British authorities recently closed it down?* Maybe they thought revolutionaries met there. Rupert peered through the window and breathed in the stench of old smoke and burnt sugar. *What kinds of debates once played out here?* The Cairenes would have lamented British colonialism, and they would have debated just which foreign agents had conspired to empower the enemy. All through the night, they would have bemoaned the lies, schemes, and hoaxes that had brought about their present state of servitude—the indignity of it all.

A procession of English soldiers attached to the command billet marched by, and Rupert turned from the hookah's lounge door. Even after the soldiers had continued off around the corner, his temple throbbed. *The dæmon that lives inside me—has it stolen into my right eye?* The idea seemed plausible, for what else might explain his blurred vision of late? Sometimes the condition felt so intense he had even considered wearing an eyepatch. *Just like a war hero.* Blinking several times over, he lurched into a druggist's shop and asked whether the proprietor sold anything of the kind.

As it so happened, the merchant did have one last item in stock—but Rupert wanted to take it out of the box to check that the product would indeed help him to focus his one good eye that much better. When he donned the eyepatch and wrapped the cord around his head, he found the item to be less than ideal. Indeed, it made his dominant eye feel much too strained. With a clenched jaw, he returned the product to the box.

The merchant called to a friend and asked that he block the door lest Rupert depart. Then the druggist shook his finger at Rupert and glowered at him. 'My word. You make me to open the box, and then you no purchase the item. How I sell it now? At very least, you must to pay surcharge.'

Rupert knew not to protest too much. How to stop someone from sticking him with a knife? Like a craven child, he bowed, and in the end, purchased the eyepatch. How else to regain his freedom? When the druggist let him go on his way, Rupert shook his hand and then made his way back to the Hotel Ibis.

He spent most evenings lounging in the lobby, chatting with other foreign residents and long-term tenants. Mostly, he spoke with the women—and he knew just how to do it, too. On more than one occasion, he had succeeded in making his advances. Five months earlier, following a brief affair, a lonely widow had even pleaded with him to come home with her to her townhouse in Gibraltar Harbour.

Late in the night, the eyepatch in his hand, he faltered back to his room. There, he slicked back his black hair and trimmed his thin, elegant pencil moustache. Once more, he would soon be responsible for the entire establishment. The eyepatch crumpled up in his hip pocket, he left his room and lumbered over to the reception desk to take up his post as the night clerk.

The lobby had assumed an especially exotic guise that night. No light shone but an oil lamp, which one of the other tenants had lit some time before. Moreover, the air smelled of Turkish tobacco smoke and meadow saffron. What a pleasing blend, too. Best of all, someone had left open the glass balcony doors—and for the very first time, Rupert realised just how exquisite was the view of Zamalek out on the Isle of Gazirah. Given the wisps of fog, the riverscape appeared as dreamlike as an impressionist canvas.

The hotel manager, Mr Shahzad, came along with a sheet of parchment in his right hand. 'You, there.'

'*Aiwa, effendi.*'

'This here most paramount,' Mr Shahzad told him, holding up the leaf of paper. 'This night no like no other. Now the Hotel Ibis do first ever dawn excursion to Gyzeh, and this here list out the very guests you must to wake up. These people already pay, so you go upstairs at three o'clock, before break of dawn, and you knock on doors and wake them all. Lorry come for them five minutes past three. If lorry don't reach highway by fifteen past three, then no one reach the pyramids in time to watch the Egyptian sunrise.' The hotel manager read over the names and then looked up. 'One more thing, please. One young lodger in ladies' dormitory, she sign up for excursion. But no knock on that door. If you did, so you wake up everyone else there. So, what you do? You find girl's name and bed assignment all here on the paper, so you take strong lantern, and you go *into* ladies' dormitory, and you find her bed.'.

Rupert's mouth fell open. 'No, I can't just wend my way in there and rouse some young lady like that.

'Why not? She will be expecting you. Just you no knock on her door.' Mr Shahzad placed the sheet of paper on the reception desk and departed the hotel.

Rupert found himself alone in the darkened lobby—and he did not move until the nighttime breeze stirred some of the hotel's parchment stationery. Several leaves fell to the floor, and a fit of soft, sinister, almost-imperceptible laughter emanated from the pupil of his right eyeball. *The dæmon.* Looking down to his oxblood-leather shoes, Rupert paced back and forth along the tattered rug. 'Here we are again. Just you and me. Say something, why don't you?' No illusory voice spoke up, but from the pupil of his right eyeball, the dæmon laughed anew. Like so many times before, Rupert told himself there could not possibly be any kind of evil spirit inside him. Still, he had no convincing explanation for the phenomenon. Might the whole dilemma follow from a case of repressed childhood trauma? He studied his faint reflection on the tabletop, well aware of the dullness in his right eye. 'Someday I'll be free of you. Do you hear? Free!'

Through the balcony doors, a gust glided into the lobby—and the current blew through some of the hotel's most important papers, until several counterfoils took flight and dropped to the floor.

Cairo. 29 August 1919.

Just before the midnight chimes rang, Rupert reported back to work. Then, just after the midnight chimes had died out, he leapt up from the hotel's reception desk and rubbed his right eye. The dæmon had grown unusually quiet, and the stillness made Rupert wonder if perhaps something of import were about to happen. With a shriek and a low rumble, the passenger lift ascended to the penthouse suite. *Did someone rent out the luxurious apartment on the top floor?* Rupert checked the transient ledger, wondering if the tenant might have arrived earlier that evening while he had been out. At last, he discovered her signature:

Maud Havelock

The lift reached its destination, and quietude returned to the hotel. With yet another shrill whistle, the elevator descended to the lobby. The thin metal screen door opened noisily to reveal a mature woman of some forty years. With furrowed brows, she marched into the lobby and then paused. She appeared unwell: the oil lamp's dim glow made her skin shine china white, the way an old woman's skin assumes a certain pallor when she enters into the pale light of a physician's examination room. Did she perhaps suffer from consumption? If so, that would explain why she had come to the Sahara; perhaps she believed the sunlight would do her some good. Despite the woman's malady, she possessed undeniable beauty. Her eyes shone a bright shamrock green. Moreover, her person exuded an agreeable, sensual aroma—a lovely scent as of piping-hot Irish cream coffee.

Rupert twitched his moustache, and he smiled the same bold way he did for a comely nubile woman. 'Hello. I'm Rupert.'

Oddly, the woman said nothing—and when she returned his smile, she did so with the kind of smirk a woman only ever displays when she says goodbye to a bashful fool who never became more than a fleeting friend.

Intriguing. He maintained eye contact, for no woman had ever smiled at him like that before. 'So, you're Miss Maud Havelock? Have I got the name right?'.

'I'm an Irishwoman, and we don't talk to just anyone.' Maud Havelock cocked her head to the side and whistled the tune to a familiar parlour song, 'Streets of Cairo'. She strolled over to the billiard table, where she bumped into a dish of sesame-seed butter teetering near the corner pocket.

The little dish fell to the floor and shattered. Rupert's right eye burned, as though it, too, had broken apart.

Maud Havelock fell silent, and Rupert wondered if she was debating whether or not to chide him for not tidying up the lobby. *I should've put the dish away.*

He ambled over to the grand balcony to collect himself. Though he could not say why, he mistrusted the woman. The cool nighttime breeze ruffled his hair. He flicked a speck of red dust from his lapel and checked the creases of his trousers before turning back to face her.

What a mysterious woman. Ignoring the sharp, jagged, broken pieces of the earthenware dish, she knelt on the floor and dipped her fingertip into the sesame-seed butter. He stared at her, nonplussed, until his right eye smarted—as if the woman had poked him there.

He reeled back to the balcony and studied the night sky, his heart beating hard. When he finally calmed himself and turned back, she had vanished. He wandered all about the darkened lobby, but he could not find her. When he returned to the reception desk, he realised he could not locate that night's list of Gyzeh-bound tenants. Had the peculiar woman pilfered the slip of paper? He switched on every light in the lobby and searched everywhere—even the ladies' powder room.

At five minutes to three, when he stumbled back to the reception desk, he discovered the slip of paper lying just where Mr Shahzad always placed it. *Has it been there all the while.*

For the first time since childhood, Rupert's right eyeball rolled back in its socket and remained like that for almost three seconds. Back home in New Zealand, when it had happened that one time before, a parson had come from Christchurch to examine him. Examining his pupil, the parson had sworn he had heard a dæmon chanting in an age-old Oceanic tongue.

In time, young Rupert had come to believe the dæmon must be the spirit of that ancient tyrant king who had toppled the famed statues of Easter Island. Having transmigrated about the surface of the ocean for a thousand years or so, the current must have blown the malevolent spirit toward the North Island. Later, once the entity had come ashore, the winds drove it through the streets of Wellington and onward down Artesia Way. Then, as young Rupert came traipsing along past a bed of thorny late-summer roses, the entity must have crept inside him—with the hope of taking possession of his soul.

And the evil spirit lives on. Rupert scanned the deserted lobby. The table clock on the reception desk struck three. The nighttime current grew, and the boughs of a tall winter thorn tree scraped against the window to the right of the grand balcony. *It's three o'clock in the morning. No time to dawdle.* Rupert rode the lift upstairs to wake the guests bound for Gyzeh.

Once they had gone, Rupert paced the length of the lobby. He placed his hand over his one good eye. The vision in the other remained blurry. *Am I going blind in the right?* He staggered back into his room and studied the eyepatch—

which reminded him of the unfortunate incident with the druggist. Frowning, Rupert brought the eyepatch into the lobby and dropped the box into the rubbish bin. He stationed himself at the reception desk and thought back to his childhood—that fateful summer's day when the tyrant's transmigrating spirit had entered his person. A misty drizzle had fallen that morning. *A soft day. That's how I remember it.* In the night, had he not felt a sudden throbbing ache in his eye? For a moment, he had wondered if a sandfly had made its way into his pupil.

He shook his head. *There can't possibly be any kind of fantastical being dwelling inside me.*

A set of footsteps slowly ascended the stairway leading up from the hotel's front door—and Maud Havelock returned into the lobby. In the light of dawn, her eyes shone the brightest green. Inexplicably, too, she held a lacquer-disc recording beneath her arm. Without even acknowledging his presence, she arranged the vinyl on the Victrola gramophone and worked the crank.

The song proved to be an Irish ballad, 'I'll Sing Thee Songs of Araby'. What a lovely reading, too, both the lady singer and the accompanist on a fortepiano.

Sitting back, he listened to his favourite verse:

> *'I'll sing thee songs of Araby,*
> *And tales of fair Kashmir,*
> *Wild tales to cheat thee of a sigh,*
> *Or charm thee to a tear…'*

The woman danced an Irish jig. Then, for no apparent reason, she stopped the gramophone. Her hands trembling, she dashed over to the rubbish bin and removed the box containing the eyepatch. When she learned what was inside, a girlish smile crossed her face. She wrapped the string around her head and arranged the cloth pad over her left eye.

Rupert longed to speak up but struggled to find the right words. *Maud Havelock.* The name did not seem to fit with the woman, and he wondered if it might be an alias. Still, why put on a false appearance? With narrowed eyes, he got to his feet. 'Are you feeling maybe a wee bit indisposed?' he asked her. 'Is that why you travelled to Cairo? Maybe you take some kind of medicament for your malady. Does the prescription drug make your vision a bit blurred? Is that why you've decided to wear that eyepatch there?'

Maud Havelock did not answer; nor did she turn to face him. Instead, the mysterious woman contented herself to check over her gown's sweeping skirts.

He felt flush on his neck, and he wondered if she felt offended by the idea of a hireling speaking with someone of her station. Like any proper gentleman, he remained calm and did not move a muscle. 'You've no reason to fear,' he continued. 'I've got breeding. I'm only stranded here because of my service with the New Zealand Expeditionary Force. Nothing like the Great War to bring a noble to ninepence.' He drew close. 'I don't dissemble. No, I haven't any reason to do that.' He flashed a grin. 'What would you have me call you? Would it be good if I simply called you by your Christian name? Maud?.

Maud Havelock contemplated his every aspect, as if she already knew every detail about him and did not find his words the least bit interesting. Then her lip curled. Without a word, she collected the recording and exited the hotel.

Had any woman ever treated him that way before? He felt like a foppish fool, so much so his thoughts turned to his hapless little brother, Georgie. Back home in Wellington, the girls had always looked askance at him. What a curious case he had always been. Georgie's pathological diffidence had often prevented him from speaking to anyone. All throughout his childhood, he would play his baroque bassoon so obsessively he might go for three whole days before even making eye contact with another soul. How unearthly the melodies he played, too, the music a solemn invocation.

Rupert fixed his gaze on the broken ceiling fan and twitched his moustache. *Keep on playing your song, Georgie.*

Cairo. 31 August 1919.

The light of the Egyptian dawn shone brightly through the glass balcony doors, and for a time, the lobby seemed a little less exotic and mysterious than it always had before.

Rupert extinguished the oil lamp, stretched his back, and pictured the latest party of hotel guests traipsing about Gyzeh and marvelling at the sunrise.

The English tenant who worked as the early-morning clerk reported for duty. 'What's bloody wrong with you, then?.

'How do you mean?'

'You look like you're suffering battle fatigue.'

'Stuff and nonsense.

'What the devil happened? Did some damn fool guest beset you in the night? If that'd be the case, I say we banish the bloody bastard from the bunkhouse. No, sir, we'll not tolerate any mischief.'

Rupert made some repartee and then descended the staircase.

Outside in the street, the cacophony and commotion of another Cairene day had already begun. From all directions, this boulevard and that, several motorcar engines roared. A great clamour rang out from the direction of Barquq Avenue, and a massive motorised coach from the Cairo Omnibus Company sped by.

Several fragments of tattered newspapers blew past Rupert's feet, and he pondered the news of the day—the revolutionaries struggling to overthrow the British Empire. In the course of time, he had come to sympathise with the Egyptians. Only yesterday, he had attempted to smooth things over with some of the locals. 'Honestly, I don't wish to enslave anybody,' he had said. 'I'm only here by the grace of circumstance, that's all. No worries.'

A lone, tattered broadsheet tumbled by in the current— and at the same time, across the street, Maud Havelock exited the Bank of Cairo.

He waved to her, but she ignored him. Instead, she looked up to the opulent flat directly above the bank.

From the direction of the apartment's exotic *bustan*, the scent of a traditional Egyptian breakfast pervaded the air.

Rupert detected the aroma of fava beans, garlic, and paprika. Though overcome with hunger, he saw Maud wander off into the labyrinthine marketplace and could not resist the urge to follow her. The task proved to be trying, though, for a large crowd had already poured into the bazaar. The woman fascinated him so. Mysterious and alluring as she was, he discerned in her the very embodiment of the bitter, self-absorbed woman. One who so despises humanity she lacks the power to *love*.

Up ahead in the crowded marketplace, Maud stopped before a bridal boutique that had only just opened its doors. Absentmindedly, she traced the palms of her hands over her narrow hips.

11

With searching eyes, he considered her thin, delicate figure—until he felt certain she could feel his gaze on her. *So why does she feign indifference to me.*

Rubbing her eye, Maud pointed at one of the wedding gowns on display in the little shop's window.

I wonder if she's about to marry. Yes. What a thrill to be hammered for life. He rubbed his own eye and revisited the notion that the transmigrating soul of some ancient tyrant dwelled inside him. 'Are you there?' If it were, the evil spirit failed to make its presence known.

The shopkeeper came along and let Maud touch the fabric. Then she shook her head, turned from the bridal shop, and hurried along through the endless throngs of people.

Rupert could no longer bring himself to follow. Bewildered by his own incomprehensible actions, he contemplated the morning sky and listened to the sounds of the people haggling with the merchants. The hustle and bustle of the city made him rejoice; what a beautiful thing, the business of commerce, industry, *life*.

A company of British soldiers emerged from the courtyard up ahead and marched forward through the crowd.

As a weary old Egyptian woman protested the soldiers' presence, he listened to all her heckling—and though he could not speak a word of Arabic, he had no trouble imagining the kinds of grievances the elderly woman intended to invoke. She had endured great injustices, and there could be no doubting her genuine anguish and desperation. She raged and rambled like a woman enslaved. .

Rupert cringed, fearing that the soldiers might throw her to the ground. But the soldiers ignored her, and when they vanished down the street, the old woman continued to hold forth.

Rupert imagined the woman as some kind of godly visionary—a seer bemoaning the omnipresent phenomenon of greed, deceit, and idolatry. When the old woman finally ceased, she peered into Rupert's eyes, her expression inscrutable.

He averted his gaze and then studied his feet. A leaf of wind-driven paper drifted past his heel. *What's that, then?* The slip of paper seemed to be a cheque drawn on a local bank. Flapping gently in the breeze, the form drifted back toward his shoe—as if to tempt him. Even if the cheque promised a princely sum, he felt much too weary to collect the item. *I'm going back to the Hotel Ibis.* He shuffled off in the direction from which he had come. *Oh, to sleep, yes.* He continued along, until he heard someone whistling the tune to that music-hall song, 'It's A Long Way to Tipperary'. He scanned the crowd, for he felt certain the person responsible must be Maud Havelock. Try as he might, he could not locate the vexing woman anywhere. *She's taunting me. Hoping to make me feel nervous.*

When he reached his room back at the Hotel Ibis, he climbed into bed, and it did not take long before he had slipped into unconsciousness. The tune to the music-hall song echoing softly, he became lost in dreams—the same dreams that had always plagued him, memories of his childhood sexual molestation, the crime that explained the true deeply repressed reason why he had always tormented himself with the preposterous notion that some evil spirit possessed him. And as he tossed and turned in bed, his unconscious mind played out what had happened. In his dreams, and only in his dreams, he remembered all: Father's business contact, Mr Impérial.

On the odd occasion, he would come to stay at the house on Artesia Way. What a well-to-do gentleman, too, for he had distinguished himself as the most successful horse trader in New Zealand. More than that, Mr Impérial had purchased land throughout Australia—from the heart of New South Wales to that glorious stretch of land where the Swan River flowed out into the Indian Ocean. He had also invested heavily in a series of health spas and bowling greens stretching out along an island in the Coral Sea.

Rupert despised Mr Impérial, for Mr Impérial had always passed judgement on everyone and everything—and he had done so with the most condescending tone of voice and self-satisfied manner. To make matters worse, the heartless businessman had often displayed a habit of snickering while pronouncing his unsolicited opinions.

If only the smug know-it-all had been wrong once in a while. Regarding points of law, though, he never made any mistakes. In addition, Mr Impérial knew everything about investment in oil futures and other key commodities. He knew how to establish monopolies and how to enter into mergers. He knew the art of supply and demand. Might all that explain why he had always regarded himself as superior to everyone else?

Rupert's slumber dragged on, and the black and white hues of the dream grew increasingly brighter—just as they always did before the dream turned to the memory of that awful moment when Mr Impérial had abused him. At a funeral pace, the repressed memory unfolded—and Rupert relived the whole trauma.

An hour later, when he awoke to the hazy light streaming through his window, the harrowing encounter faded from his memory as it always did. Still, this awakening proved to be most unusual; for the first time in his life, he knew that he had envisioned something terribly profound. *What was it, though?*

In vain, he struggled to remember. Sitting up, he wondered if perhaps he had experienced a ghostly visitation—the spirit of some long-dead hotel guest gently whispering into his ear as he slept. Had the ghost wished to tell him something? What if the spirit possessed a treasure map and knew all the secrets buried in the Valley of the Kings.

Shivering, Rupert mused on the subject of his brother. In recent years, Georgie had dedicated himself to learning the ancient art of rhabdomancy, or as it's more commonly known, dowsing. One of his recent letters had even spoken of the time he travelled out into the wilds of Tasman Glacier in the hope that his humble wooden staff might guide him to some lost Māori city.

Rupert climbed out of bed and stumbled over to the window. He thought of Anastasia back in England. In the last year, the sensuous young woman had come to share something in common with Georgie. Three months earlier, a pen friend from London's Westminster Spiritualist Society had written to describe Anastasia's remarkable progress. The beautiful young blind woman had acquired the power of clairvoyance. Evidently, she could locate any lost hoard—wherever the riches lay buried.

The hazy light shone brighter all the time until he closed his eyes. *A moment ago, what did I dream?* With his eyes closed, he felt his way back to bed and lay still. *It was probably nothing. Just another dream of Anastasia.*

II.

England, County of Warwickshire. 2 September 1919.

As the train rolled along through the midlands late that afternoon, Anastasia registered an agonising ache that seemed to originate from within the deepest recesses of her womb. She retched, but thankfully no one noticed. She retched again and rubbed her gut awhile. *Why this recurring anguish?* She knew the answer well enough; she could not let go of her past, her erstwhile fear that a diadem spider lived inside her. *So, how to forget the illusory beast?* Her belly churned as if she had swallowed a mouthful of artichokes. She pinched her lips together. *How to forget?* The answer had to be *spiritual*; consequently, the answer must also be *ethical* in nature. *I'll enjoy a proper resolution to all my sorrows only after I've helped to heal someone similarly afflicted.*

The train reduced speed. *We've reached Coventry already?* She tried to picture the city, but it was hopeless. *I'm blind. I shall always be blind.*

When the train stopped, Admiral Ilingworth guided her through the door and down onto the platform. Standing there, she could not help but scowl. She despised the old man for numerous reasons. As managing director of Westminster Spiritualist Society, the retired admiral had only ever exploited her. Last winter, the charlatan had even hired a team of mesmerists to transform her psyche in order to manipulate her into believing she commanded the powers of divining.

In time, she had become somewhat successful at the endeavour. Earlier this summer, the admiral had brought her out to Oxfordshire—and working with nothing more than a witch hazel bough, a faint yet steady magnetic force had guided her to a considerable hoard of Celtic trade silver buried a half mile north of Wayland's Smithy. Then, in the days and weeks that followed, she had slowly learned to master the art of dowsing. Still, the more accomplished she had become, the more she had come to feel like a slave working on behalf of heartless and ruthless thieves. Time after time, the admiral would take her out into the English countryside—where he and his associates would compel her to seek out whatever ancient plunder might serve to enrich *them*. How she longed to go free. *If I don't escape, I'll live and die as a bondswoman. What an awful fate.*

Gripping her arm, Admiral Ilingworth guided her down from the train platform. In the street, he hired a taxicab to bring them to a hotel in the heart of Coventry. 'Let's have a simple supper, a dish of poached haddock or whatever, and then I'll take you to your room,' he told her. 'You've got busy work to do come tomorrow, and I can't have you coming over faint.'

Two hours later, Anastasia stationed herself at her hotel window to feel the evening breeze against her face. The current made her eyes feel dry and gritty. She wondered how the darkening sky looked at that moment. *How about a soothing shade of red streaked with amber? Yes, that sounds about right.* When she lay in bed, she did not fall asleep for long. At eight o'clock, she awoke to an odour as of permafrost drifting into her hotel suite. *That odour— it's the Russian tundra. But it can't be.* She pinched her nose shut.

Someone knocked softly on the door. 'Open, please,' a woman said in a thick Russian accent. 'I must speak with you this instant. Please, my friend. Twelve blocks, I come. So, you open door. I bring most grave message. You begin noble crusade.'

At first, Anastasia refused to answer. For all she knew, the visitor had noticed her photograph in the evening paper and had come for no other reason than to ask that she help her track down some absurd memento. These days, all kinds of people deluged her with all kinds of strange requests.

The woman gave six more staccato knocks. 'You are there?' She banged on the door with her fist. 'Please to come speak with me. Face to face.'

Anastasia buttoned up her night robe, climbed out of bed, and made her way over to the door. 'Go away. I don't do personal engagements.'

'*No.* Grave message from the gods, I bring. The gods summon you. They wish for you to participate in big, magnificent adventure. Big, noble quest.'

Anastasia tasted something savoury yet bitter on the tip of her tongue. This sensation typically wouldn't appear unusual. Ever since going blind, all her other senses had grown stronger—and her sense of taste had grown strong enough that, when she dined, she had the power to detect even the faintest under-taste. At present, though, the tip of her tongue registered the sensation of something almost *ethereal*—an overripe unsalted olive from a garden belonging to some enchantress. *A lady of the Orient. A witch.*

Six more times, the Russian woman pounded on the door. '*Please.* Come you speak to me. Face to face.

The taste on Anastasia's tongue grew stronger. She folded her arms across her bosom and recollected the wilderness of Sinai—remembering the olives that Ernesztina's mirror-making society grew in their little garden down by the seashore.

When the woman banged on the door two more times, Anastasia unfolded her arms and rested her brow up against the lock stile. 'Who are you? What's your name?'

'I am Madam Maksimovna. Fortune teller. Born under the sign of Gemini. Maybe you hear of me. Maybe you hear of my psychic boutique.'

'I'm sorry, but no. I've never heard of you.'

'Listen, please. Everyone in Coventry, they come to me to learn amazing revelations, the secret meaning of dreams.'

Anastasia lifted her brow from the lock stile and gazed sightlessly up to where the cross rail was. *Do I open the door?* Even before she had lost the power of sight, she had always found it trying to trust others. Ever since that train journey to Arkhangelsk, that childhood trauma, she had understood the omnipresence of deceit in this world—the propensity for betrayal. *It's the deceit of Lucifer.* Sightless, she stared down toward her hands.

Out in the hallway, the fortune teller groaned in frustration.

Anastasia felt for the latch. *Here goes. Albeit with the greatest reluctance.* She wrapped her hand around the cold brass knob and opened the door. Immediately, the fortune teller's warm respiration—it reeked of borscht—slashed the oily malodorous vapours already lingering in the air. Anastasia mused over that train journey so many years ago—remembering the moment she opened the sleeping-cabin door, only to encounter the ghost girl.

'Greetings,' Madam Maksimovna said.

'What's this all about?' Anastasia asked her.

'So many things happening,' Madam Maksimovna whispered. 'All across Egypt, it's a time of turmoil. Endless riots, tragic demonstrations. A time of destiny for everyone.

The fortune teller's breath made Anastasia cringe. She felt the woman drawing inappropriately close. The woman's exhalations ruffled her fringe. *The fortune teller must be studying me.* For a moment or two, Anastasia shuffled her feet.

'You have beautiful hair,' Madam Maksimovna said. 'Even with the way you wear your, how do you say, Piccadilly fringe, you resemble the lost Anastasia. But she wasn't gap-toothed like you. Do you know about her? Yes. I speak of the *true* Anastasia.'

Anastasia brooded over the civil war back home. What had happened to the House of Romanov? Had the grand duchess perhaps survived the mayhem? According to some rumours, she had.

The fortune teller seemed to step back. Her voice an almost-imperceptible whisper, Madam Maksimovna recited a solemn Russian-orthodox prayer.

Anastasia pictured the one true Anastasia wandering the primaeval Siberian Forest. Would the czar's innocent daughter even know how to fend for herself out there? Perhaps she would be gravely injured. What if she had suffered a crisis of faith? *Maybe she's grown cynical. Godless, even.*

When Madam Maksimovna concluded her prayer, she poked Anastasia. 'All the rulers of the world must face their destiny. All kingdoms. That's why you must go back to Sinai. There, you must locate the glorious treasures Man must possess to prepare the path for the Great Jubilee.'

Anastasia laughed like an exasperated schoolmistress duped by some foolish little girl. The way the Russian woman spoke reminded her of how a member of some cult might rave on and on. *Why do the demented always believe that the end of the world must be near?* Slowly, Anastasia stepped back from the doorway. She found her way over to the reading table, where she plopped down in the chair and opened her Moon-script edition of the New Testament. *Here we are.* Lovingly, she traced the tip of her ring finger across a few of the ripples protruding from the frontispiece. Then she flipped forward to the Epistles.

Madam Maksimovna followed along, bringing her distinctive odour with her. 'Why do you think you possess great powers of divination?' the woman asked Anastasia. 'Why do you think God Almighty should grant you the power to discover silver and gold? You think maybe He hope someone should bleed you for profit? You think He hope you serve heartless thieves, corruption, conspiracy, collusion, fraud?'

Her blind eyes staring straight forward, Anastasia removed her hand from the book and wrapped her palms around her elbows. Who could say what the deranged woman might do? For all Anastasia knew, a dozen other members of the fortune teller's cult would be here any moment. Madam Maksimovna traced the tip of her finger down the length of Anastasia's arm, and as the Russian woman exhaled, Anastasia felt a faint ache deep in her bowels—something like the way it had felt when she had believed a diadem spider must be inside her, the creature gnawing away at the lining of her womb.

'What if you locate a dozen ceremonial Roman chariot burials tomorrow?' the fortune teller asked. 'Do you think your friends should share any of the riches with you? Of course not. So, why not come with *my* friends? In the desert, you will do God Almighty's work. Until everything proves ready. How else should the Saviour come save us all?'

The ache in Anastasia's core grew worse—as if the diadem spider must be stabbing her with a sharpened snail fork. 'It's not my place to serve either treasure hunters or crazed cults, for that matter,' she blurted out. For a moment or two, she rubbed her abdomen. *How to forget that awful diadem spider once and for all?* She wondered again if the answer to the question might be both spiritual and ethical in nature. *Yes, indeed, I'll enjoy a godly resolution to all my sorrows only after I've helped to heal someone similarly afflicted.* The wind wafted through a few strands in Anastasia's fringe. Then the strong, sweet fragrance of summer flowers drifted into the hotel room and swirled all about her shoulders. *God, how lovely.* Anastasia felt her way over to the corner, where she had placed her witch hazel bough atop her travel bag. The summer breeze blew softly. She took the divining rod into her arms and held it like a baby. *There, there.*

Madam Maksimovna drew near. 'I know you don't trust me, but maybe soon, if you reconsider, you come to visit my psychic boutique, and I tell you a bit more.'

Anastasia stared into space. 'Yes … no … *maybe.*'

For her part, the fortune teller said no more. The wind died down, and she departed with a self-deprecating laugh.

Coventry. 8 September 1919.

Early that morning, Anastasia awoke in her hotel room and swatted at the air. *I can't believe I'm still here. How much longer?* She slipped into a long gown with a dropped waist in the hope the unsuitable attire might convince Admiral Ilingworth to let her have a day of rest rather than yet another walkabout. For the past few days, Anastasia had done just as Admiral Ilingworth had instructed—and she had searched each and every field to which he had brought her. Day after day, though, she had failed to discover anything.

When the admiral stopped by her room to collect her, he did not even mention her gown. As usual, he guided her downstairs and onward into the hotel's garden.

No sooner had they reached their table than she realised she did not feel at all hungry for breakfast. *On the contrary, I'd prefer to starve myself. Yes, without my freedom, what does anything matter?* The distant bells of Coventry Cathedral broke into a triumphal tune, and then they proceeded to count out the hour. *Eight o'clock.* She took a deep breath and scratched the tip of her nose. *Do I detect the scent of Egyptian chamomile flowers?* She tapped the tabletop. 'What's growing in this garden? Would it be something from an Orient land?'

'Heavens, no,' Admiral Ilingworth answered. 'The hotel garden has nothing but lovely honeysuckle. Proper *English* honeysuckle.

She breathed in, but she still detected Egyptian chamomile. *How could it be?* Perhaps she had grown so charmed by the idea of returning to Sinai that a part of her unconscious mind had come to believe she had already reached the desert. *No.* Someone from the hotel staff brought the breakfast to the table, and the air filled with the aromas of grilled tomatoes and black pudding. The sweet sensation only lasted for a moment or two. Then she breathed in a second time, and she pictured the table strewn with the exotic kinds of dishes Ernesztina once served down there in that village nestled against the Red Sea shore. *The village of Al-Hubu. Aiwa.*

After breakfast, Admiral Ilingworth helped Anastasia into his rented motor buggy and brought her out to Holyhead

Road. 'We're here, love. One of the last few meadows Coventry has to offer.'

Like so many times before, it was time to take the bough by the forked end and venture off across the fields. She hesitated, however. As the admiral's attempts to place the divining rod into her hand grew increasingly fervent, she rubbed her stomach and pictured a diadem spider living inside her womb. When the admiral finally forced the bough into her hands, she let it fall to her feet.

The admiral returned the bough to her hands. 'Be strong, girl. Today you'll find something magnificent. I know it.'

A jolt of energy streaming through her hands, she felt a series of strong signals awaken deep within the witch hazel bough. *Oh, something's here.* She bit down on her tongue. Until she had felt the signals, she had hoped to have an undemanding morning. Later, in the afternoon, she would leave the hotel and track down Madam Maksimovna. *Why not?* If nothing else, perhaps the fortune teller could help her to escape the spiritualists.

Admiral Ilingworth placed his hand on the small of Anastasia's back and gave her a gentle push. 'Go on,' he said in a fatherly tone. 'Let's find ourselves something grand. How about an ancient promise ring?.

Anastasia's mouth filled with that same bitter taste from before—a sensation as of unsalted olives. *Oh, how good it would feel to be free. Yes, free.* She raised her hand. 'Perhaps it'd be dangerous for me to roam about out here in the wild. There must be plenty of blackberry bushes here and there, and they'd have loads of thorns, no?.

The admiral chided her, and he promised to keep her from stumbling into anything too perilous. After some hesitation, she gripped the forked end of the witch hazel bough and permitted the signals to guide her through what, judging by the delicate fragrance, was a vast stretch of meadow rue.

A creature hissed—a disturbance so soft only she could have heard it. And then something—it must have been a snake—slithered past her left ankle. She heard the snake rustle away, and she paused to whisper a prayer of thanksgiving.

Admiral Ilingworth nudged her shoulder. 'No dawdling. Let's not forget those accounts we've yet to balance back home in London. "Half a pound of treacle, that's the way the money goes!" So, let's soldier on. *Non timeo neque fines.*' A second time, the retired admiral nudged her shoulder. 'And just so you know, there's a patch of Timothy grass stretching out over to the west. Would that be a good place? And there's a patch of daylilies over to the east. What about that direction?'

She did not answer, for she felt certain her silence would discomfit him. Then, feigning sickness by staggering this way and that, she exhaled loudly through her nose. Sweating, she looked up to let the warmth of the sun beat down on her face. Motionless, she prayed for a summer rain—anything that might provide her with a good pretence for suggesting they go back to the hotel. *What if a mischievous fox came around, followed by a pack of foxhounds? Or what if a sparrow hawk swooped down, as if the animal felt wary of our presence and felt it had to defend its nest or something like that.*

Nothing of the kind happened. Even worse, the divining rod jumped and trembled—until the witch hazel bough felt warm in the palms of her hands. Dutifully, she held fast to the forked end. Then she let the signals pull her forward through a cluster of what felt like wildflowers. She paused to breathe in a pungent, metallic aroma, something like chloride of lime. The odour made the muscles all around her nose tighten up. *Could it be fairy rings? Yes, I think so.* She stepped back and removed her shoes, for how to advance any further if to do so might cause her to crush even one immaculate mushroom?

Admiral Ilingworth came up from behind. 'What do you suppose might be buried within that ring of toadstools there?'

She marched onward, and feeling with the sole of her foot, passed over the ring of moist, cool fairy rings without breaking any of them apart. Once she had traversed the mushrooms, she felt the divining rod point down.

Admiral Ilingworth patted her head. 'Splendid! Wait here whilst I find a fieldstone to mark the spot.'

When he darted off, she nearly snapped the divining rod in half. Determined to control her temper, she contented herself to tap the end of the witch hazel bough against her knee. The bitter taste in her mouth grew sharper. She knelt and proceeded to pick a bit of debris from between her toes.

Admiral Ilingworth returned to her side. She heard something drop beside her right foot. 'A wee pebble to light the path!' he announced. 'The day after tomorrow, I'll bring Mr Shrewsbury and son out here, and they'll dig up whatever's down there and then bring everything back to the hotel.'

'Must you be so greedy of gain?' she asked, hoping the question did not sound too rude. When he did not respond, she resolved to deceive him. 'There's no plunder here,' she said, dropping the witch hazel bough to the side.

'No plunder? What do you mean?'

'It's a nest of snakes,' she told him, for want of anything better to say. 'Oh yes, I feel it all through the soles of my feet. A nest of snakes. The worst kind, too. *Vipers.*'

'It can't be!' the admiral shouted. 'You are never wrong. You got the blighty touch. Yes, you're as lucky as Augustus with all your divine favour and that.

'*No*. You've got to believe me. When Mr Shrewsbury and

son come around, the vipers should only bite them, and we can't have that.'

'Why do you speak this way? Perhaps you're just feeling a wee bit fatigued.'

'No, sir. Can't you hear all those snakes hissing and wheezing below? There must be a dozen vipers there.' She listened attentively—until she almost believed her words to be true. The nest of vipers just had to be there—the merciless creatures awaiting that indelicate meddler who happened to trespass on their warm regal den.

At last, Admiral Ilingworth helped her up onto her feet. With a sigh, he returned the witch hazel bough's forked end into her hand. 'Why don't we move somewhere else?'

She had no reason to answer, and as she trudged onward, the signals grew increasingly faint. *Good. To hell with plunder.* For a moment or two, she twirled the witch hazel bough. And then she stopped and held herself still. Up ahead, something sounding like a dove sang. *Oh, that's lovely.* She let go of the witch hazel bough. Guided by the soft music, she lurched forward. In no time, she stood beneath the cool shade of what had to be an immense tree—a white willow, perhaps. Then, with the dove's song filling the air, she placed the palm of her hand flush against the tree's fissured bark. 'Do you hear that tune?' she asked. 'I think the dove must be forlorn. The little songbird would like to go free and fly off somewhere but can't decide which way to go.' Her lips parting, she pressed the palm of her hand against the willow—which emitted a scent not unlike that of the driftwood burning in the hearth back at the hostelry down in the Sinai Peninsula. For a time, she revisited her sojourn there. 'Maybe it'd be better if we go back to the hotel. Perhaps we could rest awhile.'

'No odds, girl. Let's get back to the task at hand.' With

a snort, Admiral Ilingworth returned the witch hazel bough to her hand.

Pouting, she refused to continue along—and the admiral wrapped his big bony hand around her wrist and pulled. When she broke away, she stopped and flipped the bough around so that she held the wrong end. *Oh!* She regretted what she had done, for that section of the witch hazel bough presently bled more than a few traces of sap. Slowly but surely, the residue spread across her palm and oozed through her fingers—until she felt as if she held a serpent in her hand. '*Quelle horreur,*' she whispered. With that, she snapped the bough in half. *There.*

Like a wounded animal, the admiral wailed. For the longest time, the shriek echoed on and on in Anastasia's ears.

Two hours later, back at the hotel, she lay in her bed—but only for ten minutes or so. Half-certain the irate admiral had retired to his own room, she made her way downstairs to the lobby. *Escape this place. Yes, go.* Beguiled by the scent of the flowers, she made her way into the garden.

What an idyllic place—especially the way the cool, soothing breeze blew through the honeysuckle roses.

Guided by the trumpeting and the occasional honk, she felt her way to the bank of a swan goose pond. There, she paused to think of Madam Maksimovna. *Might she hold the power to set me free?* The notion seemed plausible. *Still, if she's a member of some preposterous cult, how should I ever get free of* her? Anastasia tapped the tip of her walking stick against the heel of her shoe.

The waters splashed peacefully. Then the late-summer wind blew through the garden, and two or more rival families of swan geese honked at one another. What a commotion.

Anastasia held the walking stick perfectly still. *I'll have to be clever if I hope to escape both the spiritualist society* and *some cult.* If she were to fail to win her freedom, either Admiral Ilingworth or the fortune teller would punish her—as if she were a slave who had done wrong. Perhaps one or the other of her captors would bind the carcass of a swan to her body and force her to wear it until the shameful burden had broken her will. *The slave masters do that kind of thing to slaves all the time.* She gripped her walking stick a little bit tighter.

The swan geese grew quiet, and a gentleman's voice called out. A moment or two later, a fellow came over and introduced himself as an officer from the Border Regiment. 'I beg your pardon, but I realise you're blind, and I don't want you to take a wrong step and fall into the waters.'

She said nothing. *What if he thinks I'm lonely?* For all she knew, she reminded him of a schoolgirl pining for love. *Yes, that's what he's thinking.*

Gently, the officer wrapped his hand around her arm and pulled her back from the pond.

Her breath growing shallow, she lowered her eyes to the hem of her gown and asked herself whether she did feel lonely. *But of course, I do. And the loneliness, it's killing me.*

The officer let go of her arm and clicked his heels. With a steady, low-pitched voice, he made a bit of conversation and then paused—as if he had asked her a question.

She had not heard the question, for she had not listened to a word. Even if he might have loved her with all his heart, she could never content herself with a strong, perfect soldier. *I've got to find someone to* heal. *Wouldn't it be good to love* him? She fingered her Huguenot cross and pendant dove and wondered just how she would ever find someone who shared the kind of trouble she had once endured. But she knew of no one. *No one except Rupert. Yes, Rupert.*

The officer from the Border Regiment marched off, leaving her there. Had her silence offended him.

She imagined the fortune teller standing at her side, the woman reeking of Russian permafrost, her eyes engaging and shining the brightest Coventry blue. Anastasia clasped her hands together. 'Please, please, Madam. Help me find someone to *heal*, someone to *love*.'

III.

Cairo. 19 September 1919.

Back at the Hotel Ibis, Rupert frittered away the better part of the morning lazing about the lobby and watching out for Maud Havelock. The Irishwoman's endless comings and goings continued to beguile him. Finally, he dropped into his chair and clutched at his stomach—not unlike a woman who imagines something alien growing inside her womb.

The lift descended from the Irishwoman's suite, and she tiptoed into the lobby. As if to vex him, she had donned the same kind of lace bonnet that the Dutch killer, Maria Swanenburg, once wore with wings that turn up on either side.

He struggled not to cringe. *Maybe I'm a wee bit self-conscious.* Dressed in nothing more than tattered house shoes and an Egyptian robe, he blushed and then raised his eyes to the ceiling fan. When he looked down again, he gestured toward her and invited her to sit beside him.

At first, she ignored him. Then, when the Irishwoman did inch her way over in his direction, she refused to sit.

Instead, she performed a peculiar kind of pantomime. She acted as if she held a forked bough in her hands, as if she commanded the same kinds of divining powers the famed Anastasia presently wielded.

That's finesse. He leaned forward and waved. 'I know you wish to shoot me a line and hand me some or other proposition,' he told her. 'So, why not come out with it, then? What's this all about?'

'What makes you think I wish to talk to you?' The late-summer breeze billowed through Maud's gown. 'I find it funny how selfish you act,' she said, fussing with her bonnet. 'Outside, in the street, the people yearn for revolution. They long to breathe the air of *freedom*. To be sure, that's why the Egyptian people fight the British Empire. Yes, they're fighting to beat the band.' Maud marched over to the stairway and departed the hotel.

He pulled his shoulders low, for he regretted having said anything. Before, he had done his best to conceal his curiosity—and no matter how many times the Irishwoman might have come dallying through the lobby, he always averted his gaze and endeavoured to honour his duties as night clerk. The task had grown trying, though. For one thing, he felt certain Maud Havelock presently spread all kinds of ghastly rumours about him. The way the female tenants studied him, there could be little doubt she had defamed him. For all he knew, she had told several of the female tenants he must be the worst kind of deviant. Still, he persevered the best he could. With tonight's list of names in his hand, he would make his rounds and knock on this door and that to wake up all the tenants bound for Gyzeh—and each time that he reached the crowded ladies' dormitory, he would kindle a little oil lamp and sluggishly step inside. Then, holding the flame high, he would creep through the maze of bunk beds. What exceeding torment he found those moments; given Maud's incessant talebearing, he could never be sure whether this or that excitable tenant might wake up screaming.

He returned to his feet. With gliding steps, he slunk over to the stairway. *That bloody Irishwoman has got me tense and ashamed. Despondent, even.* Lifting his robe, he descended the stairway and continued into the marketplace, stepping cautiously so as not to trip on his tattered shoes.

There was no sign of the Irishwoman. She could have dashed off down just about any street or alley.

He stopped beside a carriage lying on its side and wondered if the horse had only just got free. *Yes, maybe five minutes ago.* With all the strength he could muster, he pushed the carriage back up onto its wheels. *When the Egyptian chap returns, he'll be thankful for the good deed. Maybe he'll offer to buy me breakfast.*

No one returned to claim the carriage. A chant arose in Arabic several blocks away. It had to be a political protest, a throng of people calling for revolution and the end of the British occupation.

He stayed beside the carriage. With the sleeve of his robe, he idly polished a section of the footrest. *When the owner returns to claim the vehicle, why not make friends with the chap?* For a moment, Rupert rubbed the back of his neck.

The chant of the Egyptian people grew in volume and intensity.

Rupert paced awhile. *No worries.* His ruminations drifted back to the carriage. When the owner returned for it, perhaps they would discuss the troubles of the day. Together, then, they would pull the carriage to the local's house.

The report of a rifle resounded from the area of the

chanting—and a chorus of anguished cries followed. The political protest had transformed into a riot, obviously. More rifle shots rang out, followed by more cries, and it was not long before the crowd bolted. How to mistake the sounds of all their shoes and sandals against the stone and pavement? And the cries of the fallen? How many of them would be trampled to death?

Ashamed and affrighted, Rupert knelt beside the carriage. He fixed his gaze on the footrest so intently he never even noticed Maud Havelock approaching.

'Why do you cower there like that?' the Irishwoman asked him. 'Come with me. Let's go back to the hotel.'

His pride would not permit it. He did not say a word to the peculiar woman—no matter how much prejudice his reserve might inspire. Holding his breath, he listened to the sounds of violence and agony and mayhem roaring in the distance. *So, how many souls have already perished?* As the morning breeze grew stronger, his mouth and nasal passages burned—for he breathed in the chemical riot-control agents the British soldiers had unleashed into the air.

The Irishwoman pulled on his arm. 'Why so stubborn, eh? Why won't you come back to the hotel with me? In the name of God! Just look at you diddling here with that haunting gaze, the stare of a killer. The love of God! You're acting like a spoiled child, a naughty little boy.'

Rupert held his hands behind his back. He had no reason to be offended, for he had never felt insecure about acting his age. *I'm emotionally mature, I am.* As the booming, cacophonous riot droned on, Maud Havelock took her leave.

A young Cairene in traditional Turkish dress—shirtsleeves and baggy trousers—approached the carriage. The young man took hold of the shafts and pulled it along. When

Rupert attempted to help, the young man kicked him in the thigh. *Was the Cairene too distraught by the riot to permit some foreigner to be seen with him.*

Cairo. 23 September 1919.

At one o'clock in the morning, Rupert abandoned his post at the hotel reception desk and wandered downstairs into the deserted fogbound street.

How serene the city was at that hour—dreamlike, too. And what a quiet cityscape. Other than the street sweepers, who would even be out and about at that hour?

A set of footsteps echoed. *Could it be some lamplighter returning home from his rounds?* He scanned the darkness. Wearing a pair of stout walking shoes, the mysterious Irishwoman emerged from the shadows. 'Here I am,' she said, the hem of her gown trailing through the sooty pavement.

Rupert stopped beside a dustbin lying on its side and kicked at some of the fig seeds strewn about the walkway. *Don't say a word.* He studied her exaggerated grin and just knew she intended to deceive him. Nothing about her seemed at all genuine. The Irishwoman had come to remind him of the various locals who had grown accustomed to acting like the British rather than remaining true to the spirit of the burgeoning revolution. *She's all artifice, that one. An actress.*

Maud waved to him. 'Come here,' she told him. '*Please.*'

He angled away from her and contented himself to listen to the current blowing through the winter thorn trees.

In perfect time with the rattling boughs, she whistled a tune he did not recognise. 'Take me riding,' she said, pointing toward the hack stand. 'Let's go riding through the streets of Cairo. At this hour, we'll have the whole city to ourselves.'

Several motor buggies sped by, the words *le Club Automobile d'Egypte* emblazoned on their doors. Rupert grabbed Maud's hand and pulled her back from the street.

The breeze played through Maud's gown. She waited until the car club had raced off around the corner, and then took three steps toward the hack stand. 'Come along,' she said over her shoulder.

'Only if you tell me what you want from me.'

'What do I want? I only wish to strike a bargain with you. If you'd be willing to perform a simple task on my behalf, I shall free you from the dodgy dæmon inside your eye. It's a fine opportunity, no?'

Rupert staggered back a step and rubbed his eyeball. 'How do you know about the dæmon?' He lowered his hand and drew close.

Smiling, she clasped her hands together. 'Stop acting the maggot. I'm a proper Catholic mystic. Clever like a sorceress. I know everything.'

Rupert shook his head. 'I don't believe a word of what you say. I'm nobody's fool.'

Silently, Maud turned her back to him and positioned herself at an angle to the place where he stood. Then she lifted her one visible shoe off the pavement, the way a street magician effects the illusion of levitation.

Rupert frowned. *What kind of match could she be for the dæmon revolving around within his eyeball?* Still, he longed to be free of the irksome fantasy. With no better option, he resolved to play along with the woman—at least for now.

Five minutes later, their carriage rolled off into the fogbound street. Rupert sat back and sighed. The coachman swerved onto Sharia-Ramses Boulevard—where the Nile mist had curled itself around a banking house fashioned from Memphis limestone. As the clatter of the horses' hooves echoed through the streets, Rupert closed his eyes. After several minutes, he opened them. But despite the beauty and solemnity of the various fogbound structures, he studied Maud instead. Given her stern expression, she did rather resemble a sorceress. *Christian magic indeed.* His arms held tight to his body, he forced a smile. 'What would you have me do for you, then?.

Maud cracked the faintest grin. 'I want you to flush a wild duck,' she told him. 'Do you remember the blind girl living up there in England? *Anastasia.* When my contacts bring her here, you must woo her. Make her *love* you.'

There could be no doubt Maud Havelock must have once worked for the spiritualists—especially those with whom he had enjoyed a longstanding correspondence. 'Tell me about your business with the spiritualists,' Rupert said. 'Why all the secrecy?.

'It's a long story,' Maud told him. 'Let's just say, me and my associates have parted ways with Admiral Ilingworth's faction.'

Rupert smirked. 'Tell me more.'

Maud sat back and crossed her right leg over her left. 'Westminster Spiritualist Society. They're a band of vile magicians. Do you know what they've done to Anastasia? Don't ask me how, but they've imbued her with great powers. She's learned the magical art of dowsing, or so it seems.'

Like so many times before, Rupert considered his little brother's quixotic dreams of mastering the art of rhabdomancy and finding his way to some lost city. *Georgie.* A commotion rang out behind them, and Rupert looked over his shoulder to find a horse-drawn jaunting car emerging from an alleyway. He screwed up his eyes, straining to glimpse the features of the woman holding the reins—but the wide brim of her cartwheel hat obscured her face.

Maud glanced back, too, but swung forward quickly and kicked her right foot back and forth. With not a little force, she tugged the coachman's coattail. 'Would you please veer to the left up here on Khushqadam Boulevard?' she said, her voice wavering.

The coachman passed by the post office, the majestic building's pillars enveloped within a silvery-white haze. The horse-drawn jaunting car followed along for a while, then vanished down another alleyway.

Maud fidgeted, and the more she did, the more confident Rupert felt. 'The woman in the buggy—she's a friend of yours? Or maybe not.

Maud did not trouble herself to respond. Once more, she tugged the coachman's coattail—but this time she spoke to him in good Arabic.

The coachman reached for his riding crop, struck one of his horses, and directed the team into one of the more modern districts. There, a succession of newfangled electric lampposts shone several rays of pink light through the otherwise grey fog. With their heads bent and their eyes averted, a humble-looking sanitation crew in the long white garments of Coptic-Christian dress had recently flooded the length of the street so it resembled a Venetian canal.

Rupert closed his eyes again and thought of Anastasia. Regardless of his communication with spiritualists, he knew little concerning her. Still, he knew he could entice her if he put his mind to it. Back home in New Zealand, he had successfully manipulated several unsuspecting young ladies. *Who hasn't played the thief of hearts?*

Maud tapped his knee. 'Promise you'll work for me. *Please.*'

He opened his eyes. 'Just why would Anastasia be coming

here?' he asked.

Maud stared straight ahead. 'I'll pay you for your services. Handsomely. And you require moneys. At the moment, you haven't got a quid to bless yourself with. And more than the recompense, I'll set you *free*. Honest. And when you go free of the spirit inside your body, you'll *rejoice*. "The heavens have provided," you'll tell everyone.'

Up ahead, from out behind the Fatimid-era courthouse, the horse and jaunting car they'd seen earlier sped forward. And now the vehicle stopped, as if for no other reason than to block the route.

The coachman pulled on the reins. Then he hauled himself up and hollered at the woman in the jaunting car.

She did not move. Nor did she say a word. In the fog, she seemed unreal—something like a mechanical doll, an automaton.

Maud turned to Rupert. 'What do you think of my offer?.

Rupert glanced up at the jaunting car to see what was going on. Losing interest, he looked down at his lap. *What kind of face might Anastasia have?* He imagined her as resembling a lady friend from Queenstown, and he pictured himself holding Anastasia close. *I'd have little trouble endearing her to me, even if she knew all about the dæmon inside my eyeball.* He lifted his head high and exposed his neck. *All the spiritualists, they would've discussed my condition with her. Frequently, too.* If so, she would identify with him. He pondered all those letters to and from the spiritualists. At the time, he had hoped to learn something that might help him exorcise his nemesis— but had he learned anything at all? He had not gleaned much, and he had even forgotten what it was Anastasia had once believed to be living inside her womb. *Might it have been the spirit of some mischievous bog rat.*

The coachman waved at the jaunting car. '*Yela*!' he shouted. '*Yela*! *Yela*!'

The swirling fog thinned just enough to permit Rupert to study the woman holding the jaunting car's reins. How pallid was the skin up and down her forearms. In that sense, the woman resembled Maud herself. 'Are you sisters?' he asked.

'No,' Maud answered. 'The other woman there, Miss Fitzroy, she's a bitter rival. My foe. Yes, and she's travelled to the Sahara to hatch her diabolical plot. The woman in the cartwheel hat—she's ever the conniving one. And she's come to thwart me.'

'Oh?' He fussed with his coat and trousers. 'Or what if you were the wicked one and the other the heroine?'

The woman in the cartwheel hat looked up. In that moment and for just that moment, the wide brim of her hat revealed her eyes; they shone a sickly, golden green, as if she had consumed a handful of belladonna berries.

Maud gripped Rupert's wrist. 'I've business to tend to just now. Why don't you get back to the hotel?'

'Who's that woman in the jaunting car?'

'Let's talk about it tomorrow,' Maud whispered.

'*No*. Tell me what you wish to take from Anastasia.

'Listen, please. Just between you and me and Sunday morning's tea loaf, I've got a witch finder on my trail. And what a terrible one, too. She knows her Christian magic, she does. Read for her degree at Tokyo Women's Christian University, she did.'

'Right.' Without another word, Rupert hopped down past the carriage step and landed with a splash.

Maud's refusal to speak plainly had him confounded as to whether he ought to enter into any kind of agreement with her. What if the Irishwoman were to entrap him into an especially awful arrangement? If he were to renege on the deal, she certainly did not seem to be the type to honour his change of heart. Neither did she seem to be the kind to content herself with breach-of-contract proceedings. If anything, she seemed to be the sort who might simply poison him and resolve matters that way. *Just like Maria Swanenburg.*

Cairo. 27 September 1919.

Rupert abandoned his night-clerking post yet again. Once more, he crept downstairs and faltered into the fogbound street. A woman's voice rang out, followed by a shriek. His intuition told him Maud was finally confronting her nemesis. Horses neighed. *Could it be Maud's carriage chasing after the jaunting car, or could it be the jaunting car chasing after Maud's carriage?* He raced off. *Find them.*

Given the ungodly hour, the clatter of the ongoing chase reverberated through the streets and alleyways: the horses, the jaunting car, the carriage, and the rival women shouting insults and profanities at one another.

Out past the Cairo Museum, he realised he was lost. He staggered about in the shadows and peered up and down the streets, trying to get his bearings. *Where am I?* A childhood memory nagged at him: a remembrance of that late-summer holiday when Georgie had gone missing somewhere along the Fox River. A pretty redhead from Westport had joined the search party, but she had insisted on going off in her own direction. Rupert had intuited her intent; she hoped to best everyone else by finding Georgie without help from anyone. Later, when the pioneering girl located Georgie and brought him back to camp, she launched into a big sermon on the crime of misogyny. She spoke about the crucial import of women's history. 'Ye gents oppress us only because ye know us females got our own way of keeping watch and deciding what's what,' the irate girl cried out. 'Yes, ye despise us only because ye can't control our line of thinking. And I'd wager that's why ye always conspire to entice us the way ye do.' Later on that same night, the pretty girl had confronted Rupert down along the modest suspension bridge that spanned the river. 'So, do you think you'd be clever enough for a girl like me?'

'Why must you be so spiteful?' he asked in turn. 'Leave me be.'

'No, I've got every right to be here. And I'll tell you something else. I know your kind, that's right. You think I hope you'll follow me home, and we'll cuddle up for the night. And as soon as daylight comes, you'll climb out of my bed and recite a morning song. A proper aubade or whatever. But even if you did, I'd surely hear every word, because I'd only be pretending to sleep. In truth, I'd be awake the whole time. How's that for a passion killer?' Before Rupert could answer, she struck his arm and vanished into the night.

Rupert shook his head to clear it of the strange memory. A bright purple smoke plume appeared over Cairo—but the night grew darker. He breathed in the aromas swirling through the air—incense powder and traces of dried onion, the aromas of the Egyptian marketplace. As he stumbled onward to the other end of the street, he discovered a woman's palm-straw hat. *Hello.* At once, the wide brim made him think of the woman in the jaunting car—her distinctive hat. *Might the woman hiding behind that hat present a danger to me?* The more he mulled over the question, the more tense he felt. *How to trust a woman who conceals her face? She might as well have been wearing a mask, a disguise—and what could be more sinister? Only a chancer ever thinks to dissemble.*

A vehicle approached from the dark fogbank up ahead. Rupert strained his eyes to see if it was the jaunting car. From the darkened building to his left, a lantern suddenly shone— as if someone had just awoken from a nightmare. Whatever had happened, the glow illuminated a series of revolutionary Arabic slogans painted on the wall.

Rupert continued around the corner and soon found himself in the heart of a desolate spice market. Shrouded in a heavy silver fog, the expanse appeared dreamlike. Most mysterious of all, an array of stuffed dates lay strewn across a lone table standing to the side of a shimmery-black puddle. The surreal display made him think about the pursuit of love— gatherings of people to make merry and to confabulate. He recalled a novel he had read in his youth, the tale of a brute who invited young women to his various social functions, only to offer them stuffed exotic fruit befouled with some kind of intoxicant. The depraved antagonist's crimes were hateful. Rupert approached the table and took one of the dates. The peppery scent of saffron drifted through the spice market and swirled about him. The date fell from his hand, and he looked up into the fog, where the outline of the horse and jaunting car appeared.

The woman in the cartwheel hat called out in a lyrical Irish brogue, her voice echoing through the deserted plaza.

He remained still. *I'd better keep silent.* He pulled the ends of his trousers up and knelt amid the shadows.

The woman climbed down from the jaunting car and approached, the heels of her shoes clattering against the pavement.

He returned to his feet and glanced about. Three times over, he snapped his fingers. 'Maud, are you here?' When the

Irishwoman failed to answer, he studied her strange rival.

The woman stopped in her tracks. Rupert noticed she held a weapon in her hand—a traditional blackthorn shillelagh. Did she intend to attack him? Perhaps, at any moment, she would rush forward and hit him over the head.

He folded his body over and made himself small, but he stood his ground. 'What do you want?' When the woman failed to answer, he fussed with his pencil moustache.

The menacing woman raised the cudgel and held it across her chest—the same way a pharaoh might think to hold his crook while passing judgement on a contemptible slave.

He resolved to stay calm. 'Do you mean to assault me with that weapon of yours? Yes, of course. You wish to have a row. Perhaps you're hoping to avenge some past trespass, eh? Still, you ought to know I've got nothing to do with that Maud Havelock. No, I barely even know her.

The woman turned to the villa to the left and appeared to study the third-floor balcony garden. When the nighttime breeze stirred a long thin vine dangling from one of the balusters, only then did she lower her gaze. Raising high the shillelagh, she lunged toward him. 'God wills it!' she cried out. Surprising him with the force of her charge, she caught him off guard. Tangled together, they crashed into a rubbish bin and fell. The terrific din would have roused the entire neighbourhood back in Wellington, Rupert thought, his head spinning. But this was Cairo, and the sorely oppressed populace must have been fatigued from the latest uprising; everyone slept, and the altercation continued. The woman proved to be a formidable adversary, Plainly, she had received training in the art of combat. With no better option, he rushed over to the jaunting car and took the riding crop into his hand. Thankfully, when he took up the reins, the horse complied with his commands. Five minutes later, not far from the majestic structure housing the High Court, the beast slowed enough for him to throw himself into the street. With a hiss, the jaunting car continued off into the fog. He flopped onto the courthouse steps. *Bloody hell, what next.*

The clunk and rattle of the horse and jaunting car echoed for a while. When the city streets returned to quiet, a stray tomcat emerged from the shadows and gazed into his eyes—until a long, lithe queen cat came along. The tomcat darted about, as if determined to prove its prowess.

Rupert turned away and looked across the street, where the figure of a tall sleek woman appeared in the fog. Silently, she stared at him. When he got to his feet, he smiled and waved. 'Maud, would that be you there?.

The unnerving figure failed to answer. Nor did she move in any appreciable way—not even as the tomcat chased the queen cat past her heel.

He wondered if she might be a prostitute. The longer the menacing figure remained still, the more he fidgeted. "Has something made you uncomfortable?" he asked. Determined to appear strong, he put his hands on his hips and endeavoured to think up something amusing to say. Words failed him. He struggled to stay calm. Perhaps the motionless figure standing across the street would prove to be nothing more than a fine lady from England—and she had sailed here to indulge her immodesty while preserving her reputation. *And what if some matchmaker told her to come here to meet someone?* Rupert scratched at his scalp. Perhaps the woman mistakenly believed that *he* must be awaiting *her*. At last, he dropped his arms to his sides and advanced three steps. 'I had no romantic rendezvous scheduled for this hour. So, do forgive me for moving with some trepidation.'

The woman held up her hand. 'I am Anastasia's friend … from the spiritualist society. Whatever you do, you mustn't betray her. Do you hear?.

He faltered off through an expanse of debris, picking his way over a series of placards, stones, and bricks, the aftermath of a recent riot. Once he had found his bearings, he stumbled back to the Hotel Ibis and checked to see whether anyone had noticed his absence. When he lay on the sofa, he fell asleep. Once more, he dreamt of his childhood trauma—every sordid detail, all the abuse he had suffered at the hands of Father's sinister, snickering, self-satisfied business contact, Mr Impérial.

At the break of dawn, Rupert awoke and returned to the reception desk. With the evil spirit rattling around his eyeball, he sought to reflect on the dream—but he did not feel quite strong enough. *Just forget it.* He hooked his arm over the back of the chair, as if that might help him to remain calm. And the glow of dawn grew brighter all the time until he found himself blinded by the light.

IV.

At the stroke of midnight, Anastasia rose from bed and revisited the fortune teller's wish that she travel back to the wilderness of Sinai. *If I did, what good would it do?* Stretching her arms and yawning, she pictured the desert. *How could I hope to locate anything amid such widespread desolation? The Egyptians could've buried the plunder anywhere.* The dry nighttime breeze invaded the hotel room. She made her way over to the window. *What am I doing here?* In all the time she had been living up north, she had only grown to despise Westminster Spiritualist Society. As such, she longed to travel to Sinai and work for Madam Maksimovna's associates. The idea seemed inviting.

Only yesterday, twenty minutes past midnight, the peculiar woman had knocked on the door. 'Already, we raise more than enough money for the great expedition,' the fortune teller had said. 'Every little thing ready for your arrival. So, come search the plentiful tombs. I know you will find goodly treasures.'

The idea of gaining riches meant nothing to Anastasia. Still, how good it would be to regain her *freedom?* Once she had emancipated herself from the spiritualists, perhaps she would go on to meet a fine, affectionate gentleman—but if Admiral Ilingworth continued to dominate her, what chance did she have of ever finding love?.

She rubbed her belly. *There's nothing inside my womb. No, no. Still, I've got to find some way to forget the past. Yes, I've got to heal someone and prove myself worthy of love.* She slipped into a skirt and a woollen jumper.

Somewhere out in the heart of the nighttime sky, a quiet fizz and whoosh awoke. *It sounds like the fabric of the universe slowly tearing apart.* Anastasia listened closely until the din proved to be nothing more than the rumble of a train rolling past Coventry. She imagined it was the Trans-Siberian Railway. And inside the dining car, the waitstaff would be serving the passengers the most sumptuous fare: a dish of fish rolls and potato pies, and a dish of salted Russian dumplings, too. Her stomach rumbled, for she had refused supper some four hours earlier. She smacked her lips. If she did not regain her freedom soon, perhaps she would do something drastic. *I will starve myself, and then I won't be much good to them anymore.*

The noise faded—until no sound remained, save a few songbirds' plaintive, high-pitched calls resonating from the direction of the public park.

Go now. As soon as she had located her walking stick, Anastasia made her way to the door. '*Liberté,*' she whispered. '*Liberté.*' With that, she stopped; footsteps passed by on the other side of the door. Once they'd trailed off, she felt for the latch and released it. Out in the hallway, the odour of the tundra still lingered in the air. *Has anyone else noticed it?* Slowly, the stench of permafrost blended with the bitter taste on her tongue, and she gagged. Despite that, she did not hesitate. Tapping her walking stick, she counted her steps. *One, two, three, four. Go now.*

When she reached the door to Admiral Ilingworth's suite, she paused and pointed—as if jabbing a finger in the old man's face. *Goodbye, sir.* Little by little, the bitter taste of unsalted olives filled her mouth. *Oh, that's just awful.* She wandered down to the end of the hall, where she waited ten minutes or more for the lift. When it finally juddered to a halt with a loud metallic clang, she cringed. *I should've taken the damn stairs.* Her nostrils flared in anger as she stepped inside. She fumbled sightlessly for a couple of minutes before she located the floor-request buttons. *Hurry!* As the passenger lift jerked its way to the lobby, the sudden jolt made her retch. She drew a few deep breaths and fought through the irritation. When she reached the lobby, she asked the doorkeeper to ring a taxicab.

The wait for the taxicab felt like forever. *Surely, someone from the spiritualist society should espy me standing here.* What would she say if one of the admiral's henchmen were to approach? As innocently as possible, she would tell the person that she had only just awoken from a terrible nightmare. *Yes, a dream of the Grand Duchess Fyodorovna.* If the fool did not know who she was, Anastasia would explain all about how the Bolsheviks had murdered her. For added effect, Anastasia might even allude to the jewels the duchess had sewn into her crinoline petticoat. Had the jewels deflected dozens of rounds, and if so, had the jewels prolonged the woman's agonising death? In the end, once the aide asked just what any of that had to do with her wandering the lobby at his hour, she would insist she had to journey off to Coventry Cathedral to pray for the Grand Duchess Fyodorovna's soul.

Yes, that's what I'll say.

She drew in a deep breath, exhaled, and drew in another. Growing still, she heard footsteps approaching. Instinctively, she held her breath. *I'll just tell him about the dream. Yes, that's what I'll do.* She exhaled. *If he says anything, I'll tell him all about the duchess, and maybe I'll ask him if the Russian Orthodox Church intends to bury her precious body in the Garden of Gethsemane. .*

The footsteps passed, as if the person were just another hotel guest and had not even noticed her.

Patience. When the taxicab came along, she closed her blind eyes. *Thank God.* With little trouble, she managed to climb inside. The subsequent journey through the streets of Coventry took much longer than she had expected—almost twenty minutes.

When the taxicab reached Madam Maksimovna's Psychic Boutique, Anastasia paid the fare and asked the driver to help her to the stoop. Once the taxicab had rumbled off, she felt for the door and knocked. At first, no one answered. *Could it be the fortune teller has already retired for the night? What if she's already fallen into a deep sleep?* A second time, Anastasia knocked—this time much more loudly. When nothing happened, she banged on the door with the heel of her hand. Again, no one answered. No sound greeted her but the call of a wintering robin somewhere above her. The nighttime breeze blew in gusts, and something brittle and papery tumbled past her feet. It sounded like a crumpled page from a discarded newspaper—perhaps a recent edition of the *Coventry Evening Telegraph*. Whatever it was, the piece of refuse drifted off down the deserted city street, emphasising her solitude.

At last, she turned her back to the door. For the longest time, she gazed into the darkness stretching all around her.

What a terrible feeling to be stranded somewhere. *If only I still had the power of sight.* She thought of everyone back at the hotel. If a few of the admiral's aides were to check her room, they would see she had gone missing. *And if they locate me, what should I tell them?* Perhaps she could tell them that she had lately felt that she had lost her powers. 'When you hypnotised me into thinking that I've the ability to dowse, you didn't do it right,' she would tell the admiral. 'That's why I had to consult the fortune teller and ask her what to do.' Anastasia tapped the end of the walking stick against her shoe. *Would the admiral even believe a story like that?* She pressed her lips together. *Courage.*

The October breeze blew a little bit stronger and colder—the powerful current streaming through her blouse until she felt violated. *That cool autumn current feels like a giant diadem spider's breath washing all over my body.* Teetering this way and that, she imagined herself as a female slave standing at attention so that some prospective buyer might have the chance to check her—the merchandise. *Oh God.* The nighttime breeze blowing still, she finally turned back to the door and knocked a few more times. 'Madam Maksimovna, are you there? Please come answer the door. Don't leave me here.' When no response came, she turned back to the street.

The gentle shadows of her blindness never shone so vividly, nor so frighteningly. In time, two distinct kinds of blackness stretched forth: above, the black of night; below, a colour shining more like the darkest ocean blue. She had to laugh at the plastic unreality of her blind woman's world, shaped wholly by her mind. *So, what might* this *world be?* Rocking in the wild wind, she pictured herself on some historic wharf—and soon she would be boarding some vessel. *Yes, I'm sailing off to the Orient.*

51

The bells of Coventry Cathedral pealed triumphally. *So, it's half past midnight.* She hooked her walking stick around her forearm and dug her hands into her coat pockets. As the last knell went quiet, a round of laughter rang out—the same kind of nervous jubilant laughter a beauty queen might make at the moment she hears the master of ceremonies recite her name and declare her the victor in some pointless beauty pageant. *That round of laughter, though, it must've been me.*

From an alleyway off to the right, something stirred to life. It sounded like an old man clearing his throat. Before long, a pair of footsteps approached.

Anastasia felt certain the intruder must be a drunkard, for the closer the footsteps came, the more the air reeked of spirits. The old man stopped, and she felt the warmth of his breath against her face and neck. Did he realise she was blind? Whether or not he did, she couldn't know what he might do to her. What if he was the type who grew belligerent when drinking? She drew a deep breath. 'Go away.

The old man belched. 'You look like you're loitering on a pier,' he told her. 'Aye, like you'd be waiting to climb aboard some fine vessel bound for I don't know where.'

'Yes, you've got that right,' she told him, hoping he would go away of his own accord.

She heard the clink of a drinking flask against his teeth as the drunkard took a swig. 'Where you bound, then?' he asked. 'I know. You've joined the Children's Crusade. Would that be so, love? Are you off to the Holy Land? Do you mean to liberate *Terra Sancta*?'

She blinked a dozen times over and then fixed her sightless gaze down toward her feet. *Please go away. Please go away.*

The drunkard tapped her pendant dove with his drinking flask. 'Did some medieval guildsman tell you to participate in them mad crusades? Sure, he did. Still, you was wrong to listen to that no-good bloody bastard. And do you want to know why, little girl?'

She did not answer. Instead, she felt for her Huguenot cross and pendant dove. Then she dropped the precious heirloom down below her blouse and buttoned the top button. *Please go away. Please go away.*

The drunkard stepped back, passed gas loudly, and then drew close yet again. 'You ought to know the Children's Crusade wouldn't be nothing but a front for the Barbary Slave Trade or at the very least its equivalent. And that's as true as I'm standing here. All throughout Christendom, all the peoples aiming to make themselves a profit, the pied piper of Hamelin and so on, they've banded together to encourage children like you to march off to Italy. And when you get there, do you know what'll happen?'

'I think you've had too much to drink. You're talking like a madman. And as for me, I've got a happy destiny.' She thought of Rupert. 'Where I'm going, I'll find someone to love and—'

'You got to kick the whole bloody fallacy of them crusades into a cocked hat,' the old man interrupted. 'If you don't, I'll tell you what will happen. The pied piper, or whoever, he'll go on and sell you to a gentleman of fortune. That's right, you heard me.'

As sincere as the drunkard's tone of voice seemed, she said nothing. Instead, she knocked on the fortune teller's door a few more times. *Please, Madam Maksimovna. Answer.*

Twice, the drunkard tapped Anastasia's shoulder. 'Don't get on that ship, whatever you do. No, you'll never get to Palestine. Them gentlemen of fortune, they'll take all ye children off to the Barbary Coast. Places like Tunis and Algiers. You'll end up living in a Moorish palace, and whoever it was what purchased you from the pirates, he'll ravish you whenever he chooses to do so. Aye, for the rest of your life, you'll be the worst kind of slave. You'll go from child concubine to diseased whore, that's all.'

Anastasia focused all her energy on the door before her. *Madam Maksimovna, where could you be?* Anastasia knocked a few more times. *Please, Madam Maksimovna.*

Coventry. 8 October 1919.

At the stroke of midnight, Anastasia climbed out of bed—just as she had done some four nights earlier. She pictured a diadem spider in her womb. 'Oh, diadem spider. If you were still inside me, do you know what I'd tell you? I'd tell you I've got to have love in my life. I'd tell you my inner journey and my love's outer journey are one and the same. Yes, and his inner journey aligns with my outer journey, always intertwined.' Like so many times before, she mused over Rupert and wondered what he looked like.

She made her way down to the lobby and left the hotel. When the taxicab brought her to the psychic boutique, she felt for the door and knocked loudly. *Please be home.* She detected the aroma of Russian beets and sweet cream. *There.*

She heard footsteps approaching inside, and the fortune teller called out something in her thick Russian accent. Then she fumbled noisily with the lock and opened the door. '*You.*'

'Forgive me for visiting at this late hour,' Anastasia said, 'but I just had to speak with you.'

'Yes, of course,' Madam Maksimovna answered. 'And now I help you escape the wicked spiritualists. Yes, of course. I help you the same way I help the Russian Imperial Police save the lost duchess. Maybe you think Bolsheviks gun her down? *Nyet*. Maybe now I tell you big, big secret. My cat, Gogol, he take the lost duchess across wilderness of Siberia to lovely safe house outside Minsk. Then, only a few days later, I take everyone all the way to Pavlovsk, and then maybe two weeks later, we come to England, and we settle here in the beautiful Coventry.'

'Please, I don't think it's safe for me to be idling out here on the street,' Anastasia told the fortune teller. 'Let's go on inside, shall we?.

'Do you know something? When me and lost duchess arrive here, we had only ten gold rubles and nothing more than that. No Romanov silk. Not even a little bit of *crêpe de Chine*. No, nothing.' Madam Maksimovna grabbed Anastasia's arms and pulled her into the foyer. Then the fortune teller slammed the door shut.

A moment or two later, when Madam Maksimovna sat her in the parlour, Anastasia detected the presence of something dangerous—a wild entity she could not comprehend. *Oh God, it's the ...* primal. Awestruck, she wondered if a giant diadem spider had crept into the room. 'What's that?'

'What's what?' Madam Maksimovna asked in turn. Before Anastasia could say anything more, the fortune teller's footsteps trailed off, as if she had marched into the kitchen to brew tea.

The evil spectre remained, and its musky odour made Anastasia think back a few nights to the last time the fortune teller had come to her hotel room. On more than one occasion that night, the Russian woman had mentioned Sicily, as if someday she and Anastasia ought to visit the enchanted isle. The primordial odour grew stronger, and Anastasia wondered if some creature of Sicily might haunt the premises. She recalled her school days and sought to remember what elusive fabled creatures lived in the Mediterranean. At one time, a bevy of giant swans dwelled in Sicily. *Could it be Madam Maksimovna just happened to possess the last living one? Or what about the otherwise extinct Sicilian dwarf elephant.*

She heard the fortune teller return to her side. Gently, the woman patted Anastasia's knee. 'I have good friend, Mr Dalrymple. Maybe you know the name. Soon, he bring together all the departments of Egyptology. Victoria College and Oxford, maybe one or two other big schools. Only the best. Everyone to come to excavate pharaohs' lost treasure city, but so what? Only *you* hold power to find the glorious relics. That's why you *must* go there.' A second time, Madam Maksimovna darted off.

Anastasia endeavoured to ignore the mysterious, primaeval presence lurking in the room. More than anything, she debated whether she ought to put her trust in the fortune teller. There could be little doubt Madam Maksimovna represented a band of psychics that had broken away from Westminster Spiritualist Society. *As such, why assume the Russian woman's faction should be any better than Admiral Ilingworth's associates? Maybe her faction happens to be worse.*

From the other side of the room, the strange presence approached. How to mistake its ponderous footsteps, and how to deny the sound of its deep rhythmic breathing? Anastasia sat up straight and braced herself. *What could it be?* She clutched her arms to her chest and leaned back. Something warm and fleecy, indescribably powerful, and overwhelmingly heavy brushed up against her right foot. *Reach down. Shall I touch it? No, don't do that.* She clasped her knees together lest the creature sniff at her between her legs. Thankfully, the creature made no such attempt. Like a large serpent, a certain part of the presence languidly wrapped around her right ankle. *Oh my my.* The creature felt like a giant gypsy-moth caterpillar, and the very notion of it made the whole of her bosom heave. Every impulse told her to run. Still, if she had done so, just where would she have gone? If she were to lunge in this direction or that, she would surely collide with something. *Then I'd fall to the floor, and I'd injure myself.* Sitting up straight and holding herself stiff, she prepared to call out—but the awe, the sheer horror, proscribed all. She could not make a sound. Still, she finally managed to rise to her feet.

The beastly presence bumped up against her hip. What power, too, as if the creature possessed the strength of a Barbary lion.

The manifestation dominated the whole of her shadow vision, and she wondered if the being must weigh more than a thousand pounds. Then, as the length of the animal glanced off her thigh, she registered the fierce undying heat of the beast's body—and she heard the indomitable drumbeat of its immense all-powerful heart.

From the far side of the psychic boutique, a heart-rending shriek awoke—the whistle of the steam kettle. Afterward, there could be no mistaking the sound of the fortune teller fumbling with the tea service.

A second time, Anastasia endeavoured to call out—and a second time, her dread prohibited her. She crossed and then uncrossed her legs. *What do I do about this?* She wrapped her hand around the cross and pendant dove. *Am I hallucinating?*

From the other side of the room, someone tapped softly on the windowpane. She wondered if it might be the old drunkard from the other day. Perhaps he, too, had espied the uncanny presence. She held the Huguenot cross a bit tighter.

Maybe it's only a matter of time before the wild thing consumes me. As futile as it seemed, she reached her hand out toward the window and waved. *Save me.*

The monstrous brute snorted. Then the warm, fleecy serpentine appendage coiled around her ankle slowly, insidiously squeezing her leg tighter. The colossal aberration panted and chuffed—each breath as warm as a blast of sulfuric steam rising from a prehistoric Russian mud pot. She breathed in the animalistic heat, which melted away the bitter taste in her mouth.

From the back room, the bustle of footfalls and the clink of china heralded Madam Maksimovna's return to the parlour. 'This October night, it's a beautiful one,' the fortune teller said, stopping some two feet away. 'And this October, it's not so cold. So, maybe we take our little teacups and everything outside into my garden, yes?'

Anastasia opened her mouth but could not manage an answer. Her breathing having grown quick and shallow, she dropped the walking stick—which clattered against the floorboards. The presence did not panic at the sudden noise. Neither affrighted nor angry, the warm hirsute appendage loosened its grip on her ankle, then unravelled itself altogether.

Madam Maksimovna returned the walking stick to Anastasia's hand. 'Please, we go into my garden. I take your free hand, yes, and I show you the way.' The fortune teller took her wrist and guided her to the back door—and Anastasia found herself within a vast garden filled with the same kinds of sharp, spicy aromas that might drift through some quiet exotic Sicilian village.

The autumn breeze played through Anastasia's blouse. She squeezed her eyes shut—tightly, too. Even if she had not heard its powerful footfalls, she did not doubt the primordial presence had followed her outside. How to deny the creature's monstrous odour? For that matter, how to deny the awesome sound of its heartbeat? All through her body, she felt the animal's deep, steady, throbbing godlike pulse. The warm, fleecy serpentine entity brushed up against her foot, coiling around her ankle, squeezing and squeezing. Again, the walking stick dropped from her hand. She breathed in and out. 'What does this mean?' she managed to say. 'What kind of creature would this be?.

'It's nothing,' Madam Maksimovna answered. 'Just my familiar.'

'Your familiar?'

'Yes, my little Gogol, he's squatting beside you. And he has a long tail. Over four feet, and that's no fib.'

'Over four feet? No cat has a tail that long.'

'No, you forget. My little Gogol, he's a beautiful Siberian tiger. You wish to feel his coat?' Twice, the fortune teller snapped her fingers—and the presence obediently slipped loose from Anastasia's ankle.

'*Quelle sensation géniale,*' Anastasia whispered, reaching for her Huguenot cross and tapping the pendant dove.

'Don't fear my little cat,' Madam Maksimovna continued. 'My Gogol familiar. If you prefer, you climb onto his big, strong back, and he take you to Sinai. Still, he cannot unearth the treasures there. I think only *you* command that power.'

The tiger let out a powerful growl, and Madam Maksimovna laughed. 'No you worry any,' she said. 'My little Gogol, he only says that he love you. This I know. When I was a little child since long time ago, Rasputin came to me outside the palace at Oranienbaum, and he teach me the secret language of tigers.'

The beast bumped up against Anastasia's hip and moved

such that the length of its trunk grazed her thigh. What an aroma the creature exuded: the scent of dried flowers intensified by its body heat.

'*Fleurs du mal*,' Anastasia whispered, revisiting her dreams of someday finding someone afflicted with the kind of obsession that had once possessed her. *Wouldn't it be perfect if I healed him and* he *fell in love with me?* She drew a deep, brisk breath, in and out, in and out. *Rupert.*

Like an angry god, a deity betrayed, the Siberian tiger unleashed a terrific resonant roar.

Oh, what power. Yes, what power. She felt as if she stood in the presence of the Creator Himself. Her blindness, a boon for the first time, prevented her from gazing into the eyes of the beast and witnessing its dreadful countenance.

V.

Back at the Hotel Ibis, Rupert studied the clock on the wall. *Here we are again. It's one o'clock in the morning. The dead of night.* His intuition told him that, at any moment, the Irishwoman would be coming along. For the past three nights, as he had endeavoured to execute his night-clerking duties at the reception desk, Maud had come by to demand that he enter into a deal with her.

The phone rang, but Rupert refused to answer. He suspected the caller was the woman wearing the cartwheel hat.

As he disconnected the handset, the passenger lift descended from Maud's suite and stopped with its customary clank. She stepped into the lobby and strode over to the reception desk. 'I think you ought to know you got me all discomfited,' she told him. 'To be sure, I'm smoking like a bottle of whiskey laid out over the peat fire.'

'Leave me be,' Rupert told her, standing and slicking his hair back. 'I'm responsible for this whole hotel, and I can't have you buzzing about.'

'Work with me. *Please*. We've got to stop Anastasia from discovering some great treasure. By fair means or foul, we must stop her from disturbing the past—the dead.'

'Push off,' Rupert told the Irishwoman. Arms crossed over his chest, he stepped back from the reception desk and scowled.

'If you won't work with me, do you know what I'll do? I'll kill you, that's what. My beloved Uncle Pádraig, he's supplied me with his repeating rifle. And I know how to use it.'

Rupert peered into Maud's eyes and noted her passion. In the hope it might make him appear bold, valiant, and unconcerned, he sat and feigned interest in the ledger book.

Maud wandered about the lobby. *She looks like a nervous young lady who sidles into a shop and purchases something she does not even want,* he thought. *Yes, that's right. And only because she feels obliged to please the merchant.*

When the Irishwoman stopped, she contemplated the ceiling fan. 'I know the trouble with you, to be sure. You're the type what tends to lie to himself.' With that, Maud bounded down the staircase leading to the hotel door and the teeming city streets.

When she was gone, Rupert reconnected the handset. Then he approached the little mirror on the wall and combed his pencil moustache. When the telephone rang, he did not trouble himself to answer. He just knew the woman in the cartwheel hat would be on the line. Relentlessly, the telephone continued to buzz. And given the desolation and restfulness at that hour, the drone reverberated through the hotel lobby that much more.

Vexed and weary and not a little bit confounded, he abandoned his post and dragged himself outside. *Shall I sell myself to that crazed Irishwoman?* He pulled at his ear and looked around for any sign of her. Already, Maud had vanished into the dark, fogbound night. Still, the woman's unnerving ladylike footfalls continued to click and clack through the streets. *Or might the footsteps belong to someone else?* He smoothed out his cardigan and loosened his necktie. A bit of debris blew by in the current, and when some of the refuse tangled itself in his trouser cuffs, he brushed it away. The footfalls ceased. At his back, someone cleared his throat. *Who's that?*

There in the fog loomed the faint figure of a heavily armed British soldier. 'Are you my contact?' the silhouetted figure asked.

Rupert stood tall. 'What do you want? Who the devil are you? Tell me something. Did you happen to notice a mad Irishwoman traipsing about?'.

The British soldier did not answer. Nor did he move. He adopted a flat gaze, as if he must be debating whether he had mistaken Rupert for someone else.

Rupert raised his hand. 'I'm not the chap you're looking for, eh?'

Once more, the British soldier neither spoke nor moved a muscle. Did he regret having spotted Rupert waiting there.

For all Rupert knew, the soldier presently contemplated the idea of raising his rifle and shooting him.

The darkened figure adopted a rigid body posture. 'We've displaced too many,' he said. 'What right have we got to do that? Whether we feel good and safe in calling this or that riot an act of insurrection, what're we doing here? Are we not the ones guilty of terrorism?'.

Rupert scratched at his scalp. 'If you mean to enter into some kind of arrangement with the local revolutionaries, I won't say a word. I don't believe in colonialism. Back home,

I'd petition parliament to let the Egyptians go free. Hat in hand.'

The soldier raised his rifle such that the action bar rested against his shoulder, with his hand wrapped around the safety and trigger guard. He ambled back into the swirling fog until he was gone.

The ease with which the soldier had extricated himself impressed Rupert so much he let out a gasp of elation. Then he paused to consider just how conniving a soldier would have to be to side with the enemy. Rupert shook his head and meditated on his own condition. *So, why not comply with the Irishwoman?* At once, he drew in a cleansing breath.

From the opposite direction, the tapping of soft, elegant, ladylike footfalls beat out a steady rhythm. Who could it be if not Maud Havelock? Whether or not it was, she did not approach. Gradually, the echo of the footsteps grew fainter.

Chase her down. Yes, that's what I'll do. He flicked an imaginary piece of dust from his oxblood-leather shoes and marched forward. *What do I say when I find her?* Perhaps he could determine some way to stall her. If nothing else, he would insist they go over the terms of the proposed deal. Afterward, he could ask her to explain just how she intended to apportion the expenses between them. For that matter, he might even demand she clarify how she intended to divide the profits in the event Anastasia actually located something of great value.

For an hour or more, the chase continued—and by the time he paused to check his timepiece, he had become hopelessly lost.

Later that morning.

Not far from a boys' *madrasa*, Rupert espied Maud waiting beside a darkened lamppost in the fogbound street. 'Please come here!' he shouted. 'Help me get back to the hotel!.
When he hurried forward, she vanished into the cool mist— as if to entice him into yet another futile chase.

He stopped and put his hands on his hips. 'Do you think you'll employ reverse psychology?' he asked, raising his voice. 'Do you think you'll cajole me into doing your bidding by acting like you don't even want me anymore? Would that be it?'

Down the adjacent alleyway, a set of footsteps drummed softly, followed by the sound of girlish laughter.

He walked off in that direction. 'Come talk to me. *Please.*'
In the darkness before dawn, he lurched into the middle of a footbridge spanning the Nile. He twitched his pencil moustache and looked around. *Where the hell am I?* If only he had brought along his pocket-sized street atlas. Wringing his hands, he studied the dark powerful river.

The waters only seemed to emphasise his predicament: myriad wisps of nighttime fog careened across the waves, as if each misty shred must be looking for a place to take refuge before the sun rose high enough to melt the smoky strand into absolute oblivion.

The dæmon reeled about inside Rupert's pupil, and he refocused on the waters. A garland of jasmine floated along on the current. *If Georgie were here, he'd probably fix his gaze on the wildflowers and go lost in prayer. 'Father, tell us what to do,' Georgie would whisper. 'Should we keep the faith, or would it be our destiny to accept Maud's proposition and tempt your wrath?'*

Dawn broke over the city, and a ray of light shone through the darkness and the mist.

A school of shimmery damselfish happened by, and one

with scales that shone the brightest Venetian red stuck its head out of the water. The creature nibbled on the jasmine while Rupert looked back in the direction he had come from, reflecting on the night's events. Why did that uncanny woman even require someone to entice the blind girl? *I'd think a blind girl like Anastasia would be as lonely as a dollar princess.* Deep inside his eyeball, back near the optic nerve, an oppressive heat awoke. He flinched. Again, he wondered what Georgie's reaction would be. *Like enough, Georgie would probably tell me we have no choice but to conspire with Maud. No matter how vindictive she might be.* With a weary sigh, Rupert rubbed his eyeball. 'What if she is a sorceress?' he asked, as if Georgie stood at his back. 'How could I trust her? I know what you'd say. "It'd be good if she were a sorceress," you'd tell me. "If she were, she'd probably make good on her promise to free you of the diabolical thing that dwells inside your eyeball. And just think of how good it should feel to be free of your tormentor. You'd be healed, Roo."'

Rupert grew quiet. A series of unnerving noises resonated in the darkness: the pounding of footsteps, the din of a horse-drawn jaunting car, the demoralising click of someone loading a powerful repeating rifle. Rupert debated whether he could trust a woman as maniacal as Maud Havelock. *Might she betray me?* If she did, she seemed like the type of woman to blame him for the breakdown. Laughing in his face, she would quote Shakespeare: 'The more fool you for laying on my duty,' she might say.

Rupert looked to the waters and prayed. 'Father, what about Maud? Should a person believe her at her word? Tell me true. When I call her to account, might she manipulate me with some sad story? Do you think she'd call me a mark and blame me for putting all my faith in her? Tell me what to do. I deserve to know. I'm an honest gentleman, more or less. I don't even get things on the never. Always, I pay up front. At least, I make the effort.'

The light of dawn grew brighter. Down in the water, three damselfish slowly circled the jasmine. Had they mistaken it for sustenance? The damselfish swam faster, and Rupert gripped the railing. 'Father, tell me you'll not be cross should I enter into an arrangement with Maud.' In a state of nerves, Rupert rubbed his right eyeball. He blinked repeatedly, too. When he restored his vision, he returned his gaze to the jasmine: one of the shimmery damselfish took a section of the alluring object into its mouth and plunged. And as the hungry creature vanished into the depths of the river with the garland, something fell from Rupert's coat pocket—the crumpled remains of the parchment stationery on which the hotel manager had listed the names of the tenants who had paid for that day's Gyzeh tour. *Bloody hell, I forgot to wake them.* Now he looked to the sky, where the first light of dawn threatened to break at any moment. *Damn.* All the hotel guests should have been preparing to explore the pyramids— everyone laughing and making merry and photographing the monuments. *What have I done.*

VI.

Palermo, Sicily. 2 November 1919.

When the steamship made her port of call late that afternoon, Anastasia faltered down the gangway and stepped onto the wooden pier. The unstable wharf swayed beneath her feet. She felt a sensation as of the merciless diadem spider stirring deep inside her—each one of its eight illusory legs poking and scratching at the lining of her womb. The momentary fright came as no surprise; ever since Madam Maksimovna had introduced her to Mr Dalrymple, Anastasia's fears had only intensified. She did not trust the enigmatic Englishman, for the antiquities scholar would not confide in her. All throughout the voyage, whenever the talk had turned to the ongoing excavations in Sinai, he told her nothing. Despite that, she had resolved to play along. Having frittered away so much time with the spiritualists, she welcomed the opportunity to explore some exotic treasure city. Moreover, if the post proved to be unbearable, she could always hire a guide to bring her down into the village—the place where she had lived only a few years before. *How lovely it'd be to return to that little place by the sea. The village of Al-Hubu.*

Mr Dalrymple climbed down the gangway now and drew close. 'Tomorrow, we must make a modest pilgrimage into the mountains.' He unfolded a leaf of brittle-sounding paper. His breath growing shallow, he read off a peculiar message. *Had he lifted it from some old legendarium?* The arcane text quoted a medieval dispatch from the Duke of Normandy and described a great discovery he had made: evidently, he had visited the sacred mountain tomb of Saint Rosalia and had located there a large thicket of wild witch hazel trees unlike any other. According to local Sicilian legend, they commanded great power. Over and above their potential to make possible the art of divining, each forked bough held the uncanny power to transform any adversary into stone.

Anastasia hooked the crown of her walking stick over her right forearm. 'You ought to know that just because I'd be a good Christian, it doesn't mean I'd be foolish enough to believe in fanciful legends,' she told Dalrymple. 'Anyway, you've no cause to take me on some mock pilgrimage. Also, even though I know you and your fortune teller friend secured my services under false pretences, I don't even mind.'

'This here's no act,' Dalrymple insisted.

'Sure, sure.' She thought back to the eve of the voyage, when Mr Dalrymple had asked her to accompany him to a prayer service out at Maritime Greenwich. Afterward, as the rest of the congregation filed out of the chapel, he brought her into the sacristy and placed the weighty worn hilt of a broadsword into her hand. 'That's a genuine Greek piece,' he whispered into her ear. 'That piece in your hand holds magical powers, the kinds of miraculous powers that once defended the Monastery of Saint George in Old Cairo. And down in Sinai, we've got so much more invaluable plunder awaiting us. Predynastic, *pagan* riches.' .

Dalrymple had always reminded her of a pathological liar who could not overcome his sickness. Smirking now, she placed the pommel of her walking stick back into the palm of her hand. 'Sir, do you honestly think anyone could be foolish enough to believe a witch hazel bough commands magical powers beyond those that permit dowsing?.

Mr Dalrymple did not trouble himself to answer. She heard a crackle as he crumpled the leaf of paper into a little bundle. Without warning, he forced the ball into her mouth. 'Swallow all that,' he whispered. 'Yes, just pretend it's a piece of *Liquirizia due Sicilie*. No, a magic pill strong enough to exorcise the Devil.'

The bundle of paper tasted like a piece of mouldy fennel, so she spat everything out into her hand.

'*No*. Go ahead and swallow that message, lest some intelligencer learn of our scheme.'

'Like who?' For a moment, she laughed at Mr Dalrymple's melodrama. Then she patted her belly. 'If you promise to take me to one of those quiet little cafés along *la Via Roma*, and if you get me a dish of fresh artichoke hearts, I'll swallow the bundle here and now. Would that be good?' Before Dalrymple could respond, the scent of Egyptian chamomile came drifting through the otherwise salty air. *Egyptian chamomile?* Tapping her foot awhile, Anastasia did her best to picture the port of Palermo—the fishing vessels laden with Mediterranean cod. *Why should the scent of Egyptian chamomile be a part of the scene?* A sick sensation as of vertigo came over her person. 'Something's happened,' she blurted out.

Mr Dalrymple pulled her toward him. '*Yes*. Up along the promenade, there's a veiled nun waiting all alone beside the fountain. But the nun's neckpiece is all wrong. Nothing at all like a proper chapel veil.

Anastasia shook her head. 'Are you ribbing me?'

'Listen, love. I know that woman pretending to be the nun. She's working for some rival faction. She aims to betray us to the Westminster Spiritualist Society, or else she means to bide her time and watch over us and purloin whatever we find down there in the wilderness of Sinai.'

A second time, Anastasia shook her head. *What have I got myself into?* She lifted her blind eyes to the sky. *Half the world must be mad, and the other half a band of thieves.*

Mr Dalrymple tapped her pendant dove. 'Go on and swallow that bundle of paper before the intelligencer nicks it and learns all about our sacred Christian pilgrimage.'

'Please don't humour me. Remember, I don't even care if you and yours prove to be as dodgy as all the spiritualists back home.' For a time, she revisited just what it was that mattered to her. With all her heart, she longed to be free to find someone to love. *Yes, I'll free him from the diadem spider inside him, and then we'll be together. And we'll live together in a bond of true love because I will have earned as much.*

A second time, Mr Dalrymple tapped the pendant dove. 'Very well, love. Have it your way. Swallow the wee bundle of paper, and then I'll get you some damn artichoke hearts. Let's go. Posthaste.'

'Why don't *you* swallow it?' When Mr Dalrymple thrust the paper bundle back into Anastasia's mouth, she finally relented and swallowed—and as the contents of her stomach churned, Dalrymple snickered like a little boy. Not so gently, then, he pulled on her elbow and drew her along through the pier.

Ten minutes later, at the café, the artichoke hearts failed to satisfy her hunger. Even worse, the leaf of paper she had swallowed made her sick. Before long, she imagined a stork the colour of white smoke fluttering down to the window stool. As ill as she was, she even heard it tapping its bill against the casing. 'What does the stork want?'

For a moment or two, Mr Dalrymple did not answer. He must have realised she had lost touch with reality. After supper, he guided her back into the crowded *piazza*. 'Let's get you back to your stateroom,' he told her. 'You've got to rest. You've got a momentous day ahead of you, come tomorrow.

When he let go of her arm, she stood still and listened to the crowd. As she breathed in, she detected the faint scent of mulberry. *How beautiful. Oh Sicily*! She listened to voices, the indistinct conversations, the music of the Italian language: from the direction of the mulberry tree, a little flower girl presently spoke to someone. On and on, the awkward exchange continued—the flower girl attempting to sell something to a drunken sailor.

'I don't want no bloody silk poppy,' he slurred.

His bad manners should have sickened Anastasia, but she had so many other more pressing concerns just then. She briefly tried ignoring everything.

The flower girl approached her. '*Un papavero?*' the little girl asked, holding what must have been a silk poppy up to Anastasia's nose. Oddly, the artificial bloom boasted a fragrance as of pomegranate syrup. Anastasia felt as if she had snorted a thousand or more black peppers, and she sneezed a few times. The flower girl withdrew the poppy. 'I don't want nothing,' she said, her voice earnest. 'I only bring you a message from the nun. "Don't you make no trouble," she says. "Go back to England. You keep away from the lost city down there in Sinai. No you go any further."'

Mr Dalrymple spoke up and chided the girl in Italian. By

the sound of it, he grabbed the silk blossom and crumpled it in his hand. '*Al diavolo te!*' he shouted at her.

As the little girl sobbed loudly, Anastasia felt for Mr Dalrymple and pulled on his sleeve. 'Get me back to the ship. I've taken sick.'

Palermo, Sicily. 8 November 1919.

For the first time since swallowing the leaf of paper, Anastasia felt healthy enough to leave her stateroom. When she knocked on Dalrymple's door, he wrapped his hands around her wrists and kissed her brow.

'I feared you'd never recover.'

She did not know quite what to say, so she contented herself to break free from his grasp—albeit gently. With both hands, she rubbed her belly. All through the previous night, the contents of her stomach had churned violently—as if the natural toxins and minerals within the artichoke hearts had finally gone to battle with the bundle of paper.

Later that morning, Anastasia returned to her stateroom to brew a kettle of chamomile tea.

At ten o'clock, Mr Dalrymple came to collect her. 'Let's make our sacred pilgrimage,' he told her. 'We've got just enough time. This bucket doesn't sail off until dusk.' Initially, she refused—but Dalrymple would not relent. Before long, he wrapped his arm around her arm and practically dragged her from the ship.

At midday, as she and Dalrymple reached the base of the mountain sanctuary, Anastasia belched in the most unladylike way. 'Pardon me. I'm still feeling a bit unwell.' When Dalrymple wandered off to purchase the tickets for the steam-powered cable car, she belched a second time. Later, when he came back from the ticket office, he guided her to the queue—a band of loquacious English ladies.

Anastasia breathed in and wondered if she detected a trace of Egyptian chamomile—just as she had six days before. *Has some rival already ascended to the tomb?* The very notion only made Anastasia's stomach acids churn that much faster. *Heavens.*

From up above, a noisy twin engine clattered to life: the steam-powered cable car descending from the tomb. As the knocking and pinging grew louder, she felt for Dalrymple's arm. 'Must we go through with this pointless charade?'

'It's no charade,' he said.

'Take me back to the steamship. I wish to talk to the ship's doctor.'

'No, listen. Sinai's a perilous place. You'll require a proper weapon down there, the kind of witch hazel bough that holds the power to destroy any and all adversaries.'

'*Please*. I know you disbelieve in such things as magical witch hazel boughs turning people to stone. You brought me here because you wish to make me think you've got religion, as if that should impress me and make me trust you. Ah, but you're *not* a believer. No, you can't fool me.' Gently, she wrapped her hand around her Huguenot cross and the pendant dove.

With a metallic thud, followed by a grating hiss, the cable car reached the earth. Graciously, the English ladies permitted Mr Dalrymple to help Anastasia climb aboard ahead of everyone else. Then, once all the English ladies had stepped inside, the cable car commenced its slow, steady ascent.

The chassis swayed back and forth wildly, and the whole of Anastasia's body convulsed. *Oh God*. She heard a dozen or more songbirds alight on the rooftop. As a chorus whistled and warbled, she wondered if it might be the music of sparrows. A powerful gust rattled the cable car, and when the sparrows fluttered off, she shivered uncontrollably. By now, she regretted that she wore nothing more than a simple chiffon tea-party gown.

An especially noisome English lady reeking of red wine tugged her sleeve. 'Do you mean to ask Saint Rosalia to grant you a miracle?'

'No. Why should I?'

'Because Saint Rosalia wields great powers. She heals encephalitis lethargica. That's sleeping sickness, where you turn to stone and become a human statue devoid of a soul.

'Saint Rosalia will heal just about any malady,' another lady spoke up. 'Back in days medieval, Saint Rosalia helped poor Robert le Diable. Up there in the mountains, not far from her bonny tomb, that's where he fought to take back his soul from the Wicked One.

'Robert le Diable? Who's he, then?' Anastasia asked.

'The Duke of Normandy,' the lady answered. 'The poor fool's mum sold his doomed soul to the Devil on the night she conceived the baby. That's because she was a greedy one, the baroness. Still, in the end, the poor wretch did take back his soul. And then he got himself a fine, loving Sicilian princess for his troubles.'

Anastasia smiled. 'Love conquers all,' she thought out loud, another strong gust rattling the cable car. Little by little, she felt as if she had swallowed a little piece of an alchemist's tincture, the substance pulsating with enough otherworldly energy to make her retch. *That day we arrived here, why did I stuff myself with all those artichoke hearts?* Again and again, the little cable car swayed—and she placed her hand over her navel. A second time, she retched. *Why did I swallow that ball of paper?.*

The cable car halted with a violent, cacophonous jolt, for it had reached the summit. Mr Dalrymple let the English ladies disembark before helping Anastasia out onto the rocky path.

Shivering anew, she quelled the urge to ask him to describe the sanctuary. As they entered the cool shadow of the mountain, she decided it might be better to picture the tomb the way everything *ought* to appear. The Italians would have hewn the structure from the finest *serpentino-classico* marble, the face as glorious as any of those famous façades etched into the sandstone hills of Transjordan.

One of the English ladies approached, and when she invited Anastasia to come inside with her and to pray over the tomb, Mr Dalrymple excused himself. At that point, the English lady drew close and hummed a few measures of a fine aria into Anastasia's ear.

'What's that melody?' Anastasia asked when the English lady grew quiet.

'That piece comes from a big fantasy opera some crazy Fritz wrote all about Robert le Diable.'

Anastasia hummed the tune, and then she stopped. 'Would that be the song he sings when he comes to pray over Saint Rosalia's tomb?'

'No, it's the tune to "*le Ballet des nonnes damnées*". That's the song the Duke sings when he summons the ghosts of all the ancient nuns to rise up from their graves. And then he stares goats and monkeys at all them lady spirits as they dance for his pleasure.'

Again, Anastasia wished for companionship and love. *Yes, someone as spiritual as Robert le Diable. Someone just as tragic, too.* The sweet scent of Egyptian chamomile awoke in the cool, wild wind—and she gasped and felt for the English lady's arm. 'Tell me. Do you notice a woman of the Orient anywhere about?'

'No, it's just us here … and a nun … with emerald eyes shining from behind her veil.'

'Oh?' Anastasia fussed with her tea-party gown's sleeve—both the chiffon and the cuff's beaded trim. Meanwhile, her insides churned and churned. Seemingly oblivious, the English lady guided her into the shrine—and when Anastasia reached the stone sepulchre, she breathed in the fragrance of the votive candles burning on the top marble slab. A moment or two later, when she backed away from the tomb, she listened to the hustle and bustle resounding from the other side of the room. Given all the sounds she heard, she felt certain a team of conservators must be preparing to perform some kind of chore. *Maybe the labourers intend to touch up a few ornate medieval frescoes.* She touched her face, parted her lips, and pictured how Saint Rosalia might appear in the various depictions. *Saint Rosalia.* Given her girlhood in Russia, Anastasia envisioned the pious woman as resembling one of the reformers who had agitated for worker-women rights in Saint Petersburg. Still, Saint Rosalia would look Italian: she would have olive-coloured skin. And she would be holding a white Sicilian wildflower in her hand. *Yes, a musk rose.* Anastasia placed her hand over her gut, for the churning had grown worse; inside her womb, it felt as if the diadem spider had returned. And as the hideous creature pulsated and fidgeted, she felt a nosebleed coming on. *Good gracious.*

Someone tugged on the hem of her gown then, and the sound of a mischievous little imp's laughter rang out. 'Why did you come here?' a little girl's voice asked. 'Maybe you wish to make trouble for the good people down in Sinai? Why do you serve the wicked? If you live like a chaste woman, so you never fall into the fires of the terrible Inferno. Please, go home. You must not serve Dalrymple. He's wicked, that one.' Without another word, the little girl hurried away.

The fact that the little girl had mentioned Dalrymple's name startled Anastasia. *My life's in danger.* Her nose bled. She pinched it shut and applied pressure—so much so the bones of her fingers grew stiff. *When I get to Sinai, how long before someone kills me?*

Someone passed by her side. Given the odour of wet lime plaster, the person would have to be one of the conservators preparing to fill in a few cracks here and there. The pungent odour made Anastasia sneeze. Then she tripped over something soft and fell to the floor. Fumbling about, she felt the tiny squares of tessaræ beneath her fingers. Finally, she found the thing that had tripped her. After turning the tattered cloth object over a few times, she shook her head. *It's a wimple, a nun's headdress. Immaculately white, I imagine.*

As soon as she pushed herself back up onto her feet, she let the mountain breeze guide her back to the antechamber and onward out the door. 'Mr Dalrymple, are you here?' The wind grew wilder yet, and she almost dropped her walking stick. 'Mr Dalrymple, please come now,' she cried out.

When Mr Dalrymple finally came along, he took her free hand into his own and drew her along the rocky path.

'Where are we going?' she asked, wondering if the gentleman had even noticed her bloody nose.

'I've located the witch hazel tree,' he told her. Then he stopped and pointed her to the left. 'We've just reached a stairway hewn into the side of the mountain,' he explained. With that, he grabbed her wrist and placed the palm of her left hand atop the stone newel post. 'Go on now, love.'

Her shoulders pushed forward, and she proceeded along. Twelve steps up, though, her bladder felt tight and heavy. She had to stop. Her legs cramping up, she chewed on the inside of her cheek.

'Not feeling well?' Mr Dalrymple asked, tapping his drinking flask against her thigh. 'Have some of my *liquore de limone*. It's as refreshing and as rejuvenating as advertised in this morning's *Repubblica*. So, go on. I'm sure you'll feel much better once you cop the brewery.

She sipped some, but it did not help much. When she returned the flask, she continued up the stairway. She gradually climbed to the newel at the highest point, encountering a fierce, frigid wind. For a few moments, she debated whether she felt the last vestiges of an autumn sirocco or perhaps the first winter mistral. Her teeth chattering badly, she pictured the approach of snow clouds. The current grew colder, and she struggled to picture the Isle of Sicily down below—all the noble *palazzi*, their rooftops' red glazed-clay tiles aglow in the afternoon light.

From miles away, a church bell pealed triumphally and then counted out the hour. *It's four o'clock.* She imagined the bold rhythmic clamour ringing out from a structure as grand as Avignon Cathedral: a towering Sicilian-Baroque cathedral, the majestic, timeless house of worship keeping watch over the Bay of Palermo. *How beautiful.*

The winds blew harder, so Mr Dalrymple draped his topcoat around her shoulders. 'We haven't too far to go,' he told her in a loving fatherly tone. 'There's a bountiful thicket over to the north. Soon, you'll hold in your hand the finest witch wand you ever had.' He grabbed her elbow and attempted to guide her up a narrow pathway to the left.

She stood still. Despite the invigorating scent of the

Sicilian firs and witch hazel trees, she swore she detected the harsh, desolate scent of Sinai. *Yes, and it's coming from just about every direction. Oh yes, from all around.* Scratching the tip of her nose, she swore she heard a disturbance arising from somewhere in the east. Soon, she pictured a terrific skein of Egyptian geese flying toward her. *Yes, at any moment, perhaps one of the wild geese will come fluttering past my face. Yes, the creature's almost here.* At last, something like a gentle, airy spirit sailed past the tip of her nose—and she nearly lost her footing. 'Oh, what was that?' she asked.

'Just a little blue butterfly,' Dalrymple answered.

'*Un papillon.*' Gently swaying, she pictured the rabble buzzing all about the Sicilian wild. Instinctively, she envisioned them as bearing a resemblance to the blue butterflies that dwell atop Mount Tarboosh in Sinai. A few of the troublesome creatures landed on the nape of her neck, and it felt as if they intended to nibble away at her flesh.

Mr Dalrymple brushed the two butterflies away, and then he fussed with the topcoat so that the soft warm collar might better preserve her. Shortly, they continued to the left and into a thicket. 'Up ahead, there's a faint pathway,' Dalrymple told her. 'Maybe a herd of Sicilian deer left it behind. Who knows?' He guided her along, and in time, stopped her and shifted her body a touch to the right. 'Cheers. You've reached the witch hazel bough. Not two feet away. What a beautiful crown, too.'

A rabble of butterflies darting about her scalp, she dropped her walking stick to the side and advanced a little bit further into the windswept thicket. As the current continued to rattle the witch hazel tree, a few of the boughs scraped her wrist and forearm. She knelt and felt for one of the witch hazel tree's roots, where it dipped into the creamy Sicilian clay.

More and more butterflies swarmed all about, meanwhile. They nibbled at her ankles, continued up her gown, and nibbled at her thighs. Soon, she even felt the fine metallic dust of the butterflies' wings sprinkling down her legs.

Mr Dalrymple clapped his hands. 'No more dawdling,' he called out. 'Take one of the sacred boughs. Go on, girl.'

'But I can't. You've got me feeling so embarrassed with all this melodrama. I feel a little bit like I'm in a picture show playing in some cinema house. Maybe even Strasbourg's *Palais de l'Europe*.'

'But what does any of that matter?' Twice, Mr Dalrymple clapped his hands. 'Take one of the forked boughs. Go on.

She rubbed her aching belly. *Maybe I've only imagined the malady. Maybe it's just my loneliness, the longing for love.* She clambered to her feet, reached up with both hands, and wrapped both palms around the first jagged, swaying limb she felt.

The winds shrieked, as if nature itself could not countenance the notion that a presumptuous mortal might think to arm herself with a weapon so formidable.

She let go, and for a moment or two contented herself to swat some of the butterflies fluttering about her nose. Then she felt for Mr Dalrymple's arm and hand. 'Why does your rival wish to prevent us from finding the buried treasure down there in Sinai? Would he be loyal to all those spiritualists back at Westminster?.

'Who knows?'

'I think you ought to tell me. Yes, and if someone would be stalking me, don't I have a right to know how much peril I'd be in just now? Might your rival be *mad*? Would *that* explain why she fears these boughs? She does believe in their supposed power, yes?.

Mr Dalrymple snickered like a sadistic little boy. 'Yes, so take one. What better way to affright her? Go on, and take any bough you wish.

Anastasia reached up and wrapped both palms around what felt like the same bough from before. She felt the flutter of a butterfly as it passed by, and when it bumped up against her left ear lobe, she paused to imagine the array of shimmery, turquoise-blue dust from the creature's wing presently sprinkled about there. Holding her breath then, she snapped the bough from the rest of the tree.

From beyond the tree, footsteps approached, and the scent of Egyptian chamomile grew almost overwhelming.

'I suppose we shall have to be quite vigilant from now on,' a woman spoke in an oddly sedate tone. 'Yes, yes. You've become all so *powerful*.'

Anastasia intuited the speaker to be the nun, for what other kind of woman ever spoke in such a tranquil tone? *Yes, and now we're standing face to face.* From somewhere out across the mountains, a rumble awoke—but Anastasia refused to give in to fear. *There must be a good explanation.* She presumed the racket to be nothing more than Sicily's famed Syracuse Railway rolling along.

'You shouldn't trust Dalrymple,' the nun continued, as if he weren't even there. 'Do you remember Rupert, the chap down in Cairo?'

'What about him?'

'Don't let anyone introduce you to the Kiwi. No, no. You can't trust him. For all you know, he's working for someone a thousand times worse than Dalrymple.'

Anastasia's heart skipped a beat. Rupert. *Maybe he's my Robert le Diable. What a joy it'd be to finally meet poor Rupert.* She giggled, feeling like a foolish little girl.

Forcefully, Dalrymple grabbed Anastasia's arm and pulled her along. 'Let's get back to the ship,' he said. 'Won't be long till we dock at Alexandria. By mid-November or thereabouts, we'll be in Cairo. Won't that be lovely?.

She did not answer. *Rupert.* She held the mighty bough up against her chest—until the forked end pulsated with life, something like a serpent's tongue. *Oh, my salvation.*

VII.

Cairo. 23 November 1919.

At teatime, Rupert opened his door to find Maud waiting there—the peculiar Irishwoman offering an empathetic smile.

'Anastasia should be here soon,' Maud told him. 'What fun. I just know everything should be perfect. Anyone else, he'd probably be disarming. Not you, though. You seem so trustworthy and so dependable and so *accepting*.'

'Perhaps you ought to find someone else,' he told the Irishwoman.

'*No*,' Maud insisted. 'You're already here. Why send to East Indies for pippins? As soon as Anastasia arrives in Cairo, I'll bring her to the hotel.'

He found himself torn. If he were to defile Anastasia or to manipulate her somehow, what might the consequences entail? He knew there would be a price to pay. *Nothing that sounds as simple as Maud's scheme could ever be as easy as she makes it out to be—no, no, no.* Something terrible was bound to happen. If nothing else, the zealous woman in the cartwheel hat, Miss Fitzroy, would stick a knife in his back.

On the other hand, Rupert dreaded the idea of denying Maud. If he were to rebuff her, what kind of reprisal might she and her contacts be capable of?

When the Irishwoman darted off, he lumbered back into his little room and, for a time, contemplated the sunlight shining a vibrant shade of red across his wall. *So, what do I do? I've got to decide. Once and for all.* He pictured Anastasia. In silence, he studied her imagined presence—the aggrieved young lady lurching blindly all about.

With a tortured yelp, the maniacal dæmon recommenced his shrill chanting—its voice buzzing throughout Rupert's right eyeball.

Could Maud help me put an end to the torment? Once he had helped her to spirit away whatever treasures Anastasia might locate, perhaps Maud Havelock did know some way to banish the dæmon—just as the woman had promised. *So, do I take Maud's offer? Maybe.*

At five o'clock, he travelled out to the Gyzeh Plateau to mull things over and to come to a final decision. *The pyramids—that'd be the perfect place to search my weary soul.* He reached the ancient necropolis at dusk, the sky shining the colour of amaranth streaked with ribbons of tangerine. *Gyzeh. There's no place like it.*

The dæmon revolving around inside his eyeball seemed to agree. As if overawed by the sheer spectacle of the Great Pyramids, the spirit fell silent. The lull felt like a revelation. For a time, Rupert revelled in the soft sounds of nature—the interplay between the whistle of the breeze and the purring of a little cat that had concealed itself in the shadows. As the cat's soft drone grew increasingly affectionate, he advanced along a rocky, uneven pathway that took him past a brick *mastaba*.

He stopped in his tracks; up ahead, the Great Sphinx loomed. What impossible beauty: the whole of the monument, its imperturbable visage, its wings and tail and right hind paw, too, shone the colour of bright gold Turkish coffee.

The purring grew a little bit louder. Could it be some feral cat wandering about? If so, had it espied some toothsome songbird? Rupert doubted it. *The purring sounds too gentle and hypnotic.* When the thrum ceased, he refocused on the Great Sphinx. *Go on.* A moment later, when he reached the narrow shrine between the beast's long, grandiose legs, he paused to study the crumbling visage—the jumble of pockmarks where the proud god's nose should have been. *Chin up, uncle.*

With a soft snort and a dry cough and hoarse whistle, too, the purring returned—but this time it sounded almost human: a sustained, troubled, heartfelt murmur.

For a moment, Rupert tapped on the stone altar on his immediate left. *I feel like a bloody fool.* The purring he heard started to resemble laughter, the kind a virtuous woman might produce with her eyes gleaming. He fixed his gaze on the Sphinx, on its eyes. What did the marvellous god descry as it crouched there? Rupert flicked a bit of dust from his coat and marched forward, only to stop before that mysterious tablet hewn into the creature's breast: the Dream Stele. He had read about the remarkable artefact in some of the books strewn about the lobby back at the Hotel Ibis. From the beginning of time, the Dream Stele had provided the Sphinx with the power and wisdom to rule its dominions. Rupert grew still now, for the sacred tablet filled him with wonder. Soon enough, he could swear he found himself in the presence of someone great—a seer. *Yes, a prophetess.* He studied his surroundings and shot a glance this way and that, but found himself alone. *How could it be?* He became lost in reverie and imagined a fine lady emerging from the shadows—a woman of station, a woman emboldened by the ancient Egyptian gods themselves. *Anastasia! Anastasia.*

If she were there, she would advance into the ruins of the Old Kingdom solar temple confined within the paws of the Great Sphinx. At the moment when she knelt on the alabaster floor, her tea gown would serve to reveal her exquisite figure— her long legs and the ideal curves of her hips and thighs and backside. Still, her big blue eyes, if in fact they shone that colour, would gaze off into space—as only the blind do.

He pulled in a deep breath, held it, and continued into the temple. Only when he reached one of the cracked limestone pillars did he permit himself to exhale. *If she were here, I'm sure she would have heard my footsteps.*

How intimidating the seer's presence would be. Perhaps she would discern the fact he must be a hoaxer, a deceiver, a confidence trickster who conspires with dodgy Irishwomen to prey on some unsuspecting soul. Surely, Anastasia would be cross with him. 'New lamps for old,' she might whisper, her head tipping back.

The tips of his toes tingling, he cringed and looked at his feet. Then, as he lurched back to the stone altar, the sky darkened—and a patch of clouds burning the colour of brightest cinnabar invaded the sky. At last, the clouds burst open with a ghost rain. With no better option, he dashed off into the ruins of the solar temple and lay on the alabaster floor. How good the cool smooth stone felt against his back.

The purring grew even louder—until the gentle hypnotic sound came to resemble the mesmerising rumble of a distant locomotive. *That's right, a train in the distance.* He closed his eyes and imagined himself riding on the night train to Luxor. *Resting his back on a divan in the smoking car, he listens to the train rolling along the roadbed. Soon, though, he finds himself eavesdropping on a trio: a corporal of horse and a lance sergeant entertaining Anastasia herself. Later, as the night train pulls into Luxor station, Rupert follows the party all the way down the pebbled promenade to the Temple of Karnak, where the rude British soldiers disguise themselves with stucco Egyptian death masks and gambol about ... as if the suppression of their identities has liberated them from all shame and inhibition. And they tell one barefaced lie after the next until Anastasia willingly undresses for them and ...*

The purring ceased, and Rupert opened his eyes. One last drop of soft dreamlike rain fell on his face. He raised his hand and slicked back his dark hair. The dæmon's Oceanic chant rang out anew, but not before the corner of his right eye espied just what it was that had made the cat purr so fervently. Amid the debris littering the solar temple lay the bloodied remains of a Nile Valley sunbird.

A little while later. At nightfall.

As Rupert arrived back in the city and stepped out of a taxicab in Ramses Square, he sensed someone coming up behind him. Maud Havelock stopped not three feet away and sighed in satisfaction. 'I'm so glad to have found you. Promise you'll help me.'

'What about this *bashi-bazouk* dæmon inside my eye?' he asked. 'Are you quite certain you've got the power to drive it away?'

'You've no cause to doubt my powers,' Maud told him, acting perfectly sincere as she stroked her own forearm. 'To be sure, I've never told a fib my whole life long.'

Over to the side, an elderly Egyptian minstrel took up his

goatskin bagpipe and broke into a tune—a song of protest, a number popular with the revolutionaries. Rupert paused to consider the political matters of the day, and holding his hands over his ears, marched across the crowded square, the Irishwoman following him into the desolate bazaar. The early evening breeze stirred some of the silver lanterns dangling from the lampposts, and as the lanterns chimed softly, the current swirled all about a badly cracked earthen pot filled with sprouted grain. He studied the damaged pot until the bagpipes died down. He dropped his hands to his hips and looked around. Maud had vanished. *So be it.* He crept through the marketplace and breathed in the aromas lingering in the air—fig paste and mint and fresh lemon *couscous.* Finally, he stopped, then spun around. Blinking rapidly, he studied the badly cracked earthen pot once more. Even without the damage, he could not imagine anyone paying more than fifty *piastres* for such a piece. Still, how truly priceless an item like that would be—if it held the power to imprison a genie, an evil spirit. *That's right, an evil spirit like the diabolical being that dwells inside my eye.* He shook his head. *Oh, to experience the breath of freedom.*

While heading back to the Hotel Ibis, Rupert felt someone approach from behind and press what seemed to be the barrel of a pistol against his spine. He did not have to glance over his shoulder to know who it was, so he stared straight ahead and fixed his gaze on a broken-down British motor buggy. 'You've got no reason to fear me any,' he managed to say. 'Let me face you, and we'll talk this over, and maybe you and me could come to terms.'

'Don't look back.' As she spoke, she did not even attempt to disguise her voice. 'If you look back, I'll shoot you here and now.' With the barrel, she tapped his spine. 'Did you ever read any of those dime novels from America? I got me a revolver just like the one Belle Starr always carried on her hip. Calamity Jane, too. And Annie Oakley for that matter. Weapons far more powerful than witch hazel boughs.'

'Go easy, Miss Fitzroy.' His eyes darted this way and that. Soon enough, someone would come along and notice the pistol in the crazed woman's hand. She must have been thinking the same thing, because she compelled him to continue slowly into the alley on the left. The darkened passage reeked of mashed fava beans and raw sewage, and at the end of the narrow corridor, an emaciated cat lay dead amid a heap of rubbish.

'What's the meaning of this?' Rupert asked, struggling to convince himself the maniacal woman had not even loaded the weapon.

Miss Fitzroy tapped his spine again. 'Something of great import happened while you were out and about this fine evening.'

'Oh? What's that?'

'Anastasia checked into the Hotel Ibis,' Miss Fitzroy told him in an oddly detached tone of voice. 'So, how do you suppose you'll seek to entice her? Do you mean to play a part in the poor girl's undoing? Do you think she'd favour the bold rebellious type?'

Hoping it did not make him appear indifferent, Rupert shrugged. 'Maybe it'd be impossible to deceive a young woman like Anastasia. She's a clever one, no?.

'Yes. I'd say she's wise enough to fathom the genius of solar monotheism. Still, that's not what brings the damsel here. No, she's got busy work to do.'

'So, perhaps I ought to decline Maud Havelock's offer.' Rupert attempted to face Miss Fitzroy, but she hissed like an angry crocodile.

Miss Fitzroy pressed the barrel harder against his back, inhaling sharply. 'Here's how you'll entice Anastasia. Tell her you killed *me*. *Yes*. Tell her you dispatched a woman who unnerved you. Yes, you shot me down. Just like Jesse James always does in those penny dreadfuls. Once she hears about your manly resolve, she'll pine for you. Just like all those strange desperate women who fall in love with whatever brute is wasting away down at the jailhouse.'

Rupert drew himself up to his full height and advanced all the way to the end of the alley. Looking down, he paused before the lifeless cat.

Miss Fitzroy whistled. 'What if Anastasia happens to be ill-favoured, uncomely? What if she's not even bedworthy?.

Again, he shrugged. What else could he do? A moment later, when he mustered enough courage to shoot a glance in Miss Fitzroy's direction, the woman in the cartwheel hat raised the pistol. She clearly called on her dominant eye to help her to take aim, too. Not once did her dominant hand tremble. Nor the non-dominant one, for that matter. *I'm going to perish tonight? No, it can't be. No.* He squeezed his eyes shut. When he opened his eyes, he wondered if he might say something. Speechless, he slipped his hands into his pockets.

'Hands in evidence,' Miss Fitzroy told him—and when he raised his arms and spread his palms, she cocked the hammer. 'I've got me a Russian pepper-pot revolver in my hand. Don't make me use it, eh?'

His arms growing heavy, he looked to his feet. 'Are we playing some kind of game?' he asked.

'Yes,' she answered. 'I'd be the assassin, and you'd be the wicked prince. Wicked as anyone who ever schemed to colonise bonny ole Egypt, Mother of the World.'

His arms drooping increasingly more, Rupert longed to rub at a faint itch that nagged him at the back of his neck—but he did not dare. *Run. I've got to run. Go.* He could not bring himself to do it, and he struggled to keep his arms up.

'What do you suppose your sin ought to be?' Miss Fitzroy asked. 'A wicked prince must be guilty of something especial.'

'I have no answer for you.'

'What about Marxism? Could it be you've been teaching the Egyptian revolutionaries the propaganda that says Marxism will guide the way? Or what about isolationism? Just like those chaps in the House of Lords, maybe you'd be the kind who wishes to tell everyone all about how nativism and narrowmindedness will guide us to prosperity. *No.* I know your sin. Maybe you believe in nation building. Yes, you'd be the wicked prince, the kind who thinks everyone ought to gladly emulate England once we colonise them and bog their own way of life.' At last, Miss Fitzroy pulled the trigger—but she sent the round directly into the body of the dead cat lying not far from where Rupert stood. Afterward, the maniacal woman stepped back and vanished into the gathering fog.

Late that night.

Back at the Hotel Ibis, Rupert reported to the reception desk for his shift—and at first, things went by uneventfully. For a time, he contented himself to polish the service bell.

Over at the billiard table, a glassy-eyed woman from Australia played against one of the locals. After the game, they climbed into the passenger lift and retired to her room. Other than that, there was no sign of life—no sign of the famed Anastasia. For Rupert's part, he could not stop thinking about her. Indeed, he could not think straight. The fabric of time itself

92

seemed to have slowed to a fantastically ponderous pace, as if God Almighty had ordained the thirty minutes left before midnight to take five hours to pass by.

Soon, the passenger lift brought the comely young lady into the lobby. How to mistake her? For one thing, Anastasia's unseeing eyes looked right through him. What perfect, fine golden hair, too. She resembled either a priestess or prophetess on the one hand and an erotic apparition on the other.

Arising from the reception desk, he studied her perfect figure and then returned his gaze to her face. To be certain, the young lady's blindness augmented her beauty. Indeed, the dreamlike expression in her big blue blinded eyes made her seem angelic, incorruptible, invulnerable. Had she pledged her body to the Lord above? Might that be the source of her supposed power? She did seem impossibly wise.

Outside, the wind gained strength, and as the boughs of the winter-thorn tree tapped against the window, Anastasia placed her right hand over her left breast. Did the remarkable young woman wish to feel the pounding of her heart? Perfectly poised, she strode along effortlessly to the lobby sofa, as if someone had told her the precise number of steps it would take for her to reach it.

As she sat down, Rupert found himself speechless and spellbound. He could not take his eyes off her face. How adorable she looked, how innocent and how childlike, too. But she seemed bold, too—the kind of woman who did not regret anything about her features and would neither enhance nor transform any aspect of her body, even if she could.

Her lips moved now. 'I'm moving toward the essence,' she seemed to whisper, as if that made any sense.

He shook his head. *Why'd she say that?* Without even thinking, he drew close and gazed into her visionless eyes.

What if she's pledged her body to the heavens above? He held his breath awhile. *If she's a pious woman, would anyone have enough charm to undo the vow?* He breathed out a bit and cleared his throat. 'Hello, Your Ladyship.'

'Your Ladyship? You flatter me. So, what's your name?'

'I'm Rupert. I'm the night clerk around here.'

'I am Anastasia.' No sooner had she uttered her Christian name than she held her palms upward and raised her blissful eyes and face—as if for no other reason than to expose her neck. 'Anastasia T. Grace,' she continued.

Down the hallway, from inside one of the tenant's rooms, a gramophone stirred to life and played a recording of Ottoman-Court music: a trio of minstrels plucking three long-necked lutes. She kicked her heels back and sat up straight—then curled up. There could be no doubt the music pleased her. Looking exceedingly calm, she fussed with her necklace. 'Have you noticed my Huguenot cross and pendant dove?' she asked.

'I was wondering what that was.' He peered deep into her blind eyes. The young lady sitting before him embodied everything any gentleman could want: innocence, beauty, virtue. In addition, Anastasia displayed not even the faintest trace of frigidity. He had no reason to believe she could ever show a judgemental nature or prove herself to be some kind of scold. *No, not her. Not a female like this. She's a woman to cherish, this one.*

Down the hallway, the exotic music continued to play— and she rocked from side to side. The longer he watched, the more inferior he felt. *What affectations might impress a girl like Anastasia?* He revisited his youth. In those days, he had always known to act indifferent, not too eager. And as he made his way through whatever reception, he would speak to the lustful females as if they were puritanical—and he would speak to the puritanical women as if they were profoundly depraved. His habit of doing so had always made the young ladies laugh, and most had regarded him as quite charming indeed. He retreated; flirtatious speech with Anastasia felt impossible. *No, no, no. Not this one.* He scratched his cheek. Had he ever encountered a woman so godlike? Deceiving her would be a challenge, he realised, as she was obviously wise. If he contented himself to merely tell Anastasia what she wanted to hear, she would perceive his deceit.

The gramophone ceased to play, and the hotel lobby grew quiet but for a nightingale's courtship song whistling from somewhere outside. *Or could it be a black swan?* A year ago, he had heard one calling out from the direction of the river.

Feeling defeated, he trudged back to the reception desk, checked the clock on the wall, and gasped. *Already, it's one o'clock in the morning.* Confused, he could not decide if he ought to register a sense of despondency or fury. *I've got to collect myself. Yes, but how?* With a sigh, he wandered downstairs and stepped outside. As he looked up and down the street, an aging prostitute approached and said something in Russian. He averted his gaze. 'Why do you trifle? I got scruples. I'll not profane my body vaulting with a charity dame like you. Hell, no.'

She flashed a malevolent glare and cursed him. He stood tall. *Don't get filled with pride.* He placed his right hand on his hip and strutted away from her. Then he turned back toward her. 'Aren't you a bit old as well? And *you* wish to cock a leg? That'd raise a laugh.' The prostitute grimaced in the most petulant manner and turned to a figure concealed by the mist and held forth, as if to protest the unforgivable outrage.

He soon felt embarrassed by his own conduct. *What's*

come over me? In an instant, he returned inside. *Might as well go back upstairs.* When he reached the hotel lobby, he studied Anastasia anew. In that moment, she pressed down on her right breastbone—as if she worried that it jutted out a touch too much. Rupert could not turn away, for Georgie had always done that, too: the poor wretch had always felt tormented by the asymmetry between his jagged right breastbone and his flattened left. *Poor little Georgie.*

Slowly, Anastasia rose from the sofa. She felt her way forward until she reached the heart of the lobby. There, she trussed the walking stick up against the billiard table and felt at her hips. *Did she fear they might be imperfect?* Again, Rupert thought of Georgie. He had always feared his hips were much too rounded and maidenly. Rupert recalled a fortnight's holiday up along the Bay of Plenty. One breezy night, he and Georgie had run down to the beach to gambol about with a harem of leopard seals—until a spiteful, mean-spirited girl emerged from behind a dead chinaberry tree. For a moment, the cruel little girl studied the outline of Georgie's body as revealed by his moonlit nightshirt.

'You've got an hourglass shape to your figure,' the girl finally told him. 'How should that be? Are you a collar and a cuff? Only girls should have curves like yours.' Her eyes glazed over, and she laughed at him in the most sadistic manner.

In the end, Rupert patted Georgie's back to show solidarity with him—but no sooner had Rupert done so than Georgie had melted into tears.

Rupert checked his timepiece now. Though the dawn remained a long way off, he strode over to the reception desk to check his papers and to determine how many people he needed to awaken for the excursion to Gyzeh. *Only three.* He twitched his pencil moustache and glanced back at Anastasia.

'*Réminiscences,*' she seemed to whisper. How enthralling that the beautiful young woman seemed to be mouthing the words to such a poetic, enigmatic, melancholy word. For the longest time, he studied her. *What's up with you, then?* Her expression wholly inscrutable, he could not discern what the young lady might be thinking or feeling in that moment. *Speak up and say something.*

She felt her way back to the passenger lift, and when she climbed inside, returned to her room—or so it seemed.

His shift continued without incident—and when the British chap came to work the desk for the early-morning shift, Rupert returned to his room to sleep. Not surprisingly, Anastasia invaded his dreams. He envisioned the beautiful blind woman travelling as a stowaway aboard that glorious steamship, the *Empress of Ireland. As the vessel pulls away from Saint Peter Port, Anastasia appears at the bow. And as the ship approaches the coast of Québec, Anastasia flies off to the stern and waves to him and .*

He awoke in a pool of sweat. Why had she appeared in the vision? Could it be his unconscious mind hoped to forestall the temptation to enter into some kind of arrangement with the conniving Maud Havelock? Whatever the case, he changed the bedsheet and curled up yet again. In time, the dream returned and the vision grew increasingly vivid and steadily more harrowing. *And Father's business contact, Mr Impérial, appears aboard the vessel and fans himself the way the elders do back home during the torrid days of January.*

By the time Rupert finally awoke, he had willed himself to forget all—including those details pertaining to the villainous Mr Impérial. For a time, Rupert strained to remember what it was that had so gripped him during his slumber. He wondered if it might have been a nightmare involving the

Sphinx. Gently, almost imperceptibly, someone knocked on the jamb—and when he opened his door, he bumped into Anastasia. Without saying a word, she raised her hand and felt at his cheek—the bony arch beneath his left eye. Soon, the impossibly graceful woman placed her hand over the left aspect of his chest. Her gentle touch felt miraculous. *Like the laying on of hands.* For a moment, he even wondered if he tasted something sweet on the tip of his tongue—a little drop of rosewater lemonade.

'Years ago, your pen friend from Westminster mentioned your name in one of her letters,' he finally spoke up.

'Yes, of course. And Miss Lambshead told me all about *you*. That's right. She told me all about the Polynesian spirit inside you. Perhaps I could help you overcome all the trouble. Do you know what I think? I think your fears of possession betray some kind of repressed memory, the remembrance of childhood trauma.'

The sweet taste on his tongue held steady, and he pitied Anastasia in a way he had never pitied anyone before. Until this moment, he had always believed a woman of fine beauty must possess incalculable social power—that she herself determined the very course of sexual selection. Now he realised his error. As he stared into Anastasia's big blue blinded eyes, he understood that a young lady may decide only among those inclined to make a play for her and not necessarily the ones she might fancy. *A beautiful woman is not spoiled for choice at all.* Feeling guilty, he eyed her hand and counted the perfect little freckles dotting her wrist.

Anastasia dropped her hand from his chest. What an impressive young lady. Though there could be no doubt she felt something for him, in no way did she act like a foolish lovesick little girl. On the contrary, she held herself like something strong and wise: a princess.

Outside, the streets rumbled with the noise of revolution—an agitator's rallying cries, the report of a rifle, the blast of an explosion. Still, he did not dwell on the troubles. *I think I'm in love.*

VIII.

The wilderness of Sinai. 2 December 1919.

Early that morning, Anastasia refused to exit her tent. She longed to return to the hotel. As the desert wind beat down on the tarp, she read some of the Moon-script books Mr Dalrymple had bestowed on her during the voyage from Sicily. The books did nothing to raise her spirits. From the moment she had arrived at the archaeological preserve, she had hoped Rupert might come to join her. *But why would he do that?* The more she pined for him, the more anxious she felt. Even worse, the way Mr Dalrymple endeavoured to ingratiate himself with the rest of the expedition made her suspect him increasingly more. Did he have some ulterior motive in bringing her here, and just what did the shameless charlatan expect her to find? *And if I do find it, does Mr Dalrymple mean to claim it for his various associates? What if I'm tried as a thief, and what if my fate turns on testimony provided by him? Why wouldn't he betray me?*

She had heard so much about Rupert—and the fact that he was acquainted with Dalrymple seemed to prove how ideal

Dalrymple must be. In addition, she realised she had so many all-too-real villains to contend with of late—specifically the condescending scholars manning the expedition. There could be no avoiding such feelings of contempt, because from the moment she had arrived here, the haughty Oxford men had insulted her at every turn. Each one disbelieved in the art of dowsing, and they scoffed at the notion she might someday stumble on anything of value.

She traced her fingertips across a Moon-script edition containing various landmark essays in Egyptology, and then she paused. *Has something gone wrong?* She placed the book beneath her pillow, lifted the mosquito netting, and climbed out of her camp bed. *Something has changed.* As she endeavoured to concentrate, she realised what had happened: the winter breeze had died down, and an impossible stillness had commenced. She slipped out of her housecoat and changed into a pair of worsted-wool trousers along with a linen blouse and matching *gilet*. Then she felt for the hatbox in which she kept a fine straw hat with a high crown. When she ventured outside, she cocked her ear. The desert seemed to have transformed into the lifeless landscape of some other, uninhabited world. No desert breeze stirred, and not a grain of sand shifted. Given the absolute hush, she half-expected to hear the rumble of the Hejaz Railway bellowing out all the way from the Arabian Peninsula. *Wait for it. Here it comes.* She heard no such thing, so she listened for any sign of life—perhaps the call of a desert lynx. *No, I hear nothing.* At the very least, she should have heard the everyday sounds of breakfast preparations coming from the neighbouring Bedouin encampment—a whistling kettle, perhaps. *But no.* She breathed in. *There's no scent in the air.* Full of mistrust, she shook her head. Given where she was, she should have detected the sweet scent of nature all around her. For that matter, she should have felt a ray of sunlight on the bridge of her nose. *What's happened to me?.*

With his distinctive-sounding, laboured gait, Mr Dalrymple came along. 'Hello, love. So, shall we brave the wild and find the treasures today?.'

She hushed him. 'Don't you feel that peculiar stillness in the air? God, it feels like the whole world must be a dream. What's gone wrong?.'

'What stillness?.'

She listened as Dalrymple shuffled off across the sand and heard the crunch of the desert beneath his feet as he returned to her side.

'I feel the desert breeze just fine,' he said.

She patted her trouser pockets and debated whether she ought to duck back into her tent to collect her witch hazel bough. *No, just go.* Though she most certainly required the witch hazel bough, she let the strange stillness itself guide her. *Yes, onward.* She lurched forward. Before long, she found herself far from the encampment. *Perhaps a mile and a half to the north, maybe even farther.* Her feet aching, she stopped and lowered her blind eyes to the earth. 'Where are we anyway?' she said. 'Out past the turquoise mines?'

'No, not at all,' Mr Dalrymple answered. 'We've been inching southbound. Can't you feel the sea breeze?'

In that moment, she should have felt a steady, salty current flowing all throughout her fringe. Oddly enough, she felt only the ongoing stillness. 'I don't feel any sea breeze at all,' she half-whispered. From no more than a half mile away, the triumphal peal of a clock tower rang out. She recognised the copper bell's booming, warlike voice. *The citadel.* For the first time, she grasped the close proximity between the archaeological preserve and the wondrous village where she had once made her home. Her hand over her left breast, she thought back to the lovelorn youth who had been so obsessed with her back in those days. *What was his name?*

Mr Dalrymple nudged her hip. 'We've got company. A band of English soldiers. They're marching down through the sand dunes up ahead, Egyptian charger and all.'

Anastasia heard a clatter of footsteps as the soldiers drew close, followed by the unmistakable bray of the ammunition mule.

'Don't come around here,' one of the soldiers announced. 'We've got loads of revolutionaries hiding in the village just beyond these here badlands.

'They're protesting the British occupation?' Mr Dalrymple asked, obviously feigning ignorance.

'That's right,' the same soldier answered. 'And each revolutionary in town, he's a bleeding deadly one. Two weeks ago, they killed a couple of English ladies from the mirror-making society.'

'The mirror-making society?' Her belly churning, Anastasia recalled the time she had worked there. Something in the compounds with which she had polished the mirrors, some element, some chemical, had brought on her blindness. Anastasia raised her hand now. 'What's become of Ernesztina?' *Maybe she could speak with the revolutionaries,* she thought. *I'm sure she always revered the Egyptian people. Yes, and maybe by now she might've learned what caused my blindness. Something in the compounds with which I'd polished the mirrors, perhaps. Some element, some chemical. If so, maybe she could help me to see again.*

The ammunition mule snorted and charged forward, only to stop and pound its hooves. Though tense at the beast's agitation, Anastasia reached for its forelock. *Why not hold the poor creature close? I'll console him, yes.* Her affectionate embrace notwithstanding, the restless mule did not quiet down. Instead, the creature kicked and grazed her ribs with one of its hooves. She sought to scramble out of harm's way, only to feel the beast's powerful shoulder strike her hard in the temple. As she fell to the earth, the sensation of absolute stillness returned as powerfully as ever. Someone knelt by her side. 'Anastasia, do you hear me? Say something!' She thought the voice belonged to Mr Dalrymple, though she could not be sure with all the ongoing commotion. The ammunition mule brayed, and the soldiers rushed this way and that, the clump of their boots adding to the racket. Her temple growing numb, Anastasia curled up into a ball and clasped her fingers loosely near her neck. *Sleep.*

Someone, Mr Dalrymple perhaps, grabbed her left shoulder and shook her. 'Don't lose consciousness, love. Try to be strong. Stay awake.'

Like a little girl, she giggled. 'No, go away.'

A second time, Mr Dalrymple shook her. Afterward, he moved her onto her back and slapped her across her face.

As she laughed anew, someone or other must have finally succeeded in taking back the ammunition mule's reins. Then, as the braying died down, she felt a drop of sweet water on her tongue—Mr Dalrymple was holding his drinking flask to her lips. Choking a little, she reached up and pushed his hand away.

'You must drink,' he told her. 'We've got to make progress. Do you hear? We've got to find the great treasures.'

'No, let me sleep,' she whispered, rolling onto her side. She pictured the diadem spider deep inside her womb. 'Well, then, you do you realise what you've done? You spooked the donkey. Because of you, that ass almost killed me.

All around her, meanwhile, a flurry of activity unfolded—the frantic soldiers squabbling over which one ought to run off to alert the medics. At last, someone agreed to do it, and the sound of his footsteps grew fainter as he trailed off.

She passed in and out of consciousness. From time to time, she heard fragments of conversation. On and on, the soldiers spoke of the revolutionaries and debated all the ongoing unrest in both Egypt and Sudan. After a while, she could not help but laugh—the proud soldiers seemed powerless to grasp why someone might wish to be free of the British Empire. When the talk finally quieted down, Mr Dalrymple shook her yet again. 'Come to, love.' For all that, she could not keep her eyes open a moment longer. *I think I'll go to sleep.* Laughing softly, she imagined herself a fallen Egyptian lotus petal. *Oh yes, that's what I am.* In no time, she became lost in dreams. *Ah, woe. I'm all tangled up in a diadem spider's web.*

That night, the medics stopped by Anastasia's tent to check on her condition and to test whether she had lost her memory. When they finally departed, she lifted the mosquito netting and climbed out of her rickety camp bed. Dizzy, she swayed back and forth—and just as she had felt the peculiar stillness earlier in the day, she felt it yet again now. *How could that be? What power had the desert.* Hungry, she felt for the tin of clotted cream she had placed on the wooden crate standing in for a night table—but the spread had long turned sour.

From somewhere outside, a violin shrieked out two barre chords.

Professor Milne. With the help of her walking stick, she made her way through the tent flap and along the dusty winding path down to the palm grove—the place where the field director had pitched his tent.

As she drew close, he ceased with the music. 'How about a pint of mahogany?' he asked her. 'A good strong spirit should make you feel better.'

She imagined him pointing his violin bow at a bottle lying beside his safari chair, and she shook her head. 'Not on your life, sir.' The palm grove grew quiet, and she pictured the professor sitting in his chair and applying a touch of rosin to his bow.

'Tell me about your powers,' the professor said after a while. 'Do you honestly believe you might someday locate something buried around here?'

'I have no answer for you. No, it's impossible to say. For that matter, today has been so *trying*. Something's gone wrong. As if I've lost all my senses.' For a moment or two, Anastasia considered the possibility she had fallen in love with Rupert—as if something like that might explain all the trouble. 'It's a funny feeling,' she continued. 'I feel so lost.

'Nevertheless, Mr Dalrymple says you wield remarkable powers. "There's almost no limit to what she might accomplish," he tells me.'

The way Professor Milne spoke at that moment, Anastasia detected a tone of irony and sardonicism. She felt insulted and turned on her heels. Counting her steps, she strode back in the direction of her tent.

The breeze played softly through the palms, and Professor Milne returned to his night piece.

Though it might have been nothing more than an effect of her head injury, she stopped before the flap and wondered if she ought to mistrust everyone here in Sinai. The violin music grew into a sad waltz, and she swayed awhile.

The wilderness of Sinai. 8 December 1919.

From the moment Anastasia awoke that morning, she could tell the injury to her right temple had healed. Not only did the bruise throb much less, she no longer found herself feeling muddled and unsure of herself. After a while, she pushed the mosquito netting away and dropped her feet onto the earthen floor. *Yes, I'm doing a whole lot better.* She felt here and there for her tweed coat and then slipped it over her nightdress. Yawning, she made her way through the tent flap and out into the warmth of the desert sun.

From all directions, a nightmarish stillness unnerved her. *Why do I keep having this same uncanny sensation?*

She heard a band of loud, haughty Oxford scholars happen by, and before she had a chance to duck back inside, they greeted her in their usual irreverent tone. As they laughed and jeered, they disguised their educated accents and spoke like commoners—to suggest that Anastasia was no better. Finally, one of the scholars drew close. 'Feeling better today, are you? Do you think today you might discover something for us? What about some right fine storehouse? Yes, you'll find us an ancient granary filled with ancient coins, little coins of electrum, enough to pay off all our excise taxes for ten years or more.

'No, she's bound to draw the crow, aye, because of all them diabolical spirits buzzing about out here in the wild,' a second fellow spoke up. 'I'd say them spirits have our poor girl feeling neither fish nor flesh.'

'What does any of that matter?' a third fellow asked. 'Kindly remember, they also serve those who only laze about. And no one's better at lazing about than our pious Christian maid here.'

As a fourth Oxford scholar gave her a mock lecture, her chest caved. When the band of scholars sauntered off, she ducked back into her tent and collected the witch hazel bough. As she tapped her foot, she gripped the forked end with both hands. *I'll show them.* When she went outside, she tucked the bough up beneath her left arm. *Which way do I go?* Counting out quietly, she inched her way off in the direction of the palace. The modest journey did not take long, for Mr Dalrymple had already told her how many footsteps it would take her. Moreover, he had told her what landmarks awaited her at the various points in the numbering of her steps. *And just like that, I'm here. At the ancient palace.* She held her breath awhile before leaning in toward the place where the entranceway should have been.

The desert breeze whistled through the maze of fluted columns, emphasising the barrenness of the structure—and how hopeless her cause. *Hopeless?* With the tip of her right index finger, she touched and caressed the little pendant dove dangling from her beloved Huguenot cross. *Pray help me.*

A great miracle should have happened then. A voice should have told her what to do or where to dig for the treasure, but no such voice spoke. Languidly, the desert breeze blew through her tweed coat—nothing more. She tapped the witch hazel bough against her thigh and pictured the vast ruined palace, indeed the whole of the archaeological preserve, stretching out before her. Given the seemingly absolute lifelessness of her surroundings, she could not imagine anything that might accord with what she knew of Egyptology. Before long, she contented herself to contemplate the silence itself. And the uncanny calm played on both her stream of conscious and unconscious reflections—until the enduring repose awoke a lucid memory of her schooldays, all the intrigue surrounding a German antiquary society that had come to Asia Minor to excavate and to prove true the war described in *The Iliad*. Little by little now, she forgot all about Sinai. She imagined herself teetering amid the ruins of Troy. The witch hazel bough held tightly against her bosom, she turned towards the warmth of the sun and pictured a badly deteriorated chunk of burnt bronze lying amid the rocks. *The bronze—could it be the remains of the armour that once belonged to Ajax? Or what about Achilles?*

A second time, the desert breeze whistled through the maze of fluted columns that comprised the remnant of the Egyptian palace. Given how mournful the current, she envisioned Helen of Troy—the Hittites' abduction and subsequent sexual enslavement of the comely Greek woman. And as Anastasia swayed from side to side awhile, a faint pulse awoke up and down the length of the witch hazel bough. Again and again, the bough trembled and pulsated—but she ignored the disturbance. Tears in her eyes, she pondered what it must have felt like for Helen of Troy to live as an odalisque, a sex slave. *How to describe the agony of such debasement? Would it be similar to how a eunuch might have felt?* She rolled the tip of her tongue over the gap between her two front teeth. *That's a terrible thing, castration. How sad.*

All throughout the witch hazel bough, the signals grew stronger and stronger, so she gripped the forked end. *Yes, I feel it!* She faltered her way past the palace, but neglected to restrict herself to the safe routes, the ones she had committed to memory, and soon got lost. *What a foolish thing to do.*

A falcon's shriek rent the tranquil sky, followed by an eerie silence. The whole of the desert grew *lifeless*. And the witch hazel bough grew lifeless, too—as if the source of the signal had never even existed. *Did I imagine it?* She placed the bough up beneath her left arm and did her best to find her way back toward the palace grounds. *Where do I go?*

As she cast about for inspiration, the witch hazel bough trembled again. Over to her left, she identified the unmistakable hiss of a horned viper. Astonished, Anastasia heard the viper's scales rattle as it stretched out to its full length.

Flooded with adrenaline, Anastasia quivered, imagining the serpent was eighteen feet long. *God help me.* Shoulders tight, she debated whether she ought to call for help. *If I do, though, what if the noise provokes the creature? Even worse, what if the Oxford scholars come along? I'd rather perish.* She felt the colossal serpent slither past her left ankle and wind back again. She held her breath and braced herself. *Oh, please go away.* The creature's horn tapped against the crown of her left foot, and her upper lip curled back. *Oh God, no.* The creature's horn tapped a second time, and she exhaled as quietly as possible and debated whether she might attempt to hold the snake down with the fork of the bough. Beneath her breath, she recited a few verses from the eighth psalm: 'Lord, you put everything under our feet, all flocks and herds, and the animals of the wild.' Her gesture did not seem to have any effect. The rattle of the serpent's scales grew louder and louder still, until she went into a state of shock and imagined the hideous diadem spider materialising on her shoulder.

'Why'd you have to participate in this kind of expedition anyway?' the creature asked, speaking into her ear. 'A proper archaeologist only ever contents himself with the simple knowledge that follows from the watchful descent through the layers of time. *Stratigraphy*, my girl. *That's* how a proper scholar helps historiographers fathom the myriad changes that come about with each succeeding war.

Anastasia heard footsteps approaching, and the diadem

spider dematerialised from her shoulder.

The sound of the footfalls drew closer and stopped. 'Whatever you do, don't move a muscle,' Mr Dalrymple told her. She heard the rustling and rummaging as Mr Dalrymple dug through his haversack. 'I'll draw the beastie away from you with a bit of flatbread,' he continued.

The stratagem had no effect: the rattle of the viper's scales rang in Anastasia's ears, and the tip of the serpent's horn tapped against her kneecap. Did the awful creature mean to rise up? Did the creature aim to stick its head all the way into her glory.

Her laboured breath whistling in and out, she pointed her eyes in Mr Dalrymple's direction. 'Please, sir. Make it go away!'

He drummed on the earth, as if to lure the serpent toward him. 'Come along now,' he pleaded. 'Come this way, you big bloody bounder.'

The gentleman's pleas were in vain. Beneath Anastasia's long flowing nightdress, the creature climbed ever higher up her left leg. She trembled uncontrollably. Then, as the creature's scales continued to rattle, she opened her mouth and attempted to scream, but could not manage to. She felt the viper's horn scrape against her left thigh. She laughed hysterically, and her state of shock turned to delirium. In her frenzy, she revisited the curious notion a witch hazel bough from Saint Rosalia's tomb held the power to turn living things to stone. *So, why not do that?* She jerked out of her delirium. *How to summon the witch hazel bough's magic?* She considered just how much a witch hazel bough's forked end resembles the shape of a serpent's forked tongue. *Yes, yes. Might* that *be the secret?* The serpent's horn poked at her groin, and she flipped the bough around and held it the wrong way, so that the fork-shaped end pointed downward. 'Please turn to stone,' she whispered. Both the hissing and rattling noises should have stopped, and the viper should have fallen off her. A moment later, an overawed Mr Dalrymple should have gasped for breath. 'What did you do?' he would ask. But the witch hazel bough did not have any magical properties—and Anastasia stiffened as the creature slithered along her body. While she trembled in horror, a local Bedouin girl called out her name and charged forward.

Following a brief interlude, a moment or two of unnerving silence, a polytonal melody whished, whistled, and hissed, as the Bedouin girl performed the tune on a traditional wind instrument, some kind of gourd flute, perhaps even an exquisite Persian flute.

Deep inside Anastasia's womb, the very spot where the illusory diadem spider had once dwelled, a muscle twitched— and a fit of shivering came over her body.

Soon enough, the horned viper ceased to rattle its scales. Neither did the creature let out another hiss. As the snake charmer's melody trilled, the serpent dropped its forked tongue from the warm space between Anastasia's legs. At last, the creature loosened its body's moist, sticky grip around her leg and fell to her feet.

The Bedouin girl recited a prayer then. Afterward, she recommenced with the music and departed slowly—the pleasing sibilance growing increasingly faint.

'So, the serpent has gone off on its merry little way?' Anastasia asked, shivering and trembling yet.

'Yes, that's right,' Mr Dalrymple answered, drawing close. He poked her in the arm and patted the back of her hand. 'You were wrong to set forth all alone the way you did. Don't ever do that again, love. No, no. You're much too precious.'

With that, Mr Dalrymple grabbed the witch hazel bough.

Her hands free, Anastasia rubbed her stomach and pictured him examining the bough to check whether she had damaged it. Standing as still as she could, she contemplated the ongoing quietude—the seeming lifelessness of the desert. 'Something's missing,' she whispered beneath her breath. The shivering spell ceased. Subsequently, her body grew warm. She dug her hands into her coat pockets and thought back to the Hotel Ibis—the way it had felt to sit with Rupert. *Oh yes, what a good feeling it was to sit with Rupert.* The more she contemplated the memory, the stronger her sense of devotion grew. Back at the hotel, he had made her feel so *alive*. And now she realised just why she had been feeling so discombobulated of late and why the wilderness had seemed so oddly desolate: ever since she had departed Cairo, the burden of loneliness had weighed down on her. *Oh yes, I know what's missing.* She lifted her eyes to the sky. *Rupert. He's missing. We should be together, the two of us.*

Mr Dalrymple returned the witch hazel bough into her hand and guided her back to the encampment. 'You've had a trying experience today,' he told her, once they had arrived at her tent. 'Why don't you rest awhile?'

'Yes, of course.' She felt for the flap and stepped forward. Inside, she fumbled for the mosquito netting, moved it out of the way, and climbed into bed. As she lay on her side and breathed softly, she hummed the tune to the Bedouin melody and pictured the little girl bringing the serpent to a lonely place. *Yes, somewhere far away. The ruins of Troy.*

IX.

Somewhere in the Suez Canal. Christmas morning, 1919.

R upert gripped the ship's railing and listened to the call of the white-eyed gull sailing past the vessel. The sight of such an innocent and godly creature made him feel impossibly guilty. How to avoid the sensation, though? In the hope they might free him from the evil spirit living inside his eyeball, he had entered into an agreement with Maud Havelock and her associates. And they had arranged for him a post in the ongoing excavations in Sinai.

The white-eyed gull returned, alighting on the railing. The seabird studied him awhile and then let out a long angry choking call—until Rupert almost wished he were back at the Port of Ismailiya. With its wings making a frenzied beat, the irate gull finally flew off. The voyage continued uneventfully; calmly, the SS *Rhampensit* took Rupert down the length of the canal and onward into the Gulf of Suez. An hour later, the steamship made her port of call at Orchid Isle—where the ship's surgeon had to deliver a consignment of much-needed medicaments to an establishment serving as a sanatorium for a band of horticulturalists afflicted with consumption.

Rupert collected his things and followed the medical party down the gangway and onto the pier, for he knew all about this place. Both Maud Havelock and Miss Fitzroy had once lived here—until some kind of rift had resulted in the women becoming leaders of rival spiritualist sects. As the ship's surgeon checked over his papers, Rupert surveyed the rocky beach and studied the wreckage of a vessel lying on her side. Despite the considerable distance, he could just make out the faded name on her bow: *The Lady of the Rosary*.

When the medical party continued along, he followed them down a narrow footpath composed of Moorish tiles in royal blue. When they approached the sanatorium gates, he paused to let the ship's surgeon and his staff go on ahead.

As he followed them up to the gate, he noticed a frail old woman in a black *burqa* lounging on a piece of driftwood.

'Who the devil are you?' she asked.

'I'm a passenger on the SS *Rhampensit*. Have no fear. I got business here.

'Get away!' the old woman shouted. 'You're bound to catch your death here. Know your holy scriptures. "The wise man plods the road upward to life, never the road downward to ruin." Proverbs 9:23.'

'But I'll only be a moment,' Rupert said. 'I only wish to purchase some orchids for a lady friend, and I hear ye grow the finest in all of the Orient, and—'

'I know. Another faithful servant of the Royal Engineers, are you?'

'No. Nothing like that. I only wish to purchase an orchid bouquet.'

'I've got it. *La Compagnie universelle du canal maritime de Suez* had you come here to tell us all about the many perils of living in the heart of the shipping lane. You'd prefer we crack on, so you could sell the whole of Orchid Isle to the blooming Freemasons.'

'No, you've got it all wrong. I'm on my way to meet a famed diviner. She's working for an expedition in Sinai. Anyway, I wish to take her some orchids.'

'What's to become of me and Mr Grabham here?' the old woman asked, pointing at a monkey in the tree above. 'When you shipping magnates banish us from our home, we'll all be broke to the wide. And Mr Grabham don't deserve it neither. He's a good monkey, a monkey of catholic tastes.'

'Please! Just tell me where to go to purchase some orchids.'

'You conniving Frenchmen don't care a tinker's damn about us. No, you'd prefer it if a steamship was to crash into our little isle some hellish stormy night.'

From within the sanatorium gates, the strains of fitful dreamlike music started and stopped. Could it be the intermittent beat of a cat's impossibly soft purring? Curious to learn more, Rupert passed through the gates and followed the sound down the pathway—until he reached a three-story Edwardian villa with bargeboards fitted to the gables.

The dreamlike purring ceased, and suddenly there was no sound but the wind in the treetops. As the current whistled an increasingly high-pitched tune, a pale hollow-cheeked brunette emerged from the glasshouse. The woman wore a pair of tattered black dungarees and a sombre-coloured workman's jumper. She had concealed her eyes behind a pair of sporting flared-frame sunglasses. 'Welcome to our humble little plantation,' the woman said in a vaguely Irish brogue, bowing politely. 'Would you be fond of some lady, so? Are you wanting to take her a handful of hot-pink blossoms?'

Rupert nodded. 'Yes, indeed.' With that, he followed the

116

woman into the glasshouse.

Inside, he fiddled with his collar as the humid air brought on a sweat. He took out his handkerchief and wiped his brow. There was little space to manoeuvre. The proprietor had managed to cram thirty rows of wooden tavern tables into the space—and each table boasted a large array of varicoloured orchids.

The woman paused to draw a deep breath, as if she believed the humid air held the power to restore her. The very idea seemed hopeless, though. Her skin shone so white the blue of her veins seemed to protrude through the flesh all along her arms and neck.

He twitched his moustache, inched closer, and studied her long pointy chin. He tried to examine her eyes, but the woman's sunglasses prevented it. His curiosity growing, he pictured her eyes as shining bright seaweed green. No matter how fervently he yearned to look into a pair of eyes like that, he stepped back a little. For a moment, he wondered if the woman resembled someone he knew. *Yes, but who?* At last, he gripped his own wrist. 'By any chance, do you know a woman named Fitzroy?'

'Can't say that I do. Does she live in Dublin, Ireland? Been to Dublin, have you?.

'*Please*. Miss Fitzroy, she's always running about in a flat-top cartwheel hat. You're quite sure you don't know her?.

From the far corner of the hot, cramped glasshouse, the dreamlike purring started again. The cadence sped up. The woman seemed to listen for a while before gathering up a bundle of pink-champagne orchid blossoms. She bound them with a thin white ribbon and placed the exquisite bouquet into his hands—and as Rupert held them up to his nose, she coughed up a great torrent of blood.

At once, his gut pulsed—as if he were to blame. 'Should I get help?' he asked, setting the bouquet down beside a sleek paring knife.

Staggering this way and that, she pointed toward a garden apron dangling from a rail that jutted out from the door jamb. 'Kindly hand me that raggedy ole garment.'

As he reached for the garden apron, he noticed the flat-top cartwheel hat dangling from the nail jutting out from the opposite door jamb. '*You.*' Quickly, he turned back and shook his finger in her face. 'You're some kind of intelligencer, yes? Just who might you be working for? Do you represent a faction that broke from Westminster Spiritualist Society, or do you hope to stop Maud's faction from finding the treasure before all your friends arrive?.

'Whatever are you talking about?' the woman said.

'Tell me what you're doing here. Each faction—it's a band of thieves! Wouldn't that be right? What's this all about?'

The woman remained silent and held onto her sunglasses, as if she feared he might seek to take them from her to expose her deathly golden-green eyes. The purring ceased, and as the glasshouse grew quiet, the woman coughed up more blood. With a crooked smile, she dashed off to the left and gazed into the pale-yellow glow of a candle burning on the opposite side of the glasshouse. 'Before you contract a contagion beyond remedy, I think you ought to return to your ship,' she whispered.

He smirked and refused to break eye contact. 'I'm not returning to the ship, I don't mind telling you. From here, I'm off to Orchid Isle Aerodrome. I'll be flying off to Sinai. Despite the holiday, my contact, Maud, has chartered one of those newfangled single-engine airliners.'

'*No.* Sail far away. Cross the Irish Sea and dock at Éire

and live there. Aye, a splendid life, it'd be.' With that remark, Miss Fitzroy coughed up a third torrent of blood.

Just go. He ran outside, and as he hurried through the sanatorium gates, he did not even stop to say goodbye to the frail old woman sitting on the length of driftwood. The incivility must have nettled her, for she cried out a series of profanities.

Thirty minutes later, he boarded the airliner—which pleasantly surprised him with its powerful rate of climb. He looked out the window and stared at the Gulf waters below. *I'll be there in no time.* When the airliner touched down, he disembarked and sought out his contact.

The woman, a colonist from the village adjacent to the archaeological preserve, greeted him down by the British Aerial Transport Company Limited office building. She introduced herself as Miss Wombwell. As they huddled together, he related his harrowing tale. Together, they checked the aerodrome for any sign of someone perhaps working for Miss Fitzroy. Given the date, though, the airfield proved to be deserted. Best of all, no signs of unrest roared through the sky—no revolutionaries calling out, no gunshots, no explosions.

After a while, Miss Wombwell patted Rupert's hand. 'Don't fear our adversaries. They're a band of failed Christian mystics, nothing more.

He gazed at one of the biplanes idling over to the side. 'I do fear Miss Fitzroy. I say she holds great power. Godly power, even. Like maybe she's got the Holy Ghost in those wild eyes of hers. Who knows? Maybe she does.

For a time, Miss Wombwell's gaze bounced from place to place. 'Maybe Miss Fitzroy commands the power to see angels. Just like those little peasant children who claimed to espy apparitions of the Blessed Virgin in that pasture outside Fátima, Portugal. What a tale. Even if each of the children dissembled, nevertheless, did they not beguile the world?.

'Yes, I suppose so.' The more Rupert pondered it, the more he feared Miss Fitzroy and her friends. At last, he paced back and forth.

Frowning, Miss Wombwell rested on his steamer trunk and crossed her legs. 'I know we'll triumph in our endeavours. And each of us will receive a reward for our troubles, because nothing boasts a measure of power quite like the sensual. And you hold that kind of power. I can tell you'll have no trouble enticing Anastasia. No trouble at all.' Miss Wombwell looked at the clouds. 'Up there in the heavens, the Lord has nothing to compare with earthly love.

'I'm not so sure we'll prevail,' Rupert said. 'Anastasia is quite powerful as well. The *spiritual* kind.'

Miss Wombwell pushed herself to her feet. 'Wait here.' Slowly, she strode across the airfield and into the livery stable.

Alone now, Rupert espied a little wooden hassock positioned to the side of the office building. On the footstool, someone had left behind a cracked olive-coloured clay dish heaped up with chocolate-walnut *baklava*. His mouth watered. How to ignore something so shamelessly unspiritual? He consumed the sticky fragrant pastries—until not even one solitary crumb remained.

Later that Christmas Day.

Rupert dragged his steamer trunk into the encampment and claimed the wobbly, empty camp bed in Mr Dalrymple's tent. In the evening, Rupert joined Anastasia in the candlelit pottery yard. Despite the fact he had no orchid bouquet to offer, he greeted her boldly. She did not invite him to sit. Instead, she rose to her feet and reached out her hands. As she had done back at the hotel, she placed her palms against his chest. And like before, her touch felt like the laying on of hands. He found it all terribly puzzling. *Does she wish to commune with me?* By degrees, his right eyeball grew warm and dry and sticky. *Does she think that if we were to come together as one, she might destroy the illusory spirit inside me? What's she doing?*

An expression of deepest anguish crossed her face, but the oddity of it lasted only a second. When she withdrew her hands, she felt for her walking stick. Counting aloud each one of her footsteps, she tapped her walking stick here and there and guided him from the pottery yard.

'Where are we going?' he asked.

'You'll see.' She guided him past the mess tent, onward through the better part of the archaeological preserve, and into the ruins of the palace.

The whole of the wreckage glowed almond white in the moonlight. He paused, lost in thought. His lips parted in adoration of the structure, and he wondered how it would have appeared had the roof not collapsed.

The early-evening breeze blew through Anastasia's hair and pushed on her back until she inched her way forward— into the palace.

He looked at the nighttime sky—a faint, tantalising light that might have been the star Altair. By the time he bowed his head and followed along into the maze of fluted columns, he could not locate Anastasia anywhere.

The warm dusty breeze whistled through the stony debris, and a woman belted out a measure from a parlour song: 'I'm On My Way to Dublin Bay.'

He stopped beside one of the tall cracked columns and debated whether the voice might belong to Anastasia herself. *No, I don't think so.* Unmoving, he debated whether Anastasia had heard. *But of course she did. A blind girl hears everything.* Still, she might not have regarded it as all that suspicious. Perhaps she presumed the singer to be someone from the expedition. Given his previous experiences, though, Rupert recalled all the recent intrigue back in Cairo. *The singer in question must be working for Miss Fitzroy.* When the song ceased, he exited the east wing of the palace and stepped into an ancient uneven lane paved with seashells. What a spectacle, too; beneath the moonlight, the glassy seashells glimmered like the satin in a nubile woman's bridal shoes. He dried his sweating palms against his trousers. *How do I attract Anastasia's attention?* He whistled the kind of call a Māori hunter might make back home.

A moment later, Anastasia emerged from a section of the palace up ahead and stopped beside a cracked pillar base. 'Who's there?'

'It's only me.'

'Oh, thank God. For a moment, I assumed you got lost.

He watched her grope her way towards him, the strong desert breeze rippling through her lace blouse and hobble skirt. When the tip of her walking stick grazed his left shoe, she stopped. They stood so close to one another, the tips of their noses nearly touched.

He studied the rise and fall of her bosom. *What a beautiful girl.*

Inside his right eyeball, the dæmon hissed dissonantly.

As if she heard, she arranged her free hand on Rupert's right cheek and drew her finger downward along his freshly shaven jawline. 'Please tell me about the evil spirit living inside your eye. Why do you fear such a thing? What trauma do you suppose gave rise to the pathology? A *childhood* trauma? If you tell me about *your* past, I'd be willing to tell you all about *mine*.'

At first, he did not respond, for the dæmon rattled about violently in his eyeball. The familiar scent of orchids awoke— as if someone allied with Miss Fitzroy must be sprinkling thousands of seedpods all throughout the palace grounds.

Again, Anastasia traced the side of her finger along Rupert's jawline, and with the tip of her left thumb, she touched his right eyelid. 'Oh yes, the spirit's there. Inside your right pupil.'

'Yes, that's right. The spirit refuses to go away.' Mindful of how peculiar he must have sounded in that moment, Rupert dried his palms against his trousers again.

'Once upon a time, I believed I had a diadem spider living inside my womb,' Anastasia told him, feeling for his hand. When she found it, she set his palm against that intimate space just below her belly.

He curled his hand into a fist. Gently, he rested his knuckles against her and pushed—the way a loving cat sets its brow against a person's chest and applies pressure and pushes. 'The spirit inside me won't trouble you,' he said. 'I promise, so help me God, yes, you may place your trust in me. That's no fib. I'm a gentleman. Someday, if and when I sail back home to New Zealand, I might even read law at Victoria University. At least, that's what my old man wants me to do. Anyway, when I go, maybe I'll take you with me.'

Anastasia's blind eyes sparkled. 'You'd better be truthful. If not, I'll ask the Furies to hunt you down. They never fail to exact vengeance against an oath breaker.'

From the direction of the pottery yard, a ceramics

specialist arrived. 'Anastasia, what are you doing out here? And who's this fellow? Might he be bullying the troops, love?'

Anastasia shifted toward the ceramics specialist and tapped the tip of her walking stick against one of the seashells. 'Don't be cross with Rupert. As it so happens, I'll require his services. There are bound to be plenty of louts out here in the wild. That's why it'll be good to have a proper gallant to watch over me.'

'No, no, no,' the ceramics specialist told her.

'Yes, yes, yes,' Anastasia countered. 'Let's go talk to Professor Milne now. And if he won't permit Mr Lux to stay by my side at all times, I'll have Mr Dalrymple take me back to England, where a girl should be safe.

As Anastasia and the ceramics specialist strode across the grounds, the women bickering back and forth, the parlour song returned: 'I'm On My Way to Dublin Bay.'

Rupert stepped back and studied the palace. *The song's coming from somewhere in the heart of the structure.* He should have moved toward the voice, but a frisson of fear held him in place. Beads of sweat on his lip, he knelt by the seashells, but soon regretted it; the scent of orchids was much stronger there, and it was not long before the uncanny aroma made him cough and wheeze. With a peculiar medicinal taste in his mouth, he scrambled to his feet and scanned the ruined palace. At last, he raced forward and returned inside and chased this way and that through the endless columns. *Go. Turn there. Yes, she's up ahead.* Soon enough, he stumbled into a vast hall. And as the song ceased, he reeled around. *How long before it starts up again in some other part of the building?* He put his hands on his hips and did his best to catch his breath.

When the song recommenced in the part of the palace from which he had just come, he dropped to his knees again and revisited all he knew about women. *If the lady were virtuous, speak to her like she was a courtesan. And if the lady has a bad reputation, speak to her with the utmost reverence, as if she were a woman of unparalleled honour.* As the song echoed through the ruins, his hair lifted on the nape of his neck. *I know nothing.*

X.

The wilderness of Sinai. The day after New Year's Day, 1920.

The fragrance of tropical orchids floated inside in the soft breeze. Anastasia pushed the mosquito netting aside and rose from her camp bed. *That aroma doesn't belong here.* She called out to Mr Dalrymple, then remembered his recent decision to depart. Her face tightened, for she could not shake the feeling that ever since Rupert had arrived, Mr Dalrymple had seemed all so self-satisfied. *And now Rupert's here, and Mr Dalrymple has gone.* She paced about the tent. In the place where the wind presently danced about the tent flap, she paused to think. *Do I love Rupert?* The wind ruffled her fringe. *How to heal someone like him? Do I have any chance? Maybe.* She slipped into a middy blouse and a walking skirt. Slowly, she felt her way outside.

A violin shrieked with heart-piercing power from the direction of the palm grove. *Yes, Professor Milne.* Enthralled by the melody, she followed the dusty path to the palm grove and felt for one of his safari chairs. *There.*

The professor discontinued with the music and offered

her a glass of gin and treacle. 'That'd be the finest breakfast I know,' he told her, sounding sincere.

She declined the offer and sat up straight. 'Do you detect the fragrance of orchids?'

From the rustling sound, she assumed Professor Milne had reached into his coat. 'I've got a bundle of fresh tobacco leaves in my hand. Smoked them over a heap of orchids, didn't I?' The professor must have placed the tobacco leaves on the other safari chair, because he took up his violin. 'Let me serenade you.' With a rasp and a squeal, he seemed to agitate the frog to increase the tension on the horsehair. Afterward, he played. As the violin sang out mournfully, she recalled the night before. How romantic the dimly lit encampment would have appeared. She pushed herself up from the safari chair and fixed her blind gaze in the direction of the ruined palace. Last night, as the famed professor had played on his violin, had she not heard a desert lynx dancing in the beams of moonlight pouring down through the fluted columns? She fussed with a few buttons on her blouse. When she stopped, she heard the sound of footfalls. Indeed, she felt certain she recognised them. *Could it be Rupert coming to greet me? Yes, it's Rupert.*

Professor Milne's melody grew more and more reminiscent of a timeless Greek piece—a hymn from the Byzantine Liturgy.

She shifted her feet and stared westward. The elegiac music in her ears, she envisioned wild horses—godly horses with a remarkable, impossible, miraculous stride, the beasts running about the Plains of Olympia. At last, she fixed her eyes on Professor Milne and asked herself what he looked like. *How about Otto of Greece?* Long before she had ever gone blind, when she was still an innocent little girl, she had examined a detailed portrait of the Greek king in the Hermitage. For twenty minutes or more, she had wondered if the Bavarian prince might be the most beautiful person in the world. Then she wandered off to investigate a canvas depicting a scene from Greek myth—the tale of Œnomaüs. *What's his story?* Madly in love with a dashing subversive, the despot's daughter had meddled with the king's chariot. *What precisely did she do?* To the best of Anastasia's memory, the girl had removed the pegs that hitched the wheel to the axle. *And in so doing, she caused the crash that killed her own father.*

The evocative violin music faded to nothingness. Neither did the professor move—until a gentle drumming resounded, as if the professor must be tapping his violin bow against his thigh.

'What are you thinking?' she asked him.

'I'm thinking about Mr Dalrymple. Rupert, too. I mistrust both of them. Don't ask me why, but I fear they're party to some kind of cabal. Of course, it could be I've got it all wrong.'

A second time, she heard the sound of Rupert's footfalls. She held her breath and felt at her Huguenot cross and pendant dove. *The professor mistrusts Rupert.* With a sigh, she lifted her vacant eyes to the early-morning sky. *Should I place my trust in him?* The soft drumming ceased, and a most unnerving hush persisted—as if to announce the fact she had indeed reached a most crucial moment in her life. *The point of no return.* She felt as if her whole self had collapsed inwards, everything falling into the darkness of her womb, only to be consumed by an implacable diadem spider lurking there. With a second sigh, she lowered her eyes to the earth and held the walking stick perfectly still. *In a wicked world like this, I can't trust anyone. Yes, but if I love Rupert, I've got to put my trust in him. Do I love him?* When the violin music finally recommenced with a few opening chords played *allegro moderato*, she counted her footsteps carefully—all the way to Rupert's tent.

'Are you awake?' she asked through the tent flap. 'Have you already had breakfast?' She heard a creak and turned towards the sound.

'Sit beside me,' he said. 'Here on my steamer trunk.'

He said nothing more—as if he, too, believed she had reached a crucial moment in her quest.

'What's wrong?' She rested on the trunk, guided by him, then touched his face, her fingers exploring the crease of his brow, his jutting jaw. His lips felt rigid. Had he adopted the expression of some extraordinary hero, an adventurer? She laughed. After a moment, the incongruous scent of orchids drifted past. She breathed in the fragrance. 'Let's go,' she said, shaking herself out of her reverie. 'Accompany me on another walkabout. What do you say?.

She felt him nod his head, and they both stood. She let the scent of orchids guide her all the way back to the sand dunes guarding the village. Once there, she removed her hat to let the cool erotic current blow through her fringe. She breathed in and delighted in the salty taste of the sea breeze. 'Doesn't it feel good?'

'Yes,' Rupert answered. 'If you could see me now, you'd laugh. I've got my arms up, and I'm swaying in the current. Like I'm dancing.'

From the citadel clock tower, the copper bell rang out in triumphal voice. When the sign of life from the village faded, the roar of the surf grew louder. Anastasia sighed in pleasure.

She hitched her skirts up and stepped lightly toward the sea, where the flowery scent awoke anew and guided her toward a stretch of the coast she had never before visited in all the time she had lived here years ago. The scent of orchids speeding up her heart rate, she stopped and gulped in a deep breath. 'Where are we? It feels like we've reached the Oasis of Nabq, but that'd be impossible.'

'We've reached a mangrove plantation,' Rupert explained.

'A mangrove plantation,' she whispered, breathing in the scent of the salt grass. *Yes, of course. A mangrove plantation.*

Rupert tapped on her wrist. 'We'll not find any treasures here,' he told her. 'Why didn't you bring your divining rod? Maybe we should go back and get it.'

'*Later.*' She fussed with her braided-cotton belt, where it reached through one of the loops in her walking skirt. 'Something's here.' The fragrance of orchids guided her through what felt like an endless jumble of brush. 'Where are we? Have we got hopelessly lost?'

'We've trespassed well into the mangrove plantation,' Rupert answered. 'We're not far from the nursery. I'll tell you something else. The saplings don't look healthy. Yes, it's true. Everything appears to be afflicted with yellow lesions. As if some awful pestilence has ruined the harvest.'

She fussed with the buttons on her blouse, as she often did. 'What about the orchids?' she asked. 'They must be looking good, no?'

'There are no orchids,' he told her. 'Please, let's turn back. We'll get your witch hazel bough.'

The sea breeze stirred her sailor collar, lifting and dropping and ruffling and curling it. As she reached up to flatten the cotton, she visualised an object lying up ahead. 'What's that object there?'

'It's nothing. Just an egg. A glorious, ivory-white stork egg perched atop a heap of wild vines. Probably medicinal,' he said, examining them. 'Still, there's no sign of the mum.

Maybe she's got a habit of laying infertile eggs. Either that or she's decided to break faith and leave and let the fragile life die out.'

Anastasia knelt and crawled forward through the plantation's damp low-oxygen soil and felt for the stork egg. *Find it. Yes, find it.* When she took the object into her hand, she revelled in the sensation. *Could it be a miraculous double-yolked egg?* She held it in her palm, wondering if the egg felt as smooth as Russian marble. *Or ancient lava stone.* When she plopped herself down, she arranged the stork egg in her lap. 'What a prize. Tell me something. Is the egg glowing like a firebird's feather that glows even after plucked?'

'No,' Rupert said.

'No?.

'No. The egg appears rather dense and grainy. A wee bit like flagstone, or maybe even a wee bit like a fragment of ore.'

Being smaller than a lawn tennis ball, the egg fitted in the palm of her hand. Gently, she caressed the prize. *What if I was to touch it too harshly?* For a moment or two, she pictured the exquisite stork egg dissolving into a heap of purplish-brown sand. *God, no.*

Rupert nudged her. 'Why do you play with that damn thing?'

She felt a tightness in her eyes. 'I'm thinking about zookeepers and such, the way they separate mothers from their young. What depravity.'

She rose, taking care not to damage the egg, and Rupert guided her across the sand. Back at the encampment, she arranged the precious egg inside an antique *coquetier* she had taken from the mess tent. Inside her own tent, she placed the eggcup atop the chest near the footboard of her camp bed. When she felt the sun's warmth on her hands, she positioned the eggcup to ensure the shell would be bathed in any sunlight that shone through the vent, warming her hands in the process. *In no time, I'll return to find the adorable hatchling awaiting me and calling out all so tenderly. Oh yes, a blessed event.*

Later that day, not far from the mangrove plantation.

For the first time in almost two years, she lamented the miscarriage she had experienced back in the seaside village.

'I know what's happened,' Rupert continued. 'It's the stork egg. Day by day, from this moment on, I think you'll become increasingly erratic. Regardless of what you might want to do, you'll always hurry back to your tent to check the egg remains safe and secure. Does that make sense?'

The witch hazel bough fell from her hand, and she dropped to her knees. 'Yes, you're probably correct. Deep down, I fear for the little chick.' She grew quiet. Given the miscarriage, she realised how terribly crucial it was she help the innocent stork to hatch properly. *What could ever be more sacred than the creation of a living thing?* A cramp throbbed in the pit of her abdomen. She thought of all the women who make a solemn vow of celibacy when they take the veil. '*Le vœu de chasteté*,' she whispered. *How could any woman bear such a terrible burden?* She wondered if some of the nuns diverted their energies to an art or craft or discipline. *Something like the ritual of sublimation. Or wish fulfilment.* A cool gust of wind blew across the desert and into her face. 'Take me back to the mangrove plantation,' she said, grabbing Rupert's arm. 'To the place where we discovered the egg.'

'Are you sure? But why?' Rupert sighed but finally complied and led her down to the coast and past the nursery in the mangrove plantation.

Anastasia sank to the earth. The desert breeze played through her middy blouse. She flicked a few of the medicinal vines and smoothed her hands over some others, locating the impression where the egg had once lain. *There, yes.* When she withdrew her hand, she fixed her sightless gaze on the sea and breathed softly, thinking about the miracle of life and how that new life ought to follow from an instance of true love. *First, the woman brings the dowry and presents herself to the one she wants; second, up in their bridal suite, he claims his wedded rights. And she fulfils her obligations and .*

Rupert reached for her wrist. 'I think I know what's got you feeling all undone. You didn't have any breakfast today. You should've had some bean jam.'

The cool winter breeze kicked up, and a storm of fallen leaves blew across Anastasia's face and fluttered about her shoulders. 'You mentioned earlier something about how the leaves appeared to be diseased.'

'Yes, they look terrible. Each one of them is spike edged. Even worse, each one is riddled with the same yellow lesions from before.'

Anastasia arose and let Rupert take her back into the desert. Though she felt like a slave, she continued with her dowsing. But she felt not the faintest signal. With a frown, she let Rupert guide her back to her tent.

After resting for a few hours, she stepped outside and listened to the sounds of the ongoing excavations: the noise from the digging implements striking the earth and the endless banter, too. From all directions, the dutiful scholars spoke of top plans, layer sheets, feature sheets, and fine grids. Only when the odour of smoke and burnt wood drifted across the archaeological preserve did she hear panicked cries in the distance. *Has a building caught fire? Yes, there's a fire down by the sea, in the village.*

Rupert joined her, and together they wandered up into the ruins of the palace. He made her comfortable with her back up against one of the fluted columns. Then he and two others ran off to find out what had happened.

She breathed in the noisome fumes. In spite of the awful stench, she wondered if she detected traces of something glorious and decadent—even a touch of fresh Japanese fleece-flower root. In time, the scent wafting on the desert breeze conjured the taste of crème caramel—the kind a sweet shop might sell. *No, I'd say it's the taste of Sicilian watermelon pudding.* The taste registered on the deepest part of her tongue, the part furthest back from her lips. *How could that be, though?* As the smoke from the distant blaze grew thicker, she decided the building that had caught fire must have been filled with the finest perfumes. Shivering, she focused on the place where the palace roof ought to be and imagined the whole of the ruined structure half-enshrouded in a miserable grey pall. Her eyes watered from the smoke, and she blinked. Her temples burned, and her parched throat ached. She coughed and swallowed, but felt no better.

She heard footsteps hurrying in her direction. 'Rupert here,' he said breathlessly. 'Dusk already, and the fire has only just died out.'

'So, what happened?' she croaked, desperate for water.

'It was a band of revolutionaries back in the village. They've burned down the opera house to protest the British occupation, I suppose.'

She could not manage a response. *The opera house.* She remembered the peculiar English youth who had once lived in the dressing room overlooking the dusty roundabout. *What was his name?*

Rupert patted the crown of her right foot. 'Let's get you out of here, eh?' He helped her to her feet. 'It won't do to have you breathing in any more ash.'

Back at the camp, Anastasia paused in the flap that served as the door to her tent and pictured the burnt, blackened remains of the once-majestic opera house. Despite this, she grinned. *How to be cross with the Egyptians? It's only natural they wish to be free.* She felt for Rupert's arm and traced her finger from his elbow to his shoulder. 'All throughout the British Empire, the people of the colonies must feel like slaves. What wouldn't they do to be free?'

A winter current blew through the encampment, and Rupert helped her through the tent flap. 'I'll see you in the morning,' he said.

Alone in her tent, Anastasia positioned herself before the antique *coquetier*. 'Do you hear my voice?' she asked, fantasising that the little stork was listening. 'Nightfall has come, but have no fear. I'm here.

Outside, a pair of Oxford men passed by the tent, talking about the locals, the revolutionaries, the opposition to British rule, the recent exile of Saad Zaghloul. Anastasia fell silent and clasped her hands together, picturing the eggcup. 'I hope the winter winds don't make you feel cold by night,' she said when the Oxford men had gone. 'Do you realise it's almost the two-year anniversary of the February Revolution? You've never felt cold like a winter in Saint Petersburg.' The desert breeze stirred the tent—the cool of the current making her think of the Russian tundra, the Arctic foxes. Her thoughts raced, and she experienced a spinning sensation. Her belly churned, as if the diadem spider were still inside her womb. Clutching her stomach, she imagined the monstrous creature inside her spinning dozens and dozens of silken threads in intricate patterns. She folded over at the waist to make herself seem small and listened to the desert breeze whistling through the canvas.

When the wind dropped, the faint strains of violin music whistled sweetly in counterpoint from the direction of the palm grove. Though it seemed impolite to her, she crawled away from the stork egg without saying goodbye. She struggled to her feet, felt for the tent flap, and stumbled outside and onward toward the palm grove. Professor Milne ceased to play, and she sensed his mistrust. Slowly, he tapped the violin bow against something—perhaps his leg.

She felt Professor Milne draw close. 'You remind me of some poor soul standing at a crossroads,' he told her. 'It's not such a rarefied thing to come to a crossroads, where a humble pilgrim must decide what direction to take. Still, it must be baffling to have to choose. No, most of us wouldn't know what to do. That's because we're somewhere *between* good and evil.'

'Yes, sir.' She sensed the professor staring deep into her eyes, perhaps struggling to learn her secrets. Slowly, she retreated two steps.

'In the morning, you ought to take up your witch hazel bough and have another go,' the professor said.

'Yes, sir.' Counting her steps, Anastasia faltered back toward her tent—and as the violin music let out a resonant refrain, she made her way inside.

She passed by the wardrobe trunk and detected the odour of something putrid. *What could it be?* She knelt before the antique *coquetier*. 'Are you well?' she asked the little stork egg. 'What's wrong? Maybe you know what a wicked world awaits you.' As she debated what else to say, a few more Oxford men passed by the tent—and their lewd comments made her brood over the problem of misogyny. *All across this awful world, it's only ever girls that women leave on hillsides to die.* She sought to tell the stork egg but could not find the words. *What's wrong with me? It's probably just my nerves.* She breathed in and out. The awful stench lingered in the air. Had some desert animal crept into the tent, only to cough up a puddle of vomit? At last, she focused on the double standards that oppressed young ladies. Her palm over her left breast, she turned her eyes toward the space between her legs. 'In our misogynistic world, a girl must remain chaste,' she told the stork egg. 'Every gentleman prefers a virgin. Who wants a girl after she's been ruined? A girl must be inviolable, undefiled.' Anastasia's hands shook, and she grew quiet. Determined to keep her spirits up, she serenaded the stork egg:

> *'If you have a daughter, bounce her on your knee,*
> *And if you have a son, send the bastard out to sea!'*

When she concluded the couplet, she held her hand out to touch the stork egg and gasped in horror: the shell had shattered into pieces, and the tips of her fingers touched a sticky puddle at the bottom of the eggcup. *Oh God, that's the yolk sac, and that's the odour I've been breathing in all this time.* Minute by minute, the odour seemed to grow a thousand times worse—until she forgot where she was. Disoriented, she felt certain that she must be living inside a desert grotto. There could be no doubt what had happened: a tiny milky-quartz dripstone had fallen from above, and the tuneful chime of the impact had reverberated just loudly enough to wholly overwhelm the delicate shell. And the precious object simply cracked apart. When she finally came to her senses and remembered where she was, she crawled outside and slammed her fist against the earth. *It's not fair.* Even though she had been perfectly sensible in the way she had schemed to preserve the stork egg, she had failed. 'So, what about the scales of justice?' she asked. 'What about the quality of mercy?'

A pair of ghostly footsteps crept by. Could it be an Egyptian revolutionary? Still suffering from confusion, she permitted her thoughts to wander in all manner of eventualities. *Maybe an Egyptian thief came around to steal a crust of bread. Yes, a crust of bread with which to feed his famished children.* As the footsteps trailed off, she chose to believe it had been a countertenor—some poor castrato who had been living in the opera house. *He's gone off into exile. Or perhaps he's resolved to join a monastery.* On and on, her gut churned. She pointed herself in the direction in which the illusory footsteps had vanished, and she imagined the wayfarer returning to her.

'Do you know who you look like?' the apparition asked. 'The way your blind eyes gaze out on the world, you suggest you're that peasant girl. Bernadette.'

'The little girl from the village of Lourdes?' Anastasia asked. 'We're nothing alike. Bernadette longed for communion with the Madonna and nothing more. Bernadette never longed to create *life*.

From one of the neighbouring tents, the Oxford scholars broke into pleasant conversation. As was their custom, they spoke of the British Empire and the unfolding revolution, the chaos of modern times and the joy of battle.

A second time, Anastasia slammed her fist against the earth. When she wandered back into her own tent, she felt at the contents within the eggcup. 'I'm so sorry I couldn't save you, but once we encountered one another, the die was cast.' Sobbing, she wiped the sticky mess from her fingertips. 'I'm so sorry.'

XI.

The wilderness of Sinai. The day before Valentine's Day, 1920.

Overwhelmed by misgivings, Rupert awoke that morning with a terrific tension headache. He resolved to avoid Anastasia for a while. He required time to think. *How can I betray someone so noble?* His decision to avoid her could not have come at a worse time, for Anastasia had grown desperate to make amends for the tragic stork egg.

'The doomed stork egg must have been a portent,' she had told him only yesterday. 'It was the Lord's way of preparing me for impending discovery.'

Even now, Rupert found himself mystified. *What does she hope to find?* He knelt on the floor and looked around his tent. Try as he might, he could not picture the expanse filled with great treasures—a hoard unlike anything ever unearthed. *What Anastasia hopes to find must be something simple. Something natural.* Consequently, she had grown more passionate about him accompanying her all throughout the wild. As the days had passed by, though, he had found it increasingly difficult to comply. His conscience had got the better of him. *So, what do I do about it?* He dropped onto the edge of his camp bed, thought of home, and fretted about Georgie. Before long, Rupert realised he had lost all sense of time. He searched for his pocket calendar but could not locate it. *If it's almost Valentine's Day, how long is it till Mothering Sunday? Or has Mothering Sunday already come and gone?* He closed his eyes. All across New Zealand, the good Christian populace would have already made the yearly pilgrimage back to their home parish. With a nostalgic smile, he pictured a large jubilant crowd gathering in Wellington's city centre. *All about the statue of the Iron Duke. How lovely.* A moment later, when he opened his eyes, he rummaged through his steamer trunk. *I've got to have a little pocket calendar somewhere.*

When he could not find a calendar of any kind, he slipped into his old regimentals. Five minutes later, his tunic unbuttoned from top to bottom, he made his way into the pottery yard. *I'll wash potsherds and lose myself in work, that's what I'll do.* As he picked up the first piece, he stopped; deep inside his right pupil, the illusory dæmon recommenced his Oceanic chant. The taunting fed his misgivings, and his headache throbbed even more. *So, do I bring Anastasia to ruin, or shall I forgo all my dealings with Maud Havelock?* The Oceanic chant ceased. He shook out his hands. *Bloody hell, how terrible it'd be to choose wickedness and to help a band of thieves conspire against someone as innocent and beautiful as Anastasia.*

A veteran ceramics specialist sauntered by, humming a medley—and Rupert imagined it was a selection from the baroque opera *Cupid and Psyche. A story about how sacred the institution of marriage was.* He winced. *I'm a bloody rat.* At nine o'clock, the morning light shining blindingly bright, he leapt up from the pottery pail. *Anastasia!*

She appeared near the acacia trees. The late-winter breeze played around her. She raised her angelic eyes to the sky, as if she had just espied something hovering there. In that moment, Anastasia bore a resemblance to one of those little Portuguese peasant children telling anyone who would listen they commanded the power to descry a great apparition in the sky—'Our Lady of Fátima'.

For a moment, Rupert shuffled his feet. Even if the children had dissembled, who could accuse Anastasia of putting on false appearances? He studied her carefully—and, as usual, he noted her undeniable *sincerity*. Once more now, he realised he did feel more than a touch of genuine affection for her. For a time, he debated whether he should call out to her. His headache spread to his jawbone. Like a morose, rejected suitor, he sat back down and continued to scrub the potsherds. By the time he glanced back in her direction, she was gone.

Gradually, he felt the force of something cracking apart his eardrums. *Had a storm cloud unleashed a thunderclap too deafening to hear?* He twitched his moustache awhile and looked to the sky. The clouds seemed harmless and natural, each mass of water vapour glowing a mundane almond white. He rubbed his eyeball and fixed his gaze on the clouds yet again. Could it be the sun itself might be burning in such a way as to create painful electrostatic phenomena.

An illusory, dreamlike explosion rocked the heavens. Or had it happened at all? What if the sound had been nothing more than an aural hallucination? One thing remained certain: the commotion had not sounded anything like a peal of thunder.

He did not dare to ask if anyone else in the pottery yard had heard anything. *Might there be some rational explanation for the clamour? What if some newfangled sounding balloon had burst apart?* As the aircraft had gone gliding off along the farthest reaches of Earth's atmosphere, perhaps the harsh cold had triggered the malfunction. Whatever had happened, his eardrums seemed to crack apart a little bit more—and another explosion filled the air, as if there must be a whole formation of faulty sounding balloons flying about. *How long before the debris comes falling to earth?* He leapt to his feet, paced about the pottery yard, and sought to restore himself the best he could. The ache in his jaw spread to his neck. He found himself walking in circles. When he realised just how foolish he must have appeared to everyone, he returned his gaze to the sky.

Off to the west, one of the clouds rolling down from the direction of Rosetta had assumed the shape of an orchid bud. The oddity of it made him think of Orchid Isle. What did he know about the sanctuary's strange history? Wringing his hands, he puzzled things out. First, a band of pioneering women from Westminster Spiritualist Society must have founded the idyllic settlement. And if the women had been suffering from consumption—and they probably had been— they would have grown disillusioned with the spiritualist society and its powerlessness to heal them of their affliction. In any event, the women must have divided into rival sects: the embittered group intending to bleed Professor Milne, and the more faithful party obsessed with stopping his expedition from unearthing any ritual burials and thus disturbing the dead. *Does that make sense?* If only Maud would come around again, he could ask her.

Another explosion thundered and rolled, and various rays of light shimmered through the clouds like a solar effect that a band of peasant girls might mistake for a Marian image.

He remembered a woman named Veronika who had appeared to him in a black *burqa*. What if she was responsible for all this mischief? If she had mastered the art of Christian magic or some such discipline, she would be powerful enough to conjure any kind of manifestation—and what better way to keep him from helping Anastasia to unearth a sacred burial than by driving him to madness.

Deep inside his right eyeball, the dæmon chanted—its voice shrill. Rupert hunched his shoulders and clasped his head. 'Please stop. I have enough troubles just now.' On and on, the racket continued—reverberating throughout the pottery yard. Blinking and rubbing his eye, he wandered amid the maze of tables sheltered by the sailcloth shade. A shaft of sunlight fell through a long perforation in the material, glinting off a row of orchid-shaped pendants lying on one of the tables. He shielded his eyes from the blinding gleam radiating from the finely polished gold and stared at a table boasting an array of scarabs and *stelæ*. When several veteran ceramics specialists passed by, he resisted the urge to say something or to ask for assistance. If they knew about his headache and came to see him as unhealthy, would they not send him back to Cairo? He looked all about. *The girl in the black* burqa. *She's here.* He twitched his moustache. *I'd wager a penny to a pound she's got herself a pocket mirror in her hand. Yes, and she's reflecting the sun's glare into my eyes.*

When he failed to locate the woman anywhere about, he faltered over to the next table and studied some of the artefacts strewn about there. *I'm not going mad.* He lifted his gaze; out on the horizon, a strain of magical, cream-white orchid trees arose from the earth, and they grew as tall as obelisks, lofty enough to reach into the clouds. *It's a mirage, nothing more.* He refused to let the visions unnerve him. There had to be a logical explanation; the woman in the black *burqa* had burdened him with subliminal messages, obviously. *Or what if she's drugged me?* The idea was plausible enough; she could have slipped into his tent last night, only to pour a strong flavourless narcotic into his water bottle.

A table filled with exquisite Egyptian amulets caught his eye. For a minute, he studied a piece shaped like an orchid seed pod split into three graceful curvaceous fragments. When he finally looked up again, he almost lost his footing. By now, the colossal orchid trees had wholly enveloped the pottery yard. While he struggled to steady himself against the table, a wondrous orchid bee the size of an albatross fluttered by. Illusion or not, he charged off through the maze of tables and out into the towering orchid trees. As he gasped for breath, the pungent earthy aroma nearly suffocated him—and he collapsed amid an illusory orchid tree's tangled roots. Someone approached from behind, but he resisted the urge to see who it was. Instead, he hurried forward through the encampment and out into the ruins of the ancient palace. Whoever had come up behind him followed at his heels the whole way, and when he paused to rest, he felt the touch of a wispy yet invulnerable woman's hand on his shoulder. 'Veronika.'

'Ring up the Royal Horticultural Society,' she urged him. 'Tell them all about the mad orchid trees blooming all across the desert.' At once, she coughed up a torrent of blood all over his arm. No matter how weak he felt, he endeavoured to break away. If he could make his way into the ruins, perhaps he could lose her amid the fluted columns. He continued to struggle, so she held him that much tighter. 'You must be the one to report all these exquisite orchid trees,' she told him. 'Yes, my friend, it's got to be you. I'll tell you why. Down there at the Royal Horticultural Society, not one of those fine titled ladies should even think to speak to someone like me, what with the Irish War of Independence dragging on back home.'

From somewhere beyond the multitude of faint orchid-shaped clouds, another uncanny explosion rumbled and crashed. The din made him fall down. Writhing about, he felt as if a thousand or more microbes must be crawling through the cracks in his eardrums. As for the dæmon's endless chanting, the racket grew increasingly sinister—as if the diabolical being presently preferred to chant between clenched teeth. Soon, the fantastical orchid trees rematerialized. Conjured by the spectre himself, the orchid trees suddenly surrounded the whole of the palace.

Rupert rubbed his eyeball. 'You there inside me, how do I get out of this mad orchid jungle? Don't just sit there on your tuffet. Help me. Don't you realise this mad Irish bird here must be dying of consumption? Haven't you noticed the way she dithers? And what about that churchyard cough she's got? If I run with her one moment longer, they'll be dragging me away feet foremost, yes, and where does that leave you?.

A strong desert breeze rose, and when the orchid trees vanished, Rupert picked himself up and staggered forward into the palace. There, he wrapped his arms around one of the fluted columns. *Saved.* From high above the clouds, one more explosion roared—and the noise made his hands tremble. *Saved?* He let go of the column. *I'm godforsaken.* With whatever strength he could muster, he let out a girlish shriek and staggered off toward the throne room.

Fifteen minutes or more passed before Veronika called out his name. When he failed to answer, another five minutes or so ticked by. 'Where have you gone?' the woman asked, her voice emanating from behind one of the fluted columns. 'Are you feeling lonely? If so, you could always profane Anastasia.

Ah, but you'd never do that. You know I'd never forgive you. No, I'd exact payment for something like that. Yes, I'd make you pay … with your life.'

He knelt on the throne room's glassy white plaster-lined floor. 'Please go away,' he whispered.

'Go home!' Veronika cried out, the woman's voice resounding from the other side of the ruined chamber. 'Live with your mother and languish like a misfit, a failure, someone torn apart by self-loathing. I know how you'll stave off the hunger for love. Like a sick little child undone by perversion and inhibition, you'll engage in solitary vices. You'll hire a splendid toymaker to build you a lifelike doll, and you'll sleep with it every night like some deviant. I know. You'll visit the dressmaker's shop and ask the clothier to design a gown for your dolly. Yes, a wedding gown with beaded-lace *appliqué.*' The woman's malicious laughter echoed throughout the throne room. 'Don't forget to give your dolly a bridal wreath,' the woman continued. 'Yes, give your beloved dolly a bridal wreath made out of olive leaves. Or what about a lovely handfasting knot?' When Rupert failed to answer, the maniacal woman threw a handful of little pebbles in various directions.

Quietly, he picked at the plaster-lined floor. As the taunts continued, he glanced at his timepiece and thought of Georgie. *Yes, I'd say today must've been Mothering Sunday. And given that Mothering Sunday would already be darkening into night, what might Georgie be feeling at the moment? Poor little Georgie; he should be feeling heartbroken.* Rupert closed his eyes and did his best to envision his brother. *All day long, poor Georgie would've espied so many people streaming into the city. And as polite society celebrated yet another glorious Mothering Sunday, poor Georgie would still be tormenting himself with sundry memories of the schoolyard, all the cruelty.* Rupert's muscles grew heavy now, so he curled up into a ball. 'Please, Veronika, leave me be,' he whispered.

Late that night.

Rupert sat up in his camp bed. *I can't sleep.* Lips slightly parted, he scanned the darkness all around. Discreetly, he had moved to another tent. Still, Veronika would learn where he was soon enough. If he drifted off, he felt certain she would come around. *What might she do?* He wondered if she schemed to whisper into his ear as he slept. Perhaps she intended to mesmerise him with all kinds of preposterous bible prophecies. *If nothing else, she'll drive me to madness.* His right eye ached and burned, and the white was bloodshot. He considered the presence inside him. *How should I ever convince myself it's not there?* He climbed out of his camp bed and wept. When he knelt on the floor, he thought of Maud. *Unless I fully commit to thwarting Anastasia, no one should ever help me go free.*

Footsteps approached the flap, and he tried to convince himself to throw his shoulders back. When all efforts failed, he concealed himself beneath his new camp bed. Moving stealthily, a woman continued into the tent. She inched along quietly, as if she had removed her shoes. He did not even take a peek to see who it was. *Who else could it be but Veronika?* At last, he looked but espied nothing save the woman's threadbare stockings. *What kind of woman treks through the wilderness in her bloody support hose? What does she want.*

Without making a sound, the intruder tiptoed over toward an old laundry basket he had left in the corner. Did she wish to take an article of his clothing to use against him in some kind of spell? Whether or not she had taken something, it was not long before she picked up her stride and departed.

He climbed out from beneath the camp bed. His right eye growing dry, he continued outside and searched for Veronika. *She has to be nearby.* He checked the neighbouring tent, but it was empty. Convinced the woman in the black *burqa* must be hiding somewhere in the shadows, he darted all about this way and that. 'Veronika, are you here?' he asked. Three times over, he checked his new tent. All the time crying out Veronika's name, he bounded off between the neighbouring tents. *Where could she be hiding?* Before long, he tripped over a guy line—and when he fell to the earth, he slammed the side of his chin against a rock. A moment later, some thirty feet to his right, the shape of a woman in silhouette staggered away into the darkness of the night. His body ached all over, and he considered lying where he was until the break of dawn. Why not content himself to watch the darkness bleed into the light of day—perhaps some haunting shade of magenta streaked with amaranth red. *No, get up.* He pushed himself up to his feet and lurched back to his former tent, where he found Anastasia waiting on his old camp bed. 'What're you doing here, love?'

'I've got a question for you.'

'Ask away.'

'You wouldn't ever think to betray me, would you?'

'No, love. I'd never forswear any vow. No, I'd never renounce on an oath or violate any pledge.'

Anastasia rose to her feet and made her way forward. 'If you did betray me, wouldn't it be a little bit funny?.

'How so?'

'In the end, my love for you would be my undoing. And everything I'd ever hoped for, it'd end up … all for naught.'

She felt for him, and she placed the palm of her hand flush against his chest. 'We must grow close now. I feel it. I know it. We must devote ourselves to the matter at hand. Soon, any day now, we'll find the treasure. I promise you.

XII.

The wilderness of Sinai. 2 March 1920.

Ten yards east of her tent, Anastasia felt a frantic rush of signals pulsating along the witch hazel bough.

'What's happened?' Rupert asked.

'I haven't got time to explain.' The signals guided her off through an expanse of sagebrush adjacent to the encampment. For two hours, she continued the search, with Rupert faithfully following along at her heels. At midday, the faint fluctuations guided her to a few dunes in the middle of nowhere. Then the vibrations brought her back toward the ruins of the palace, where she stopped to rest. She heard a rattle beating and clapping from the depths of the earth. 'What's all that noise?'

'It's a spotted leopard snake,' Rupert told her. 'Damn. It's bloody long, too. With a blunted tail.'

For the first time, she heard the serpent's hiss. 'So, the terrible thing means to dispatch me?' When Rupert failed to answer, she pictured the creature undulating ever closer. Perhaps it had no intention of harming her. What if it had only noticed a bit of debris glowing in the glare of the sun? She willed herself to remain calm. 'This can't be happening,' she said a few times over. 'Ever since early this morning, I just knew this must be the day when I ought to discover at least something.'

Rupert drew close. 'Don't make any sudden movements. Maybe the serpent will go away.' His panicked tone of voice almost made her laugh. She probably would have, too, if her belly did not churn so violently. *Has the diadem spider returned to my body?* Rupert must have noticed the way she held her hand over her gut, for he gathered her into his arms and held her in the most affectionate embrace.

She wondered if she heard a whole chorus of hisses, and she pictured a thousand or more horned vipers in every direction—each creature peeking up from the earth and trembling in adoration, as if each one believed the spotted leopard snake to be the spiritual double to their kingly forebear, the primordial serpent of Mesopotamian legend.

Twenty minutes or more passed by before the spotted leopard snake finally continued along. Up and down the witch hazel bough, the occult signals reignited with a series of erotic pulsations. A feeling of elation swept over her body, and she reeled around. When she came to her senses, she remained still. Given how frustrating the day had been, she half-expected the signals to guide her off to nowhere unusual—an ancient Bedouin well, perhaps.

Rupert pulled on her sleeve. 'Let's go,' he implored her. 'Don't you wish to find something grand? Maybe we'll stumble upon King Solomon's mines, or what about some long-lost exploration shaft?'

She ignored Rupert's sentimental talk and lifted her eyes heavenward. 'I do feel something,' she told him. 'Soon, I'll find what I'm meant to find.' The dream of her impending triumph left her cheeks burning. She understood it as guilt, for though she predicted success for herself, she still had no idea how to heal him. Until that moment, she had always believed the answer would come to her. *But no. Maybe it won't.*

Rupert nudged her. 'Why the blank expression? Have you got a guilty conscience about something?'

She felt for Rupert's arm. 'A caring healer longs to know what medicaments, potions, and herbal concoctions should save her patients from whatever grave, miserable pathogen or disorder. And she succeeds in the end. And a caring healer like me longs to know the spiritual way to heal. And yet I fear I'm bound to fail.' For a moment or two, she could swear she heard the beating of wings resonating from somewhere off to the east. *Could it be a cast of powerful hungry falcons? Yes, I think so.*

The vibrations streaming along the witch hazel bough remained steady, meanwhile. Like a living thing, perhaps even a serpent, the whole of the bough seemed to undulate— as if determined to escape her grasp. *How to ignore something so miraculous? Oh, my goodness.* The vibrations guided her all the way out across a narrow fault line and onward past an oasis filled with brush exuding the aroma of wild mustard. 'Where are we?' she asked. 'A place of total desolation?'

'Yes, more or less,' Rupert answered. 'Up ahead, there's a clementine tree, but not much more than that. A few desert herbs, nothing more.

She pointed her eyes eastward and wrapped her free hand over the pendant dove dangling from her Huguenot cross. When she breathed in, she wondered if she tasted something sweet. *Could it be candied fruits? No, what about Sicilian gelato?* Twice, she tapped the witch hazel bough against her hip. Then she licked her lips. 'Please take me over toward the wild herbs you mentioned.'

'For what reason?'

'*Intuition*,' she answered.

'*Intuition?*' Gently, Rupert took her elbow. He pulled her along some twenty-two steps to the east. When they stood before the desert herbs, she knelt and dropped the witch hazel bough by her side. She reached out her hands, the way a young lady might do when warming her fingers before a hearth. A second time, she could swear she heard a beating of wings. *Has a pair of falcons descended from the sky?* Sure enough, two forceful entities glided by. A falcon let out its distinctive melancholy, heartfelt, piping call—followed by another falcon answering the call in an even more plaintive key. *How beautiful is a falcon's strong wild call.* She felt something soft and graceful glide past her cheekbone and imagined it a feather having fallen from one or the other creature's majestic crest. When she finally felt for the little plants and caressed their long, thin stems, she doubted the herbs were herbs at all. After a while, she touched the blossoms. 'I think we've discovered a cluster of little Egyptian lilies.' She laughed. 'I think I'll plant them in a pot and place them next to my tent. With a little bit of water and just the right kind of potting soil, I'll get them strong and fragrant again, and won't that be pleasant to breathe in their lovely scent?' Slowly, she rolled up her sleeves, dug both hands into the earth around the base of the stem, and proceeded to pull the desert plant's roots up from the fieldstone to which they had attached themselves. In a perfect world, the rock might have been shaped like a stork egg, too—but the fieldstone had sharp unnatural contours, not unlike a pyramid in miniature. For a few seconds, she paused to imagine a vast army of Nubian slaves constructing some extraordinary monument. 'How many countless people do you suppose the pharaohs worked and starved to death building all their amazing structures?' she asked now.

'Why do you say that?' Rupert asked in turn. 'Perhaps you ought to concentrate on the business at hand, love.'

'For that matter, I wonder just how many people the pharaohs obliterated in establishing their empire.' Anastasia reached up beneath her straw hat and fussed with her fringe awhile. She felt for Rupert. 'If I could heal you of that presence inside you, please know I'd do so.' When he failed to answer, she lifted her eyes to the sky and mouthed the words to a silent statement of supplication: 'Pray tell me how to save this young man here.'

Rupert touched her wrist. 'Keep digging, why don't you?'

She felt for his hand and held it tight. Her body quaking, she recalled her schooldays back in Russia—a lecture pertaining to the history of medicine. The instructor had argued some of the greatest physicians and apothecaries of the past had acquired all their knowledge by testing their medicaments on enslaved people. As a consequence, whether the concoction happened to be an extract from a botanical plant or a toxic substance from the Isle of Corfu, countless unknowing slaves had to perish so the researchers might learn the proper dose for this ailment or that.

Rupert took the Egyptian lilies from her hand and dropped them to the side. He placed her palm on the tip of the unearthed piece. 'Dig,' he said in a loud voice.

She wondered why he seemed so eager to excavate the rock. *Does the shape fascinate him?* She tapped the immovable stone. *What if it's hollow? If so, does it contain a few exotic seedlings? Maybe so, and every bit as deadly as belladonna lily.*

Rupert pulled her hand away and helped her move over

to the side. 'Please let me have a go,' he told her. As she sat back, she imagined him feeling the peculiar stone. Would he prove strong enough to lift it? He dug and dug. Without a word, he pulled her close and placed her palm around the tip of the unearthed piece. Afterward, he planted a kiss on her temple. 'Have you any idea what you've discovered?' he asked. 'I think maybe you've stumbled upon—.

'A small capstone.' She trembled all over and fanned herself.

'That's right. Hence the pyramids.

'Yes, one of those little cult pyramids lost in the soot and sand.' She wrapped her hands around the stone, and her emotions ran wild with ecstasy. She giggled until she realised how undignified she must have sounded. The sensation did not last, the jubilation quickly turning to a sense of profound sorrow. She placed her hands over her face and dragged her fingers down her cheeks. *Whoever awaits us below, I've disrupted his slumber. My God, I've profaned someone's tomb.*

Rupert exhaled loudly. 'What if this structure buried beneath us here proves to be the storehouse where the Egyptians went and hoarded all the treasures?' He gasped, as if a sense of awe must be sweeping over him. 'What if we come to find something down there that changes everything we know about the world?.

She felt for the Egyptian lilies and held them up against her left breast. 'Oh, my crying eyes,' she whispered. With her free hand, she felt for Rupert's thigh and squeezed. 'I guess we've got no choice but to tell everyone. Or would you prefer we enter into some other course of action? *No*, why don't you go collect Professor Milne and bring him out here? I'd think he'd be happy with the discovery.'

'Right.' Rupert backed away, further and further—until she heard a thud as if he had stumbled into the clementine tree. He snapped his fingers. 'Are you quite sure you're content to stay out here for a while on your own?'

She pulled at her straw hat and fussed with her fringe again. 'Go now. Get the professor. Tell him what we've found.' When Rupert hurried off, a hissing awoke—and her eyes darted all about. She clutched the Egyptian lilies tighter and pictured a spider-tailed viper emerging from the brush.

The hissing ceased. Had the creature noticed her kneeling there? More to the point, did the animal instinctively know her to be blind.

Her face tightened. *Yes, the serpent knows.* In the eerie silence, she pictured the serpent's tail. *Maybe it'd be an orange bulb adorned with a jumble of little appendages.* She took a few rasping breaths. *Go on with you. Please.* She dropped the Egyptian lilies and clenched her fists. 'Begone from my sight,' she said, noting the irony.

The viper rattled the tip of its tail, as if the creature believed her to be foolish enough to reach for it. She rubbed her stomach a few times. *Perhaps the viper believes me to be hungry enough to crave something that hideous.* The serpent came closer and rattled again. *What a harrowing sound.* Slowly, she eased herself to her feet. *Could I make it back to the clementine tree? Even if I could, what good would it do?* She turned due east and envisioned Rupert sprinting back toward the fault line. How long would it take him to reach the encampment, and how long would it take Rupert to convince the disbelieving professor she had stumbled onto something of note? She became lost in reverie and pictured Rupert making his way back into the heart of the encampment. *Out of breath, he collapses before the mess tent. And he cries out like a beast, as if nothing else could constitute a better way to gain Professor Milne's attention in that moment other than the sound of complete animalistic desperation.*

At her feet, the serpent continued to rattle its tail. *If only another creature, maybe a common desert finch, were to distract it.* She listened for a wild fluttering of feathers but heard nothing. On her ankle, though, she felt the sharp, burning paroxysm of the serpent's bite. She swooned. And when she fell to the earth, she slammed her right temple against the miraculous capstone. *Everything always happens to me.*

The wilderness of Sinai. 8 March 1920.

From time to time that day, Anastasia woke and found herself lucid enough to grasp what had happened to her. In those moments, she might reach out to feel the mosquito netting against her fingertips. She was back in her little camp bed. *The expedition nurse must've treated the snakebite.* Anastasia slipped in and out of consciousness until, late that morning, she awoke and felt strong enough to rise. After a struggle, she climbed out of her bed. A moment later, she forgot where she was. For a while, she wondered if she might be a nursemaid whose task it was to care for Agamemnon's army. 'I've gone blind,' she called out. 'The enemy, the Hittites, they've cast a spell on me and ….

'Anastasia,' a woman's voice called out.

Anastasia reached out and felt for the woman's shoulder. 'Do you work for that antiquary society presently excavating the ruins of Troy?.

The woman laughed. 'Listen, please. I'm the expedition nurse, and we're in Sinai.

'Yes, that's right,' Anastasia continued. 'So, I'm sleepwalking?'

'I think you're awake,' the expedition nurse answered.

'Still, you're quite feverish and delirious from the snakebite. The effects of the venom, all the neurotoxins. So, let me help you back into bed.

'What's happened to the people of Troy?' Anastasia asked. 'Did anyone survive the battle? What about Œnone? If she's lying half-dead somewhere, we've got to find her. Yes, we ought to locate Œnone. Wasn't that the Hittite woman scorned by Paris? Everyone forgets her, but that's not fair. Everywhere you go, people remember Helen of Troy. Never Œnone. So, let's find her. Maybe she's gone off to Oxyrhynchus or—'

The expedition nurse grabbed Anastasia's arm, struggled with her, and sought to cajole her back into her camp bed— and when she could not manage to do so, she let go. 'You stay here. I'll find someone to help me put you back to bed.' Without another word, the nurse ran off through the tent flap.

On and on, Anastasia groped about in this direction and that. Blinking, she wondered if nightfall had arrived. *How good it would be to feel the warm glow of the evening star shining down on me. Yes, indeed. For that matter, how good it would be to feel the cool of the evening breeze wafting across my body.* Someone came up beside her, so she sank to the floor and remained still. 'Who's there?' she asked. On and on, she listened—but there was no response, as if she had only imagined the visitor. Little by little, all the venom streaming through her veins burned hotter. A torrid sensation awoke all throughout her temples, too, and she wondered if she had sustained some kind of scalp wound. Her state of delirium intensified, meanwhile, until she did not doubt the presence of someone standing on the other side of the tent. *A young gentleman. Yes, a young gentleman with an astounded heart-struck expression on his face.* She raised her hand. 'Have you come to examine the ruins of Troy?' she asked the imaginary visitor. 'After so many years of abandon, I suppose the whole place must seem awfully inhospitable. M–M–Maybe we should …'

The visitor approached and gathered her into his arms. 'I'm so sorry I left you alone out there in the wild.

She recognised the visitor's voice as belonging to Rupert. 'Am I dying?' she asked him.

A long, pregnant pause followed, as if he did not know—or he did not wish to answer.

She drew a deep breath and grinned. 'Tell me something. Have I been talking in my sleep? If so, I hope whatever I said wasn't too embarrassing.'

'It was nothing,' he told her. 'An odd French phrase, an odd Russian word. I couldn't make any of it out.'

She touched the pendant dove where it lay against her chest. While the early-morning breeze played through her fringe, she paused to imagine how beautiful the desert appeared. 'It's nighttime, yes? So, I suppose the desert must look glorious beneath the glamour of the New Moon. On a night like this, the last of the winter stars must be shining bright.'

'It's early morning,' Rupert told her. 'Do you remember your discovery of that little capstone? The cult pyramid?'.

'What an awful burden to be blind.' She pursed her lips. 'Do you know something? Not one point of light, not even the constellation Hydra all agleam in the night sky, could ever shine bright enough to permit me to see again.'

Rupert said nothing. He caressed her forearm. When the nurse returned with a few assistants, they put Anastasia back into her bed. The expedition nurse administered a sedative, and Anastasia heard Rupert leave before she fell asleep.

She did not awaken until nightfall. *Yes, I feel the cool of nighttime.* Determined to stand, she pushed the mosquito netting away. No matter how trying it was, she climbed out of bed and felt for her walking stick. Thankfully, someone had placed it right there on the floor. She took the walking stick in her hand and paused to knead her left breast. As a dire consequence of the snakebite, her heart felt swollen. Despite this, she felt her way forward. When she faltered her way through the tent flap, she paused for a moment to picture the encampment—the alluring glare of lanterns glowing from all directions. From across the sand dunes, the cool nighttime breeze made her shiver. Off in the distance, dozens of excited voices spoke and laughed. The sounds came as no surprise; by now, everyone must have had a glimpse of the capstone. *What might the professor be thinking just now?* In all likelihood, he and all the other dedicated, sophisticated Egyptologists would be thinking of the precious cult pyramid itself and the ancient art of mummification. *What else?* Perhaps the Egyptologists had already gathered together all the gunny sacks they could find, in anticipation of plundering whatever wondrous treasures awaited them below. The nighttime breeze built up again. She fixed her blind gaze in the direction of the waters. *What might the surface of the Red Sea look like on a night like this?* She imagined the whole body of water shone the colours of black grease and green pickle, purple jam, and powder blue. She drew in a few deep breaths. An explosion of laughter and merriment rang out from the heart of the encampment—the expedition's ongoing celebrations. Given the venom streaming through her body, she felt nothing. She wondered what potent substances the expedition's medical staff had injected into her bloodstream while she had lain unconscious.

Whatever the treatment might have been, it must have contributed to her stupor. Time passed, and the hour grew late. From the direction of the palm grove, the pleasing scrape of the professor's violin played. She let the music guide her toward him, until it stopped—and she heard footsteps approach.

'You shouldn't be out and about so soon,' the professor told her. 'Let me take you back to your tent.

'*No*,' she told him. 'Play some music for me. *Please*.

'No, no,' he insisted. 'You're not well. Let's go find the nurse. Have you ever spoken to Miss Peregryn? She'll know what to do.'

Anastasia shook her head. 'No, I feel just fine. Let me hear a wedding song. Let's pretend it's my wedding night. Ah, but who'll dance with me? No, why don't you play me a lovely little anniversary song. Yes, and we'll pretend my husband died a few months ago. No, let's maybe pretend I'm a tragic Oriental girl. Yes, let's say my husband proved himself to be the worst kind of tyrant. And our union was never anything more than a temporary pleasure marriage.

The violin music failed to recommence. 'You don't know what you're saying,' the professor told her. 'That's why you've got to rest.

She leaned forward and envisioned the oasis she had stumbled on some six days earlier. Her expression slack, she pictured the moonlit clementine tree swaying this way and that in the nighttime current. At last, she pictured the alluring moonlit capstone itself. 'What's buried inside the cult pyramid? If it's some ancient ruler, why did he have himself concealed the way he did?.

'Who knows?'

'Do you think that maybe he feared someone might someday profane it if he didn't hide it away? Given the events of the day, I suppose his fears were warranted.'

Professor Milne remained quiet—and she presumed the heartless scholar must be studying her face. *Yes, he's peeking into my blind, diseased, poisoned eyes. Yes, that's just what he's doing.* She sighed. 'Are you trying to make me feel indignant?' She wondered if she might find her way back to the capstone. *How many footsteps would that be? Think.* She could not remember.

Professor Milne took her by the wrist, as if he intended to help her back to her tent—and when she resisted, a struggle ensued. After a while, she staggered away on her own, but she nearly bumped into one of the trees that comprised the palm grove itself. Professor Milne came up beside her. 'You've fulfilled your paramount charge, and yes, you've proven yourself to be a game young lady. Please know that I'm proud of you for finding the pyramid. Now let me take you back to your tent.

The nighttime breeze filled the air with the scent of aromatic gum resin. The scent did nothing for her. *If anything, it smells sickly.* Various palm leaves stirring at her feet, she made her way through the thicket and stumbled off in what she believed to be the direction of the capstone.

The professor grabbed her wrist. 'You shouldn't be out and about.'

She did not resist. Standing perfectly still, she imagined all the labourers unearthing the cult pyramid in the coming days and weeks—until the capstone loomed high above an ever-deepening pit. In the end, the whole structure would positively shimmer in the sunlight—and by night, the dazzling moonglow would bounce off the intricate limestone casing. *Praise be. And how good it feels knowing those awful highbrows from Oxford must witness my triumph.*

On the other hand, what if the ancient structure contained

nothing sacred nor momentous? The professor let go of her wrist, and she stumbled about the palm grove, lunged some ten feet over to the side, and brought her foot down on an oddly smooth rock shaped like a pristine little stork egg. *What a miracle. Yes, a miracle.* She felt for the rock and held it against her breast.

'What've you got there?' Professor Milne asked. 'Put the rock down. Let me take you back to your tent.'

'Do you know why a girl has no choice but to send her noble blood to market?' she asked. 'I'll tell you why. She does so because she longs to make a baby, and what could ever be more precious than that?'

Professor Milne took the rock from her hand. 'I agree with you. There's nothing quite so proper as the inclination to pass on one's bloodline.'

She laughed, albeit resentfully. '*No,* that's not what I meant at all. I simply meant that life is such a precious *gift*. A gift from the Living God.'

A thud pounded, as if the professor had dropped the rock to the earth.

She lifted her unseeing eyes to the sky and pictured the late-winter stars shining down on her. Even if their sparkle seemed a little bit dull that night, what would it matter? She felt at one with the deity, the whole of the cosmos.

XIII.

The wilderness of Sinai. 23 March 1920.

Early that morning, Rupert realised he had fallen ill. The symptoms resembled the same ill effects that had sickened so many others by now: the cough, the fever, the chills, the malaise, the clammy skin. There could be little doubt the labourers had been growing ill as the expedition unearthed the cult pyramid. Across the course of the past week, all the various members of the expedition had been debating a number of theories. Professor Milne wondered if a natural gas reservoir might be to blame—either a deposit of mineral oil or some kind of methane emission. Others feared the pyramid itself must be the source of the outbreak, with an array of minute cracks in the ancient structure having released a potent fungus into the air.

Rupert climbed out of bed and staggered about his tent. As bad as his condition had grown, he longed to return to the pit. For a time, he sought to change out of his nightshirt to the extent his failing muscle coordination would permit him to do so. Still, he had to try: Maud and the others would surely expect him to stay abreast of any and all progress, and Maud would never forgive him if the professor were to spirit away the treasures before she and her associates had even planned the heist. At last, Rupert fell to the floor. Powerless to dress himself properly, he wrapped himself in a handwoven Bedouin-style throw blanket Anastasia had bestowed on him sometime before.

When he finally departed his tent, he paused to marvel at how desolate the encampment seemed—everyone either working out by the cult pyramid or else ailing in the sick tent. *Where's Anastasia, then?* Rupert staggered along and soon found her sitting in the ruins of the palace. Her presence complicated matters considerably and made him shiver and blush. Clearly, she had not yet fully recovered from the snakebite: her eyes were a touch too watery, and given the way she incessantly patted her heaving bosom, it seemed as if she suffered a fair amount of chest pressure. *Still, she looks better than I feel. That's a good sign.* He entered the ruined palace and drew near. 'Are you getting better?' he asked. 'Sure you are.'

'How do *you* feel? Why aren't you helping out with the pyramid? Has something gone wrong?'

'I feel bloody miserable,' he answered. 'Like I'd be dying.' He laughed sadly and regretted ever entering into any kind of arrangement with Maud Havelock. 'I helped to dig up your magnificent pyramid. And now I find myself falling apart. Who knows? Perhaps the gods of Egypt foreordained all.'

Anastasia waved her hand in front of her nose, as if she detected a deathly odour on him. 'You ought to go down to the sick tent and ask for a bed.'

Before Rupert could say anything, Professor Milne approached. 'Come along now,' he said, addressing Anastasia. 'Let me guide you down into the pit. Would that please you?'

Whether or not she felt up to it, she nodded eagerly. 'Yes, let's go down into the pit.'

If Professor Milne noticed Rupert there, he did not say anything to him. Breathing heavily, Professor Milne took Anastasia's hand and guided her onward—Rupert following along at their heels. When the trio reached the pit, the professor guided Anastasia down a makeshift sandbag stairway descending thirty-nine feet into the earth. There, he placed the palm of Anastasia's left hand against a section of the masonry.

A fiery gleam in her eyes, she caressed the limestone. 'You've descended so far so quickly. What kind of digging equipment did you use? Did you damage the structure?'

'Heavens, no,' Professor Milne assured her. 'Trust me when I tell you that your pyramid intimates absolute perfection. The whole structure is immaculate.'

Rupert drew close. 'What do you feel, love? Do you detect the presence of some awful pharaonic curse looming over the premises?.

As if to dissemble astonishment, she held her right hand over her face so that the tip of her ring finger rested against her nose. 'A curse?' She whispered something unintelligible.

Rupert shook his head. He wondered if the snakebite might have affected her good judgement. The professor took Anastasia's hand and guided her over toward another section of the masonry, and as they strolled off, Rupert wrapped the blanket tighter around himself and retreated to the sandbag stairway. Silently, he surveyed the length and breadth of the remarkable structure.

Inside his eyeball, the evil spirit's Oceanic jarring chant recommenced with a low-pitched grunt. The entity sounded as doleful and as strident and as sonorous as a dying god—at least a dying king, a forlorn ruler undone by some tragic flaw. Rupert buried his face in his hands, for the excitement that had attended the discovery of the pyramid felt all wrong. He shook his head, for he realised who must be waiting on the other side of the door: a prideful, condescending king. *That's right, and he'll be rubbing elbows with his know-it-all counsel.*

From up above, a series of nightmarish metallic groans and whistles and shrieks rang out, sounding like an army of ancient silver-and-gold automatons. *What the hell?* The Bedouin blanket fell from his person, and he stood there naked. Once he had wrapped himself up again, he lumbered up the sandbag stairway and listened to the frigid desert wind blowing through some of the earthmoving vehicles and excavating machines the professor had employed in digging up the pyramid. *Right, that's all it was.* His steps dragging and his breath turning to the odour of warm rotten onions, he staggered back to his tent and collapsed into his camp bed. *I think I'm dying.*

Later that day.

Rupert awoke, pushed himself up onto his elbows, and looked all about. *Has someone just been here?* There could be little doubt: the floor was strewn with juniper berries, cashews, and three little pieces of what appeared to be dried lime.

Veronika, the woman in the black *burqa*, entered through the flap—with a knife in her hand.

Too weak to protest her trespass, he climbed out of bed and pulled on his old regimentals. 'What do you want?' he said, collapsing onto the lone chair.

Veronika slid the knife into the sheath at her waist. 'I've come to give you a bulletin, and it's not the kind you're likely to read in any of the newspapers. Miss Havelock and Miss Fitzroy have killed each other.'

Rupert covered his mouth with his palm. 'What happened? Did they shoot one another? At the same time?' Trembling, he sat back and fixed his gaze on the vent. 'What happened?'

'I don't know all the details. Back home on Orchid Isle, they had a row. Yes, and they fought like Kilkenny cats.' Veronika removed her belt and slipped out of her *burqa* to reveal an Irish-lace blouse and a long gathered-waist skirt.

As she checked herself over, a shadow passed over the tent rooftop. Rupert ran outside to find that a falcon had come to alight atop the dolly. The very presence of such a powerful bird of prey made his body sweat and his teeth chatter. Looking perfectly indifferent, the falcon preened its feathers. He ducked back inside.

'Let's return to Orchid Isle,' Veronika told him. 'When we get there, I'll teach you the way a proper horticulturalist arranges the pollen inside an orchid's womb.'

He paced awhile. There could be little doubt that Veronika intended to entice him into following her to Orchid Isle only so that he would no longer have the opportunity to serve whoever remained from Maud's faction.

Veronika clapped her hands. 'We'll feed my newborns a colony of fleshy mushroom spores, just like they do at the Royal Botanical Gardens. Won't that be fun? We'll feed my little ones the spiciest spores in all of the Orient.'

He flopped down on his rickety camp bed and gripped the corroded bedrail so hard a layer of rust broke off. His hand badly discoloured, he rubbed his palm and fingers on the linen. 'You've no cause to trifle with me. As a matter of fact, I really think I'm dying.'

'I know,' the woman continued. 'You care nothing

for orchids. No, you value only antiquities. An ostracon, some fine Egyptian faïence bottle, whatever. So, you bring everything to the pottery yard and you polish it up. Later, you send all the treasures of the Orient to some museum in New Zealand.'

When he finally lifted his gaze, he found Veronika had gone. With a sigh, he went outside to look for her. As he searched, though, he stubbed his toe against one of the angle-iron stakes holding up his tent. He took a deep breath; the desert breeze reeked of mouldy pumpkin rind. As if repulsed by the odour, the falcon launched off the tent dolly and took flight. Rupert followed the creature all the way back to the clementine tree—where a commotion sounding like a train of snorting, growling, bleating dromedaries awoke at his back. *Have the revolutionaries come for us?*

He saw a caravan descend on the whole area—and fifty or more merchants gathered around the edge of the pit to marvel at the pyramid.

One of the English volunteers approached Rupert. 'You wouldn't believe how good everything's going. All blessed day, we've been working like old boots. I'll tell you something else as well. We've discovered the doorway.'

Before Rupert could respond, a piercing shriek rang out from the encampment—and a falcon swooped in low, the rush of its powerful wings fanning the nape of his neck.

The falcon's presence spooked the dromedaries—and they snorted and growled and bleated all the more. Some of them took off running this way and that, their hooves trampling the earth.

As the merchants gave chase, Rupert wrapped his arm around the clementine tree. *We've found the bloody doorway.* The discovery made everything seem so fateful. In no time, everyone would know what king awaited them inside the mysterious cult pyramid. 'I wouldn't be at all surprised if it's a visionary king,' Georgie would say, if he were here now. 'Maybe it's the king who invented the idea of democracy.' Rupert went lost in thought now. *What if Georgie was right?* Thousands of years ago, the visionary ruler would have been the first person to ever pretend to extend power to the people. From the moment of his accession, that king would have been the first ruler to fathom the various ways that cabals, conspiracies, and highborn oligarchies may come to attain and to hold on to absolute power. *And all in the name of democracy.* Rupert let go of the clementine tree, and he focused his gaze on the cult pyramid's capstone. 'Listen, you shouldn't believe in democracy,' he longed to tell Georgie. 'Democracy only ever fails, and that's because no one ever remembers what the public thinks or desires. No, trust me. In every parliament committee room, it's the scourge of bureaucracy, the state officials, who command all the bloody power.'

For a moment now, Rupert remembered his father's smug, sinister business contact, Mr Impérial—for he had wielded great influence within New Zealand's various corridors of power. At last, Rupert collapsed amid the clementine tree's mangled roots. The backs of his hands cold and clammy and flush, he wondered if he had ever felt more dismayed.

Some thirty minutes passed by. Once the scholars had restored order and the merchants had subdued the last of the dromedaries, Professor Milne brought Anastasia back to the pit. As they passed by the windswept clementine tree, Rupert greeted her and followed along. When she reached the sandbags, she continued below. Once more, she placed the palm of her left hand against the casing. As she tapped her fingernails against the limestone, a large, powerful falcon descended from the sky and came to alight atop the capstone. She looked up, as if to permit her blind eyes to picture the bemused creature ogling her from above. When she let go of the casing, the creature quickly fluttered down and wrapped its feet around her right forearm—the way a tamed falcon returns to its master.

Intimidated, Rupert sagged. Still, he drew close and poked her wrist. 'What's the meaning of this?' he asked.

She did not answer. She gasped for breath and placed the back of her left hand against the falcon's breast—as if to feel for a heartbeat. With the tip of its tooth, the weapon that enables a falcon to paralyse its prey, the winged creature nudged the outline of her right nipple where its shape sensually protruded through her blouse.

Rupert twitched his moustache. 'I swear this hawk here's got something to say. Like it's got a message to share. Something profound.

Plainly nettled by Rupert's words, Anastasia backed away several steps and remained silent for a time. During the strange interlude, the labourers, the whole of the expedition, stopped what they had been doing—and everyone gazed at the young lady, rapt. How to interpret the falcon's miraculous devotion to her? As the winged creature dug its talons deeper into her right forearm, she let the tip of her nose brush up against the creature's strong, hardened crown.

'What's this all about?' Professor Milne asked.

'I think the falcon detects the faint trace of something bestial having been inside my body,' she answered. 'The diadem spider. That'd explain why the falcon has befriended me, and more than that, he cherishes this cult pyramid. I think he believes the king who invented the art of falconry dwells inside. The tyrant who enslaved all birds of prey.

'That's absurd,' Professor Milne told her. 'Honestly, you can't expect a band of proper scholars to believe in such preposterous ideas. No, no.

Anastasia breathed in and cringed. When she touched the falcon's breast, the animal shook its soft downy crop and took flight. She dropped her hands to her thighs and looked sightlessly at the sky. 'Deep inside the cult pyramid rests the ancient tyrant who invented the art of falconry,' she muttered beneath her breath. 'Of all things.'

An older gentleman from the pottery yard approached. 'What about the treasures?' he asked her. 'What does your intuition tell you? There's bound to be great riches inside, no? What about a cache of golden figurines?'

She did not answer. Instead, she stroked some of the scars the bird of prey had left on her right forearm.

Rupert studied the structure. *So, what awaits the expedition deep inside this cult pyramid?* Boldly, he placed his ear against the masonry—and in his sickness, he could swear he heard the sound of a show trial babbling indistinctively from inside. *What better way to goad the ignorant electorate?* He felt even more indisposed and was overcome with a series of shaking chills. *I'm bloody well dying here.* Slowly, he removed his ear from the masonry and peered into Anastasia's eyes. 'It's rather sad you've discovered this place. Do you even know what history's kings and tyrants and political grandees were like? They entered into loveless arranged marriages. Marriages of convenience. They disbelieved in *love*, and that's why they felt no shame with regard to quitclaim deeds and such. For that matter, they had no real quarrel with adultery. Nor any other type of betrayal.

Anastasia breathed in and licked her lips. '*Betrayal*,' she whispered. '*Betrayal. Betrayal.*' She let out a brittle laugh, raised her blind, glassy eyes to the sky, and offered a sad smile.

Late that night.

When Anastasia stopped by, Rupert invited her into his tent. Once he had sat her on the edge of his bed, he trimmed his pencil moustache. 'How may I serve you?' he said, clipping away.

'Take me back to the pyramid,' she said. 'Please, I wish to touch the door.'

'Maybe that's not such a good idea.' He put down his scissors. 'Just think of the wicked king and all his ministers, all those bastards haunting the other side of the entryway. That bloody tyrant, maybe he'd be rubbing shoulders with the bloody bastard minister who invented the art of running for office. For all we know, he's the politico who first came up with the decadent idea of always thinking about the upcoming election and how to persuade the marks with publicity stunts and such rather than good ideas.'

'Are you fond of me?'

'Yes, of course. On my oath.'.

'So, take me to the door. This instant, I say. And don't try to dissuade me. Show me you're faithful and loyal and *dependable*.'

As ill as he still felt, he could not deny her. Once he had returned his little shears and shaving mirror to his steamer trunk, he guided her outside and all the way back to the clementine tree. She reached her hand toward the pit, and Rupert wondered if she could picture the pyramid's immaculate limestone glowing its bright silver beneath the moonlight. He heard an exultant cry, initially unaware it was Anastasia. Gently, he tugged her sleeve. 'Why are you feeling so giddy?' he asked, heat rising through his chest.

She did not explain herself. Instead, she pointed in the direction of the makeshift stairway. 'Let's go.

'No, let's stay here,' he whispered. 'There's nothing down there but the door, and it's probably just an everyday slab of stone. Nothing more.'

She glided the tips of her fingers across his chest. 'I wonder if some artisan carved an elaborate cartouche into the jamb. And maybe some kind of inscription, too.'

For a time, Rupert pictured the ancient doorway, an array of hieroglyphs etched into the entablature. 'The inscription is probably some preposterous curse. "If you profane this holy shrine, let an army of genii destroy you and leave you no heir!" Something like that.'

Anastasia cast her blind gaze to the earth and retched. She grimaced as if she registered a terrible taste in her mouth. Had her powerful sense of smell detected some sickening odour creeping up through the space between the door and the casing? Rupert wondered. With the tips of his thumb and first finger, he held her perfect chin. 'Have no fear,' he told her.

'Tell me something,' she whispered, wiping her mouth. 'What about the people who brought me here? Are you working for them? What will they do with the contents of the pyramid?'

Rupert winced, and when he failed to say anything, Anastasia groped her way over to the east—where she bumped into the water barrel in which the labourers stored their pickaxes. He followed after her, and when he held her close against his open shirt, she lifted her brow and let her nose brush through a tuft of hair on his chest. He trembled as she kissed him just below his neck dimple. While the nighttime breeze rattled the boughs of the clementine tree, she pulled him down to the earth and touched the button above the fly of his woollen trousers.

He pulled back. 'Sexual congress? We can't. We're both of us quite ill, and it wouldn't be a good idea to poison one another.'

She did not answer, but smoothed her hand over the place where the serpent had bitten her. Rupert struggled to pull back a little bit further, for the more he thought about the venom streaming through her body, the more he dreaded the idea of touching her. He detached himself and stood up, lingering beside the sandbag stairway.

She lay on her back. 'Describe the pyramid just now.'

A beam of moonlight shone across the door, and the slab of stone shone like a fine black sapphire. 'The pyramid looks quite wondrous,' he said. Entranced by the enigmatic beauty of it all, he inched his way down the length of the sandbag stairway and rushed over to the monument's doorsill. Given the magical way the moonlight shone down in that moment, the stone slab should have miraculously opened. *So, why doesn't the door open?* Three times, he patted the stone. Perhaps the king and his counsel believed the expedition to be a band of unworthy subjects having come to petition them for some petty favour. Rupert patted and patted the stone slab. 'You've got it all wrong. I've come to pay tribute. So, let me come inside.'

But the door failed to open—for surely the inhabitants knew he had told them a fib. Meanwhile, as the moonlight continued to pour down, the odour of fungus and disease crept all about. *Could it be some everyday mould?* Like a fool, he breathed in and held the awful fumes in his lungs.

From above, Anastasia clapped her hands quickly—as if

infuriated by his having rejected her. 'Come back to me this instant,' she shouted. 'You can't just leave me all alone up here.

Like the worst kind of lout, he ignored her. Once more, he fixed his gaze on the stone slab. The way the Moon shone in that moment, he wondered if the stone shimmered like black jade—or perhaps even fossilised wood. With all his might, he pushed. When the door refused to open, every impulse told him to vandalise the barrier blocking his way. For a moment, he searched for the perfect kind of flat rock with which to scrape a host of rude caricatures into the obsidian-like surface. When he failed to find an implement that might do, he clenched his fists. *Why not write a series of insults and heartlessly derisive epithets?* He recollected his schooldays— all the things the sadistic little boys and girls might say to Georgie. *All those insults.* After a while, Rupert tapped on the door. 'What's an insult, anyway?' he asked, as if someone might be listening on the other side of the stone slab. 'Maybe an insult wouldn't be anything more than a projection of the party's own insecurities. *Insults.* It's all transference, the stuff of scapegoating. Wouldn't that be right?.

The Moon waned, and the stone slab shone like something lustrous and alien, something rarefied. Rupert thought back to his school days, the meteorite the schoolmistress kept on her desk, the mesmerising way the stone and nickel and iron glistened in his eyes. He considered how a schoolmistress seeks to indoctrinate her children, perhaps even deceive them. The king and his counsel might approve of all that. They would want her to demonise any and all rivals. And the king and his counsel would surely want her to compel the children to question any rival's air of legitimacy. More than anything, they would want her to encourage the children to hold the nation's rivals to a standard utterly impossible to meet.

In myriad colours, the glamour of the Moon continued to bounce off the pyramid's doorway—creating a pattern resembling dazzle camouflage. *I'm beguiled, I am.* As sick as he already was, Rupert almost expected a voice to speak up from the other side of the stone. One last time, he patted the stone barrier. 'Would a person have any reason to believe in your bureaucracy-approved education, Your Majesty? Do you wish to know how bloody petty academia would be? It's nothing but straw-man arguments. No, your instructors can't even tolerate the notion of playing the devil's advocate once in a while. And how about *you*? Do you even know how to adjudge things from someone else's perspective?'

A woman's long, lithe shadow passed over the cult pyramid. Anastasia had approached the edge of the pit. 'Come back!' she cried out. 'Have you any idea how perilous it is to leave a blind girl all alone in a place like this? What if a swarm of sand rats come for me? What do you suppose they'll do? They'll nibble away at my ankles until ...'

He espied a faint light in the sky. *Could it be the star Alphard? Yes. It's hovering over her shoulder.* Anastasia stepped back from the edge of the pit, and her glassy eyes made her appear wholly transfixed. As her shadow lifted, he cocked his ear. *Has she sauntered off into the desert?* From above, the silence endured. No sound swept over the desert other than a faint whistle—a cool breeze, the last vestige of winter. Again, he studied the stone door, questioning if he heard footfalls on the other side.

The Moon traversed the sky, and the fickle light made the stone slab appear as worthless as imitation quartz.

Shall I return to Anastasia? If he did, perhaps she would push him onto his back and climb onto his body—wholly ignoring their poor health. He marched toward the sandbags but reeled back around and fixed his gaze on the door. With purpose, he slammed his fists against the stone. As in a story from olden times, some entity inside the pyramid should have heard and answered him. Lost in quiet colloquy, though, not one spirit troubled itself to call out to him. By degrees, he stepped back. *What might they be talking about inside there? If nothing else, they'd be debating the art of war itself.* He glanced at the earth and fussed with his moustache.

'Let's send out our army,' some fine counsel's voice should have said in that moment. Remember, the enemy of our enemy must be our friend.'

'Yes,' the king should have announced. 'Remember, too, if we spread our sphere of influence, we'll have more places to which to send our exports.'

The call of a desert owl rang out, but the sound did not seem at all real. If anything, it sounded comical—the noise that a mischievous comedienne might make. Rupert looked up, only to find Anastasia wrapped around the capstone. The venom-addled woman had come back down into the pit, and she had climbed to the top. 'Our expedition has exposed the whole of the pyramid,' she said.

'How did you get up there?'

'I felt my way. With my hands.'

'You shouldn't have done that. You're almost twenty-five feet directly above me. If you fall, I'm not sure I'll be strong enough to catch you.'

Once more, she made a funny sound—the call of a desert owl.

Rupert strained to see her eyes, her face. 'Don't let go, whatever you do. And take care not to lose your toehold.

A third time, Anastasia called out like a desert owl—as if out of spite.

XIV.

The wilderness of Sinai. 18 April 1920.

At midday, a fierce burning desert wind swirled across the encampment, and as the sandstorm grew, Anastasia made her way to Rupert's tent and felt for his hand. 'I know what this upheaval must be,' she told him. '*Al-khamsin.*'

'That's right. Ain't nature grand?' Holding her hand tightly, Rupert guided her down to the truck park—where everyone else had already taken shelter within the expedition's various pantechnicons. When he found an empty one, Rupert helped her up inside and closed the hatch behind them.

The merciless gale grew into a deafening cacophony. The hot, relentless sandstorm threatened to bury the northernmost reaches of the archaeological preserve—including the cult pyramid. When the hatch blew open, Anastasia felt a hot, infernal cloud of peppery dust and sand explode around her. As the debris whipped about, she imagined the refuse was a collection of torn star charts and tattered, crumpled climate maps.

A second time, Rupert closed the hatch. While he helped

her to brush the dust and sand from her person, she listened to the din emanating from outside—the roar of the sandstorm, the chorus of panicked voices shouting at one another, the clatter of tin pails, and the sharp snap of linens dangling from some nearby clothesline. She felt at the space all around her. If she had known this would be their shelter, she might have prepared it. *I would've built us a bed of Egyptian lilies.* She felt at her snakebite, its faint, lingering scar. Though the wound had not healed completely, she felt good and strong enough to reach for Rupert. On the chance that he might be looking her way, she offered him a gap-toothed smile. *If only he'd take me, here and now—yes, I'd gladly lie beneath him.*

He did not make a move. Even more disheartening, someone outside in the swirling sands knocked. As soon as Rupert opened the hatch, one of Professor Milne's associates spoke up: 'Get along to the pyramid,' he told Rupert. 'The sandstorm threatens to bury it, ruining all of our work! So, the good professor wants us to drape a massive sheet of oilcloth over the whole damn pit, and we'll require all hands up there if we're to have a sporting chance.'

Anastasia felt for Rupert's hand and squeezed. 'Yes, you ought to go. Don't fret about me here. I'll manage.'

'Right.' Without even saying goodbye, Rupert climbed down from the van and shut the hatch behind him.

Left alone, she rubbed her stomach a few times—until the air current seemed to grow stronger. *Oh God, what if the storm blows the whole van over?* She held herself tight, drooped her head, and listened. Outside, the sky filled with quite a commotion; it sounded like a thousand or more birds of prey, a cast of hungry, wrathful, merciless, godlike falcons. *Yes.* She became lost in thought. Perhaps the falcons had commanded the sandstorm to come for no other reason than to blow the backfill back into the pit—for would they not yearn to bury the remarkable structure anew? If they believed the Egyptians had buried the father of falconry inside, or at the very least the tyrant's spiritual double, every falcon would surely associate the cult pyramid with a kind of slavery. For all she knew, each winged creature had resolved to forgo any feeding at all—until the cast had fulfilled its sacred, vital charge.

From far away, a raucous din clinked and clanked; it had to be the mess tent, all the lanterns clattering in time with the pots and pans. She rolled her shoulders. *Already, the high winds would've left the whole place as a jumble of tables and chairs and kitchenware.* Her belly rumbled, for she felt hungry. At the same time, she wondered if the mess tent's corner guys might come loose. *What'd happen then?* She pictured the billowing roof threatening to collapse and the Bedouin cook grabbing hold of the aluminium upright—until another strong gust came along, and the upright levitated two feet or more before returning to its place. Her stomach rumbled anew, and Anastasia wondered if she could make her way there. Once she had found either a crust of bread or a plateful of Yorkshire pudding, she could take shelter beside the wrought-iron bake oven. *No, don't go.* The hatch blew open, and a torrent of hot soot and sand enveloped her. When she finally managed to shut the hatch, she lamented Rupert. *What if he and the others don't survive the storm? What if the storm buries them alive?* As the hot desert gale continued to lash the wooden pantechnicon, she pictured the mess tent's tin upright falling to the side. *What then?* Once the roof had collapsed, the whole of the mess tent would lurch forward like a big ball of tumbleweed. The depths of her gut growling, Anastasia pictured the mess tent enveloping poor Rupert, the young man writhing about this way and that—plentiful amounts of watermelon and figs, cottage pie and fairy cakes, field beans and olive oil, spiced Red Sea fish and savoury *kibbeh* drenching him in a damp, sticky residue.

Anastasia clutched her arms to her chest and lay low. *I should've brought a pillow.* Her neck aching, she sat up again. *Al-khamsin* roared louder, and she thought back a few days to mid-April or thereabouts. Had she not heard an unearthly moan in the sky late one afternoon? *I should've taken it as a portent. God, I should've known the storm drew close. I should've insisted everyone prepare.* A loud, mighty gust shook the pantechnicon, and her stream of consciousness quickly cycled back to the present. She prayed for a lull in the storm so that she might step outside. If nothing else, she could call out to someone and ask for a bit of flatbread. Naturally, her thoughts returned to the mess tent. She pictured the current driving it down some gently sloping hill before tearing through an array of windswept wild shrubs.

A second loud, mighty gust shook the van—and a few pebbles flew in through the vent and pelted her in the face. She felt at the space all around her. When she discovered nothing, she thought of her Moon-script books back inside her wardrobe trunk—her prized second edition of Madam Helena's *Isis Unveiled*. Anastasia laughed wistfully. *What sheer delight it'd be to trace my fingertips across that book. Yes, I'd lose myself in fantasy and get lost on the page.* Again and again, she rubbed her hungry belly.

Outside, for the second time, the sky filled with the cacophony of wrathful, shrieking falcons blown by the high winds. Had they noticed the expedition's efforts to preserve the pit, and had the birds of prey grown furious because of it? Perhaps a hundred or more falcons had already come to roost in the boughs of the clementine tree for no other reason than to glare at everyone.

Anastasia clenched her jaw and listened. *Are the falcons' cries growing more and more maniacal? Just what, if anything, do they believe? Would it even be possible for them to think the tomb housed some wicked soul? Maybe so ... and maybe a scholarly chap like Professor Milne doesn't even know half as much as they do.* A dozen more mighty gusts shook the pantechnicon such that the entire van teetered before returning to its place with a violent thud. *God, it's like punishment from on high.* She held her hand over the neckline of her gown and wrapped her fingers around her pendant dove. Outside, the falcons grew quiet—and the silence unnerved her. *What if they conspire to do something drastic? Perhaps the falcons hope to invade the tomb and spirit away the tyrant's body.* She imagined the birds of prey lugging the tyrant's remains off to her tent and dropping the evil falconer into her wardrobe trunk. Trembling, she pictured the maniacal birds of prey sprinkling her favourite pot-pourri all over his face. *And then what?* She pictured a few of the falcons endeavouring to avail themselves of her wrought-metal padlock to secure the wardrobe trunk for good. Still, even if the falcons managed all that, the crazed mummy would burst forth soon enough—the padlock breaking into pieces, both the locking lever and the driver flying everywhere. The whole idea made her cackle like a little girl in the grips of hysteria. *Stop.* She closed her eyes, held herself as tight as she ever had, and sought to convince herself the deafening sandstorm made a soft, tender sound—the sound of a genie lovingly blowing in her ear. *Oh yes.*

From somewhere outside, perhaps forty feet away, a voice sounding like Rupert called for help. *Was that an aural hallucination?* She clenched her jaw. Then, as the call for help came again, she opened the hatch and climbed down from the van. Guided by the sound of his voice, she trudged into the fierce gale. 'How goes the battle?' she asked, when she finally reached him.

'What're you doing out here in the elements?' Rupert asked in turn.

'I want to help save the pyramid. I'm a game girl. I'm strong.'

'Go back to the truck park before something bloody awful happens.' Rupert brought her over to the side and placed the palm of her hand around what felt like a thick hemp rope. 'The professor had us arrange this twine here so we could find our way back through the eddy. Just follow the rope, love.' Without another word, Rupert marched off in the direction of the pyramid.

The sound of his footfalls died out, and she faltered her way along the length of the rope—but in the same direction he had taken, through the wind-ravaged encampment *toward* the cult pyramid. A moment or two later, the burning sands stinging her body, a large object soared by, whipping wildly in the violent, merciless current, flapping and groaning like a colossal oilcloth. *It's the tarp for sheltering the pit. But if the tarp has gone free, how long before the sandstorm buries everything anew?* She groaned. Still, she lumbered along. *I've got to stand guard over my precious discovery.* In the end, the hemp rope guided her to yet another rope—and that one in turn guided her all the way to the clementine tree, where a few of the clementines fell on her scalp and a few others promptly bounced off her shoulder. *I'm here.* She let go of the rope, knelt on the earth, and crawled off towards the pyramid. As she drew closer to what she adjudged to be the edge of the pit, the earth grew unsteady—and she realised a whole section must have failed, such that down below, a great earthen mound had built up all about the narrow passage bordering the pyramid's south wall. *Oh my. What if the collapse buried Rupert?* On her hands and knees, she ventured to the place where the sandbag stairway provided access into the pit—and she crawled all the way down.

At the very bottom, someone greeted her—and she recognised the voice as belonging to an unpleasant little fellow from Cambridge Divinity School. The little fellow did not help her to her feet, so she pushed herself up. 'I fear Rupert Lux has met with death by misadventure,' she said. 'Help me search the heap where we've had the cave-in.'

'So, you doling out the orders now?' the insolent fellow asked her.

'*Orders?*' She did not know what else to say. Despite the winds and sands, she pictured the cowardly chap avoiding her blind gaze by looking at his feet. *Yes. That's right.* She pictured him stroking a tuft of mousy brown whiskers at the tip of his chin and imagined him as having a rather weak chin at that. She resolved to ignore him, and she continued along. Feeling her way, she soon reached the place where a section had failed. 'Rupert, do you hear my voice?' she asked, her question drowned out by the storm. Like a woman searching for her baby, she burrowed downward and scooped out as much of the fill as she could—until her tattered, blackened fingernails bled from all the abuse.

Up above, the little fellow from Cambridge Divinity School called out to one of his friends—a bone specialist from Victoria College. 'Look at the young miss down there,' he continued in a snide tone. 'I do believe she means to exhume that kiwi bloke.' As the two academics broke into a fit of laughter, she tore through the earthen mound. Not until she felt half-certain the two louts had marched off did she admit defeat.

All around, the sandstorm produced the most frightful clamour—a sound as of some great, impossible vortex, the kind of maelstrom that obliterates flotillas. *Like the Spanish Armada.* She called out for help, but who could have heard above all the noise? Over and over, she called out for Rupert, too—but he never answered. The skin all around her snakebite tingled and burned until she felt a stripe of blisters forming across the trunk of her body and reaching deep into her cold, empty womb. *Take shelter.*

Later that day.

Anastasia awoke back inside the pantechnicon. When she sat up, she endeavoured to gauge the hour. *Did I sleep straight through the sunrise? Has dusk already arrived? If so, the sun should have already appeared soft and fluid through the dust clouds.* She lay back down. *How did I get here? Did someone bring me here?* She curled up again and pictured the storm-tossed dunes all aglow in the hazy, tranquil light. When she collected her wits, she exited the shelter. The storm felt and sounded as fierce as ever, but she found her way back to the hemp rope and ventured off toward her tent. *Why not offer my precious dowsing rod as a sacrifice?* With a heavy sigh, she raised her unseeing eyes to the sky and whispered, 'If I burn up my witch hazel bough, would that placate all you falcons? Would it convince you to call off the storm?' She let go of the hemp rope. In defiance of the high winds, she crawled away.

I've got to call on my shadow vision. She crawled low to the earth and pushed through the storm until she located her storm-tossed tent. She fumbled for the flap and entered. *Quickly.* Once she had located her witch hazel bough, she felt for a tin of paraffin oil and made her way through the flap. While she counted out her steps, she groped eastward—until she reached a patch of wild artemisias. There, she drove the witch hazel bough into the earth. And despite the endless gales, she managed to kindle a fire. '*Tout est fini!*' she cried out. When the blaze spread up and down the length of the witch hazel bough, the dancing flames scorched her forearms. Still, she did not draw back. *I am the priestess, and here's my sacrifice.* She did her best to envision the hungry fire. Perhaps it would cycle through a myriad of otherworldly colours—wild strawberry and dark lava, soft gold fusion, and the brightest tangerine. *How good it'd be to witness something like that.* On and on, the fragile wind-tossed fire crackled and burned, then dwindled. Like a woman overcome with adoration, Anastasia stroked her arm. *Yes, it's done. My dowsing rod is gone.* The sands playing through her tousled hair and ripping through her blouse and skirt, she whispered, 'Let the tempest die out.'

Nothing changed. On and on, *al-khamsin* tore through the encampment. If anything, the storm seemed to grow stronger. *Why should I be surprised?* As the current roared, she wondered if she heard the strains of music—the professor scraping his bow across his violin strings. With a sigh, she pictured the palm grove in complete disarray: empty mahogany bottles and safari chairs strewn about. *And here I am acting all prayerful.* At last, she managed to push herself onto her feet. *The whole preposterous idea of making a sacrifice must've been nothing more than the venom confounding my mind. What was I thinking?* She scrubbed a hand over her face and staggered onward through the artemisias.

The winds grew stronger yet and a touch more vengeful, too. A downy softness touched her—a cloud of plumes accompanied by the distinctive cries of pelicans. *Great whites,* she thought.

Don't get to feeling overwrought. Don't get lost in hysterics. Despite her resolve, there could be no avoiding a nervous collapse; given the intense events of the day, she came to hear the roar of the sandstorm as a portent of death. Over and over, she cried out—until the voice of a young Englishman called to her.

When the young man reached the place where she had fallen amid the artemisias, he helped her to her feet.

'Who are you?.

'I came up from the village to see if anyone required help out here, that's all,' the young man answered. 'Why'd you make a fire out here?' he asked.

She realised he must be referring to the charred remains of the witch hazel bough, so she opened her mouth to answer.

'Are you blind?' the young man asked, tapping her wrist.

'Yes, I am blind,' she said.

The young man gasped.

'Is that so awful?' she asked.

'No, no. There's something falling out of the sky. Oh yes, I think it means to swallow us! Like some kind of vengeful angel! An angel shaped like a monstrous jellyfish!'

She lowered her eyes to the earth. Her ankles held tight, she knelt and placed her brow against the crown of her right foot. 'Don't say frightful things like that. You've got to help me find my friend, Rupert. And—'

'It's almost here!' the Englishman said.

'Don't talk like that,' she said.

'It's a flying moon jelly descending from the heavens,' the young man said. 'Yes, I think it means to consume us both.'

Anastasia lifted her eyes to the sky and pictured a godlike being there—a colossal shapeshifting enigma. The merciless

188

being fell on them—and both she and the frantic young Englishman cried out in unison. When she fell to the side, she recognised the creature as the wayward oilcloth with which Professor Milne had intended to preserve the cult pyramid. The coarse texture of the canvas was unmistakable. Still, the oilcloth whipped and snapped and contorted in the most violent manner—until the flapping of the canvas fanned the smouldering witch hazel bough into flames, and the material caught fire. The smoke made her cough. Still, she struggled to break free and to take the young gentleman's hand and to pull him from beneath the tangled bundle. In the end, they helped one another to escape. Once they had crawled off, she paused to listen to the crackle of the fire commingling with the howl of the sandstorm.

He tapped her right wrist again. 'You wouldn't believe how gloriously bright is the blaze,' he told her. 'It's lighting up the night.'

She shook her head and coughed. 'Nightfall has come?' She felt for the young man's arm. 'If the fire happens to be burning as brightly as you say, do you suppose it means that God Almighty has forgiven all my sins?.

The young Englishman failed to answer the question. *Well, how would he even know what I'm talking about.*

The winds wailed on and on, almost as if the sandstorm and its lamentations would last forever.

She scrambled to her feet. The young Englishman took her hand, and she squeezed his thumb. 'Get us back to the hemp rope.

When they finally located it, they continued down to the truck park, where the young man helped her into one of the vans.

Some other pair had already taken shelter there, and they

snickered maliciously. Anastasia determined the pair to be the expedition's Arabic translator, along with a big brute named Mr Molland. Plainly, both scoundrels derived great pleasure from the Englishman's physical appearance.

'Might you be some kind of dandy?' Mr Molland asked the Englishman. 'Might you be a gentleman of the back door? Aye, might that explain all your finery?.

When the two academics burst out in a fit of high-pitched laughter, she pulled on the young man's arm. 'Let's return into the sandstorm,' she said.

'Yes, the two of you ought to push on,' Mr Molland continued. 'You fine young ladies ought to get yourselves over to the Bedouin rainwater cistern. You'll give yourselves a good bath, eh?'

'Whatever you do and wherever you go, Anastasia,' the Arabic translator sneered, 'don't let your girlfriend there use *our* washrooms. We can't have a chap like that lazing about one of our cast-iron tubs. No, no. Soon enough, he'll proposition this fellow and that. And we can't have such buggery.' With that remark, the whole of the wooden wagon rocked back and forth.

She intuited what had happened: Mr Molland had positioned himself on all fours to simulate the thrusting motion of someone engaged in the act of sodomy. 'Here's how the ponce sods off,' the big brute blurted out now. 'Yeah, buggery, that's the Englishman's pleasure. Just think of it. A chap who prefers unnatural sex acts. For shame!'

The sadistic bigotry sickened Anastasia—and she felt the sensation of the diadem spider slowly returning into her womb. And now the entity scraped at her insides with each one of its eight long, hideous legs. A burning sensation spread throughout the place where the snake had bitten into her flesh. *My God.* Her insides churning, she longed to speak up and to chide the two academics but could not manage it. If she had felt stronger, she would have pulled on the Englishman's arm a second time. *But I can't.*

On and on, the inhuman, insidious taunts rang out—the jeering, sadistic, animalistic laughter, too.

At last, the young Englishman crawled back toward the hatch. 'Perhaps the two of you feel the love that dare not speak its name, but the sensation has you affrighted. Why else would you hector me the way you do?' The hatch opened, and the young Englishman bustled off without even shutting it behind him. Nor did he say goodbye to her, as if he believed her to be on good terms with his tormentors.

With downturned mouth and heavy arms, Anastasia fixed her lifeless eyes on the opposite wall and thought of Rupert. *Was he killed out there?* Her jaw went slack. *Maybe he was meant to die, or else he would've died from whatever illness afflicts him. Maybe a dozen or more must die soon. And all because I had to discover that accursed pyramid.*

Mr Molland placed his big sweaty hand on Anastasia's leg and shook her. 'How you feeling, little girlie?'

Even after he had repeated the question, she could not bring herself to answer. Instead, she reached for the place where the snake had bitten her. *That's a wound too long in healing. Heavens.* The winds rattled the pantechnicon. She felt the serpent's venom streaming through her veins. Mr Molland touched her again, and she swatted the lout's hand. When she sat back, she listened to the roar of the sandstorm. *Oh God.* The awful cacophony sounded like a million incensed, ravenously hungry falcons. *Yes, that's right, a cast of falcons.*

XV.

The wilderness of Sinai. 23 May 1920.

Rupert awoke early to find Professor Milne hovering over him. 'What do you want?' Rupert asked him, shaking off a series of terrible dreams dominated by Mr Impérial.

His skin a bit mottled, the professor removed his hat and fanned himself. 'I want to know how you're getting along these days. Are you ill?'

'Am I ill?' Rupert sat up and placed his feet on the floor. 'Yes, I do believe I am. Sick as a dog.'

Professor Milne sneered and stuck his finger in Rupert's face. 'I order you to take a place in the sick tent. As of this moment onward, consider yourself under quarantine.'

Smug academic, Rupert thought, but at nine o'clock that morning, he staggered off into detention. When he reached the sick tent, he paused to read the crude paperboard sign attached to the eave.

'*Welcome to our humble rest home.*
Please don't beset the invalids. It makes them neurotic.'

For a considerable time, Rupert refused to continue

through the door. *Haven't I forgotten someone? This last month or so, haven't I forgotten something?* He shifted his weight. Though he had not given too much thought to the deceased Maud Havelock, he did not wish to fail her faction. *I've got to stop Anastasia from disturbing and profaning the tomb. I've got to prevent her from enriching the louts who manipulate her.* Still, he doubted he would be strong enough. As the expedition had laboured to unearth the cult pyramid anew, his health had continued to deteriorate. Now, whether the malady followed from a fungus within the ruin or from some other reason, he felt certain he had no more than one month to live. A recent development compounded all: Professor Milne had calculated that in no more than one month's time, the expedition would be ready to remove the stone-slab doorway and open the structure. The professor's calculations unnerved Rupert.

Only yesterday, out in the pottery yard, his growing sense of foreboding had compelled him to confront the scholar. 'Before it's too late, sir, we've got to bury the tomb. Something as wicked as pestilence awaits us inside.'

'What you're feeling is nothing more than toxic fumes from some natural gas reservoir,' the professor had insisted.

Anastasia had made her way over then. 'Rupert speaks the truth,' she said. 'It's like this. Thousands of years ago, all the falcons cast a spell on the father of falconry. Yes, to have their revenge, the falcons turned him to stone that he should live like that for all eternity. Honest, I've seen it all in my dreams. The ancient falcons conjured the little pyramid to house their nemesis, and now the various falcons of our time believe we mean to release him from his spell and let him die easy and …'

A sensual breeze rolled in from the sea and crept into

Rupert's robe. His eye burned, so he stepped back from the sick tent. As he did, the evil spirit inside his eyeball recommenced its shrill Oceanic chanting. 'Why must you put me through the mill?' he asked the uncanny being. 'Tell me what's what, old man. And don't give me any cock-and-bull story. How do I heal myself of this pathology?' No ancient Polynesian deity answered. Even worse, the chanting droned on. Rupert staggered this way and that, for the illusory cacophony reverberated all throughout his being.

An hour later, Rupert awoke to a cloud of metallic-blue carrion flies darting all about the jumble of dirty stockings that littered the floor. As he rubbed his temples, he heard the steady dissonant modulation of goat bells. 'Does anyone else hear goat bells pealing?.

'Don't be daft,' one of the others told him. 'All that ringing in your ears is only the bubbly natural gas buzzing about your bloodstream. You're feeling the collar, just like the rest of us. Happens all the time. We dig for gold and end up finding some potent chemical deposit.'

The goat bells holding steady, Rupert rearranged his woollen army blanket and lay back down.

One of the other ailing archaeologists, a fellow by the name of Neville B. Grimes, strolled over to Rupert's bed. 'If you don't mind my asking, did you ever have it off with Anastasia?'

'What a disgusting question.' Rupert swatted at some of the carrion flies and rolled onto his side.

Neville snickered and shook the bed. 'That'd be the hooker. You of all people having your way with a bird as fine as that Huguenot girl.' .

'What do you mean by that?' Rupert asked, pushing himself back slowly.

194

'I mean, you're a sodomite, only you don't even know it. I'd say it's down to the fact you can't accept your own sordid nature. Back home at Saint Christopher's College of Medicine, all them mad doctors call it 'primal repression'. They got loads of clever books all about it, don't you know?'

When several other sardonic fellows spoke up to wholeheartedly agree with Neville's slanderous comments, Rupert climbed out of bed. 'Have a good laugh, gentlemen.' Calmly, he buttoned up his nightshirt and made his way outside into the glare of the sun.

From behind a boulder the colour of white smoke, a scorpion crawled forward—as if for no other reason than to catch a glimpse of his right eye. Perhaps awoken by the scorpion's perilous presence, the dæmon broke back into its wild Oceanic chant—and the goat bells resumed.

Three times over, Rupert rubbed his right eye. 'Stop!' As the cacophony continued, the weight of the illusory falcon returned; the invisible creature had come back to roost on his shoulder. In no time, his knees failed him. Writhing about in the dust, he stubbed his toe against one of the ceramic bedpans lying about the sick-tent grounds. When he grew still, he scanned the mint-blue sky. 'Dear Lord, silence that awful din! Make it stop!' If anything, the pulse of the dæmon's chant only grew louder and faster. Rupert rubbed his right eyeball. 'Someday you'll be sorry. I'll send you away, and that's a bloody promise.' He smote the earth, sending the scorpion scuttling off into the rocks.

The chant ceased then, and no sound remained but the dissonant peal of the goat bells—but they grew louder and faster, as if a stampede of a thousand hollow-horned beasts must soon descend on him. Breathless, he crawled off into a patch of wild Egyptian beans. Then, as the noise of the stampede grew almost deafening, a nondescript woman in a blouse and a long walking skirt approached. 'Who might you be?' he asked her, fixing his gaze on the fistful of grape leaves in her hand.

'Get away. You don't recognise me face? To be sure, I'm your lady friend from Cairo.'

'*No*,' he almost shouted. 'You're *not* Maud Havelock. No, you can't fool me. What do you want?'

The woman dropped the grape leaves at her feet. 'What did our rivals tell you? Did the girl in the black *burqa* say something? Did she tell you I'd be dead? And what about the cult pyramid? Did she tell you we must have respect for the dead and never disturb ancient burials and such?' The woman stepped forward. 'Dalrymple has told me to bring you a most paramount message.' The fallen grape leaves fluttered about in the cool, gleeful late-morning breeze. 'He wants you to remain true to our little agreement. And if you do, you'll be greatly rewarded.'

'Greatly rewarded?' Rupert slouched.

'Greatly rewarded indeed,' the woman whispered, sitting beside him. 'Stay true to us and we'll reward you with the most priceless of flowers. A lady slipper orchid. And when the noble precious bud opens, the blossom will take the shape of the splendid ancient leather house shoe that Nitokris lost to the Prince of Egypt on the night she attended the Pharaoh's winter revelries.'

'Nitokris?'

'Yes, Nitokris, the loveliest virgin maid in the history of the Nile Valley. You've never heard of her?'

As fatigued as Rupert felt, he could not bring himself to say anything. Indeed, he rather resented the fact someone wished to speak to him at this inopportune moment. After a while, he crawled back into the sick tent—only to bump into a wooden crate on which one of the nurses had heaped a consignment of antitoxins.

The woman claiming to be Maud Havelock followed him inside and put the crate back in place. Then, once she had picked up all the fallen phials and had arranged each one where it should be, she flashed a motherly smile. 'Why so galled?.

Rupert refused to answer. Instead, he shuffled over to his camp bed and fluffed his tattered pillow.

She strode across the tent. 'How could anyone refuse an offer such as mine?' she asked him. 'What a terrific insult. If you sold that orchid, you'd be as wealthy as a king.'

Silently, Rupert staggered off to the other side of the crowded sick tent and lay on the floor. *Don't listen to another word. I've got to rest. I've got to get better. Stay here. Don't go.*

Nightfall.

Barefoot and dressed only in his nightshirt, Rupert exited the sick tent and tottered off through the archaeological preserve. *I must find Anastasia.* A part of him longed to confess his deceit that very evening. *Why not?* He had come to disbelieve that anyone from Maud's faction could help rid him of the entity inside his eyeball. Try as he might, though, he could not locate Anastasia. *Maybe she's gone off to the pyramid.* He marched off in that direction, but when he reached the pit, the site proved to be deserted. The seemingly moonless night made him weep for a moment until he cursed the darkness. Other than the dim glow of a solitary tin lantern dangling from the clementine tree, no light shone.

A twinge awoke throughout his right-shoulder muscles,

and Rupert paused beside the night watchman's little American pup tent. The way the portly old man gasped and yelped in his sleep, Rupert wondered if the poor night watchman, too, might be dying. *Could it be some kind of bloody curse?* At last, Rupert inched his way over to the uneven sandbag stairway. *Did I hear something?* He stopped. The night grew brighter, the glorious Moon having emerged from the clouds—and even if he hallucinated all, the ponderous weight of an illusory falcon settled on his shoulder and nudged him with the hook of its beak. Could the uncanny creature hope to keep him from going any further? The invisible, diabolical falcon rasped and pecked at Rupert's ear. *Shall I return to the door? If I do, perhaps something unspeakably gruesome will happen.* He pictured the faint traces of a face, an ungodly visage resembling the tyrant's death mask, gradually emerging from the silvery moonlit stone. *I can just see the face, its features, the silvery eyes.* Rupert imagined them as taking after those of a diseased person, someone plagued by cataracts. *I'm quite sure the face will speak up and say something, but what?* He imagined the inscrutable visage asking him this: 'Are you my equal?' Rupert shivered now, for he thought of the peculiar countenance as having the most unnerving voice—one with a tone sure to leave him feeling unbearably self-conscious, as if the voice were sure to sound like a recording of his own intonations. *And who wants to hear a recording of his own voice rather than feel its timbre through the bones of his face?* Rupert pictured the face adopting a grin. 'No, *you* are not my equal,' the face might say then. '*You* are no one to disturb my slumber. No one. Do *you* command the power to charm an electorate with promises of sound wisdom and moderation, only to assume power and govern as a spiteful radical? Have *you* the power to rig elections? Have *you* the power to see no evil and hear no

198

evil and to employ such a policy as a means to justify undying entitlement spending and economic stagnation? Have *you* the power to beguile the public and convince them to ignore the many consequences of democracy and all its decadence?'.

Back inside the little tent, the night watchman's snoring grew much too rapid. Rupert stumbled over and peeked through the flap. 'Can't you even smell the contagion, you fool?' When the night watchman woke, Rupert knelt at his side. 'You've got to get out of here, mate.

Slowly slurring his words, the night watchman muttered some profanities before climbing out of his bedroll. 'What're you doing here?'

'I'm trying to find Anastasia.'

'She's not here.'

'I know.' Rupert glanced over his shoulder and studied the pit for a moment. 'Maybe we ought to bury her accursed pyramid before the damn thing unleashes a terrible plague. What do you think?.

'Go back to the sick tent where you belong,' the night watchman told him. 'And I'll give you some good advice as well. If you don't know sleight of hand, don't play *any* card games. All them blighters down there in the sick tent, they know every trick. Some of them have been fixing sporting events for years.' With that, the night watchman cscorted Rupert back to his camp bed.

Once the night watchman plodded back to his little pup tent, Rupert lost himself in slumber. A series of dreams soon disturbed his rest—remembrances of home, with all those tormenting memories of Father's business contact. 'Mr Impérial, yes, I remember,' Rupert whispered in his sleep.

The dream grew increasingly vivid.

Rupert rises from his camp bed and returns to the pyramid. There he descends to the door and knocks. And soon enough, Mr Impérial opens the door and greets him. 'Come inside,' the smug businessman says. Mr Impérial guides him to the heart of the tomb and down a winding stairway, into the bowels of the earth— perhaps deeper than any explorer has ever descended. At last, Rupert stops and taps the ancient wooden banister. 'What's this all about?' he asks. 'Where are you taking me?' For the longest time, Father's evil business contact says nothing. Instead, he flashes a knowing grin and drags Rupert further down the stairway. 'I'll take you to where Anastasia is waiting. And she'll tell you why you must die, and she'll tell you why she must give herself to someone better. She'll explain to you what your unconscious mind already knows. She'll tell you that, all those years ago, I succeeded in taking your manhood away from you. And that's what makes you inadequate and unfit for marriage.'

From that moment on, Rupert struggles to go free. Still, no matter how hard he kicks, he finds he's no match for Mr Impérial. And a moment passes by before they reach the Earth's core—where Anastasia appears, the young lady dressed in a regal Polynesian gown. And she sits Rupert beside an underground oven composed of fire-heated rocks and tells him every vile thing Mr Impérial said she would.

XVI.

The wilderness of Sinai. 2 June 1920.

The breeze blew in from somewhere out on the horizon. Anastasia stood along the edge of the pit and waited while Professor Milne's team prepared to remove the slab that served as the cult pyramid's door. *Today's the day. We're going inside.* The sky filled with frantic cries: a cast of irate, maniacal falcons. The clamour reminded her of the jackals howling that night Rupert confessed his deceitfulness. She blinked uncontrollably, for she found herself as puzzled and as panicked as she had felt that night. Now she debated whether she ought to undress down to her foundation garments. *If I did, what would the falcons think? Perhaps the gesture would placate them, because they'd recognise something of themselves in my wild abandon.* Little by little, she came to her senses.

From below, a dozen or more voices cheered. Had the labourers succeeded in drawing aside the monolith that had sealed the tomb? She whispered a simple prayer of thanksgiving and readied herself. Then, tapping her walking stick here and there, she found her way over to the sandbag stairway. The falcons' protestations grew louder and louder, and as the current moved through the length of her summer gown, she raised her face to the sky. *The falcon will never forgive me. At any moment now, perhaps the whole cast should swoop down and tear me to pieces.* She let the walking stick fall to the earth, and she crossed her arms across her chest.

Footsteps ascended the sandbag stairway. 'Let me help you down,' the professor said, returning the walking stick to her hand. Anastasia lowered her blind gaze from the sky. The professor took hold of her left elbow and helped her to the base of the pit. From there, he guided her to the door. 'Shall we step inside?' he said.

When the party proceeded through the door, she let Professor Milne help her forward into the corridor. *Oh my.* In the cool of the shade, she paused to touch the cold masonry. At the same time, she breathed in the faint musky remnant of some unknowable odour—until the tip of her nose burned.

'Do you smell something funny?' Professor Milne asked her.

'No,' she lied.

'Honestly? I always assumed a blind lass like you might've detected something, since you should've honed all your other senses to make up for your … limitations.'

She should have taken the comment as a patronising insult, but she barely registered any kind of emotional response. Ever since Rupert had confessed his deceit, she had found herself numbed—as if he had turned her to stone. Despite all, she continued forward. *Don't stop. Keep going.*

When the party reached the cool of the grand gallery, she heard the shuffle of footsteps darting off in this direction and that.

'My assistants,' the professor said. 'They're arranging

candle lanterns to illuminate the full breadth of the space.

She imagined the light all around her radiating a dreamlike glow—perhaps even a sweet, subtle Persian indigo. She craned her neck as if she could see the ceiling. With a grin, she imagined the ancients had painted some of the constellations there. At last, she lowered her sightless gaze toward the floor. *Just how big would this room be?* She adjudged the treasure room's dimensions to be that of a stately parlour room. *That sounds right.* Staring straight ahead, she imagined an alcove there. *And inside, there'd be a cage, and within the cage would be two falcons, both creatures blinded by dark velvet hoods that some falconer had draped over each captive's glorious feathery crown. And even after all these thousands of years, neither captive has starved to death … at least not yet.*

The floor seemed to move—and for a few moments, she imagined herself sailing on a ghost ship—perhaps even a godless slave ship. When the floor ceased to move, she pictured the enchanted tomb. *How beautiful it must be.* She imagined a chryselephantine idol fashioned by some ancient hand, a statuette of some kind, positioned atop the sepulchre. *Or what about an Egyptian ibis studded with jewels of sapphire?* She leaned forward. 'What do you see?' she asked the professor. 'Describe the tomb for me. Please.' .

'Ah, but there's no tomb anywhere,' he told her. 'The whole place is empty. That said, we're standing not ten feet from what appears to be an immovable life-size sandstone likeness of some portly damn fool pharaoh.'

She pictured the figure as Oberon—right down to his regal cape. Giggling, she made her way forward and placed the palm of her left hand on the sandstone figure's chest. Carefully, she felt for a heart scarab—the costly kind of talisman an ancient high priest might have embedded in the sculpture's left breast. *If this thing had indeed served as a pharaoh's spiritual double, a fine talisman has to be here. What else might've served to silence the wicked entity if and when the gods demanded it speak up and confess the pharaoh's sins?* She discovered nothing, so she moved her hands to the statue's hips. Each one felt as smooth as pearl, and that sensual fact alone made her heart beat harder and harder. *Yes. Oh, yes.* She rolled the tip of her tongue over the gap between her two front teeth and wrapped her left palm around the effigy's throat.

An aroma like *escargots à la bourguignonne* invaded the air. Had the strange likeness just exhaled? A second time, the uncanny being seemed to breathe out—but this time, the exhalation smelled like spoiled garlic-mushroom oil. Moreover, it sounded like a groan. Gently, she felt for the double's lips. *There.* Her fingers detected an ill-formed mouth. She rested her brow against the pharaoh's left breast. 'This here would be the place where the heart scarab ought to be,' she whispered, letting the root of her nose come to rest against what felt like a flaxseed protruding from the king's soft, stony chest. *Could that flaxseed be a mole?* She redoubled her efforts to grasp what had happened. 'Who turned you to stone?' she asked. 'Did someone condemn you to live for eternity this way? I imagine you must yearn to breathe your last and go to your reward, yes?'

A summer breeze whisked down through the corridor and washed through the whole of the grand gallery so that the flames crackled within the various candle lanterns. *Oh, that's lovely. It sounds a bit like the flapping of fairy wings.* For a moment or two, she pictured Cobweb and Moth and Peaseblossom and Mustardseed flittering all about—the four little sprites dancing like girls from the Monte Carlo Ballet.

What a terrific ballet company, that one.

The breeze died out, and when the stone figure seemed to groan a second time, she raised the crown of her walking stick and tapped its chest. 'If you command the power to speak, say something,' she whispered. When the entity failed to speak up, she dropped her walking stick and wrapped both hands around the statue's throat again. 'Have you got any wondrous treasures for us to plunder?' she asked, her voice cracking. 'What about a cache of eternity rings?' When no answer came, she let out a muffled shriek; the absence of plunder convinced her the figure looming before her must indeed be the worst of penitents. 'Well, then, what crime did you commit?' she asked. 'Tell me every detail. What trespass?' Though the voice might have been nothing more than a hallucination, she felt certain she heard a whisper—and the timbre thrilled her so much she swooned.

Late in the evening, she awoke in what felt like the camp bed back in her tent. From the direction of the palm grove, the familiar sound of Professor Milne's violin played. He performed a night piece, a simple lullaby. *No, it's a piece from that fantasy opera,* Oberon. As she lay there listening, she counted the days to Midsummer's Eve. *When the date comes, perhaps I'll gather a handful of Midsummer flowers and arrange them beneath my pillow. Even if the weight of my skull crushes the delicate petals, my dreams are sure to come true on Midsummer Night. That's what little girls believe, anyway, little girls and queer little boys.* When the alluring violin music concluded, her thoughts drifted back to the likeness held captive inside the cult pyramid. *And what about the absence of any treasures?* She thought of the fools who had always believed she might someday find something of great value. *Mr Dalrymple and the rest will be crestfallen.* She sat up. *I wonder if any of them even stopped by to check on me. Probably not.* She lay back down and shook her head.

The desert breeze surged, and a series of odours wafted through the tent—one of them vaguely reminiscent of a gentleman's hair pomade. She wondered if Rupert had stopped by the tent to check on her. *No, he probably feels much too guilty to watch over me.* She felt for her Huguenot cross and touched the pendant dove. *I wonder if he'll ever speak to me again, but what does it matter?* She did not think she could ever forgive him for conspiring against her. *If he comes to me tonight, I'll put him to shame. I'll remind him that I always hoped to cure him of his malady.* At last, she pictured Rupert stopping at the foot of her bed. 'Someday, somehow, I'm sure I would've puzzled out a way to convince you to forget all about that entity in your eyeball,' she said. 'Someday, somehow, I would've cured you of all your hysteria.'

She heard swift, determined footsteps entering her tent—so she arose a second time and felt for the mosquito netting. 'Who's there? Rupert, if it's you, go away. I have nothing to say to you.' The footsteps stopped at the edge of the camp bed. 'What's the meaning of this?' Anastasia asked.

'I've just heard the news,' a rather shrill womanly voice spoke up.

'Who are you? Do you work for Mr Dalrymple and all of them, or do you work for the rival faction?'

'What difference does it make?' the woman asked. 'Perhaps I'd be dressed in a black *burqa*, or maybe I'd be dressed in a gown with a velvet bodice. Either way, you've failed to find any great treasure. At the same time, though, you've committed a great sin. Yes, you're no better than an Egyptologist who disturbs a deceased pharaonic soul's blissful slumber.'

Anastasia thought of Rupert again. As lonely as she felt, she longed to be loved by someone—and she had always fancied him. *So what? I'll find somebody better.* Again, she felt for the mosquito netting. 'Please go away.

'No.'

'But I've got to rest now.

'Then rest. Sleep.' Slowly, the footsteps trailed off to the side—as if the intruder must be searching the length and breadth of the tent, stopping now and again, the strange woman perhaps rifling through Anastasia's wardrobe trunk.

Anastasia lay back down. 'Are you hoping to find plunder I might've taken from the pyramid? Even if I'd discovered something, I wouldn't have taken it. A proper Christian woman knows right from wrong. At least a proper Huguenot woman does.'

The intruder froze. 'What do you mean to do about that king down there in the cult pyramid?' the woman asked. 'Whosoever the king might be, he's living down there in greatest agony. Of course, he should be as dead as Queen Anne. But he's *alive*. And I'm sure he wants you to return to him. Who knows why? Maybe the poor fool believes you hold the power to free him from the hex. I know. Maybe he thinks you'll come put a touch of something magic on his lips. Maybe a touch of magic thyme honey. Yes, he imagines something like that ought to do the trick.

Anastasia debated sitting up yet again and pushing the mosquito netting away and climbing out of bed. Instead, she remained where she was. *Careful. I must not provoke her.*

The intruder tapped her foot a few times over. 'If only you had discovered an everyday burial. There wouldn't be much of anything to do. Ah, but you've got a great labour to perform now. In finding what you have found you must determine some way to release the captive from his spell, his never-ending inability to perish from this world.' The intruder tittered like a mischievous child and exited Anastasia's tent.

The wilderness of Sinai. 8 June 1920.

At dusk, Anastasia mustered the strength to climb out of bed. *I'm* not *dying.* Dressed in her nightgown and nothing else, she felt for the tent flap and stumbled outside. *I wonder how the sky appears just now.* In that moment, the sky probably shone a bright exotic hue—the colour of orange marmalade bleeding into orchid pink. She pointed herself toward the horizon and wondered if her eyes presently reflected the light of the gloaming. Whether or not they did, she counted out her steps and found her way back to the clementine tree. *How many more steps to the stairway?* Though she had forgotten, she made her way over and inched her way down to the base of the structure. Soon, she felt her way to the door. *Did anyone notice me?* Step by step, she faltered her way down the corridor and back into the grand gallery. There, the distinct aroma of *escargots à la bourguignonne* guided her forward.

For the second time, she touched the king's lips. *There you are.* A tingling in her fingertips, she dropped her hand to her side. Quickly, her earlobes grew itchy and hot. She sensed the presence of someone else standing to her right. *But who?*

Someone drew near. 'Do you think he deserves his torment?' a woman asked her. 'Don't you believe he's committed great crimes against the falcons? That was a crime against nature, no? A crime against the sensual world.'

Anastasia did not trouble herself to ask just who the

woman might be. How to keep track of all the rival factions and their competing aspirations? She focused her attention on the place where the stony likeness had revealed itself. *Might he be the tyrant who invented the art of falconry?* She touched the king's chest, and as she had done the other day, groped for the elusive heart scarab. When she withdrew her hand, she rubbed her abdomen. She felt sick and struggled to maintain her balance. *Has the diadem spider returned to my womb?* Her belly throbbed until it felt as if she had swallowed a bread knife. *Oh God, the guilt. What do I do?*

The woman who had spoken a moment before circled around both Anastasia and the strange figure.

'Help me to free this person,' Anastasia said. 'How do I do it?' Anastasia reached out with the end of her walking stick and tapped a section of the stone likeness. *Might this be the inventor of falconry? Maybe, maybe not.* She blinked.

'Do you believe it possible for the falcons of antiquity to have transformed some great luminary to stone?' the woman asked. 'If so, how could it be he lives on?' If the woman knew the answer, she did not say. Instead, she hummed a priestly incantation—which soon morphed into a nostalgic tune. After a few measures, Anastasia recognised the air as an excerpt from a celebrated D'Oyly Carte operetta, *The Gondoliers*—Don Alhambra's song, 'There Lived a King.'

When the woman concluded her singing, Anastasia thought she heard the king exhale. A familiar scent returned, too, and Anastasia propped her walking stick against the king's leg. 'Oh yes, *escargots à la bourguignonne.*' She paused to think. *The alluring scent—have I only imagined it?*

The woman clicked her heels and belted out yet another song.

'The harp that once through Tara's halls
The soul of music shed,
Now hangs as mute on Tara's walls
As if that soul were fled.'

Anastasia sighed deeply, noisily. 'Have you come to gloat? Do you mean to judge me and chide me for all my sinful pride and so forth?' When no answer came, Anastasia backed away from the sandstone figure. To the best of her knowledge, she stood directly in front of the other person. 'I don't know what to do about this formation here. Do I simply ignore it? Tell me what to do.'

Gently, the woman pushed Anastasia back—until Anastasia felt the contours of the sandstone figure's pot belly up against her spine.

The woman cackled and snorted. 'Stop opening and closing your mouth without saying anything.' Before Anastasia could respond, the woman belted out another quatrain.

'No more to chiefs and ladies bright
The harp of Tara swells:
The chord alone, that breaks at night,
Its tale of ruin tells.'

When the woman concluded her lament, Anastasia smoothed out the wrinkles in her nightgown's silk-knit fabric. 'Why did you come here?' she asked.

'I only came to tell you to free this king here. Don't you think he'd wish to rest in peace after all these thousands of years? It's a crying shame what's happened to him. That's why you ought to release him from the spell. Do it, why don't you? That'd be the right merciful course to take. That'd be the

210

Christian thing to do.'

Anastasia reeled around slowly and tapped the formation's chest. *Could it be the ancients went and fashioned this sculpture as a way to deceive some god awoken by some arcane superstition? Does that make sense?*

A second time, the woman clicked her heels. 'I don't mean to get you thinking all arseways. Honest. My heart bleeds for you, and that's why I can't just wash my hands of this whole sordid affair.'

Anastasia felt at the contours of the representation. *Does the stone contain some ancient king's spirit?* She shook her head. *Who knows?* The desert breeze cried out from down through the corridor, and while the warm wind moved through her fringe, she contemplated the stone likeness. *Without a doubt, a proper mummy should've awaited me down here. And the ancients should have wrapped the body in byssus cloth. And the ancients should have placed him on a feather bed with silk curtains and a frame of cedar overlaid with gold. A bed fit for a king.* She pictured the mummy holding his sceptres, a crook and flail, across his chest. The breeze died down, and as the air stilled, she tapped the stone likeness. If a person was there, how would she know how to release him from the spell? *Perhaps a great witch would know.* She thought about Titania. *What might* her *counsel entail?* Anastasia pictured Titania speaking into her ear. 'Call on your heart,' she might say. 'The little butterfly inside should tell you what to do. Yes, your soul should tell you. By cock and by pie, I swear it. Yes, and after you've redeemed yourself, you'll return to the Christian life.' Anastasia wondered what Puck might say, if he were to come along in that moment. 'Don't listen,' he might say. 'This king here, he went and enslaved all the falcons. Let the despot pay for what he's done. This king here, he sinned against the natural world. The good, warm, wild, *sensual* world!'

Anastasia placed the palm of her left hand over her left breast, and she felt her soft, steady heartbeat. 'How do I break the spell?' If her soul knew how, it did not say—so she pressed down on her pounding heart. 'Tell me the counterspell!'

Her ankle smarted near the place where the snake had bitten her, and she fell to the floor. What a feeling of devastation, too. Until that moment, she had believed she must be growing stronger—this changed her opinion. Little by little, she felt ill. *No, no. I'm* not *dying.* She scratched at the snakebite scars, the two little puncture wounds, until she knew the skin there must have grown raw and red. *All of that venom streaming about inside me yet, it's not killing me. No, no.* With her ankle throbbing, Anastasia felt feverish and erratic. Slipping in and out of delirium, she forgot who she was and imagined herself a slave girl. 'Why don't you go ahead and put me to death?' she asked the stone figure. 'If a slave girl no longer has the strength to perform her labours, what good would she be?' When no answer came, she pictured her heart beating inside her body. 'What about the spell?' Her soul remained utterly silent. For the longest time, she concentrated and pushed herself to envision what might happen if she were to dream up some way to thwart the curse. She pictured the king crumbling apart, the sound of the implosion something like bread soda dissolving in water.

At last, she stepped back. 'I disbelieve this peculiar formation to be anything at all,' she said. 'No, it's nothing at all. Some kind of ancient ruse and nothing more.' Finally, she exited the cult pyramid and found her way back to her tent. How to sleep, though, after all that excitement? Stumbling about, she slipped into a walking skirt and jumper, then felt for the tent flap and made her way back outside. She reeled around. Had the last gleam of twilight already bled into soft blue darkness? If so, no light would be shining at present save the Moon's curious glow. *Yes, it's nighttime.* Feverish, she wondered if she felt a snake crawling up her side seam. *No, the serpent is down there by the kick pleat.*

She felt the breeze on her face, forgot all about the illusory snake, and imagined the desert wilderness stretching out before her. *How long before life on Earth concludes?* Her skirt flapped. 'Should life on any other planet ever take root?' she asked, half-certain someone was there waiting to answer her question. 'There's no place else so *sublime* as this world,' the person would say. 'As a consequence, what would it matter if life sprouted in some other galaxy? Even a land of fantasy could never compare to Mother Earth.'

Anastasia lifted her eyes to the sky and pictured the Moon shining down on her as brightly as ever. Then she dropped to her knees and crawled off, only to roll down into a shallow depression. When she sat up, she felt at the crater's dimensions and patted the earth here and there. *What could it be?* If only she commanded the power of sight, maybe she could examine the soil. If it seemed a bit blackened, she might have concluded that someone had scorched the expanse for some reason. *Might this big hollow be the remnant of some elaborate Bedouin sand oven?* She clenched her fists and pushed herself up onto her feet. How to tolerate such a terrible scar on the natural world? She kicked at the earth until she believed she had buried the unseemly blemish.

From the direction of the Red Sea shoreline, a terrific, unnerving explosion boomed.

A bomb. She shifted her stance to face the seaside village. *Did the explosion come from there?* Her unseeing eyes searched the sky. *It's the Egyptian people. They long to go free.* She lowered her eyes to the earth and pictured the mysterious crater she had filled in. A second explosion thundered out, a bomb louder than before. The resonating din made her tremble all over. *The revolution*! *The revolution.*

XVII.

The wilderness of Sinai. 19 June 1920.

Rupert arose from his camp bed early that morning, only to find Anastasia awaiting him at the sick-tent door. Her blind, angelic blue eyes seemed dull. He twitched his feet. *Has she come to demand some kind of explanation?* He slipped his morning coat over his nightshirt and, dragging his bare feet, exited the sick tent. 'There's something quite paramount you ought to know,' he told her.

'Oh?' No matter the bright summer glow, her eyes refused to shine.

'When I came out here to join you in the desert, it was because all them bloody thieves had promised to ding the dæmon out of my eyeball. And I had to find some way to go free of the evil spirit, didn't I? That's why I don't repent of my coming out here.'

'So, I ought to forgive your deceit?'.

'On my oath, I had no idea you'd fancy me. What's more, I promise to perform some kind of penance. Maybe someday, I'll find something grand to do. The kinds of amends that'd

215

make you proud. A rite of atonement to transform me into a better person, a good person.'

She let out a forceful breath. 'If I'd found something of value, you would've helped them take it all. And then, if those heartless people had proven themselves willing to uphold their end of the sinful bargain, you would've accepted every penny of their recompense. And you would've abandoned me. Blithely.'

'Please forgive my deceit. I beg you.'

'*Sure.*' A flush appeared in Anastasia's face and neck. Her expression blank, she tapped the end of her walking stick against the earth.

The June breeze grew warm and erotic. *Just the way it always does with the approach of Midsummer's Eve.*

She breathed in and shrugged. She had put out all the signals to a young man who simply did not know how to respond. 'I'm going now.' Tapping the end of her walking stick here and there, Anastasia meandered on her way.

Rupert returned inside, only to find a pair of labourers playing a game of cribbage on his camp bed—and they had arranged the cribbage board atop his pillow. He dropped down onto the floor. As he rifled through faded photographs and newspaper clippings from home, he thought of Georgie. *What might he be doing?* Whatever it was, he would not be haunting some tearoom in Auckland and talking to a beautiful nubile lady like Anastasia. For a time, Rupert pictured Georgie down at Christ's College, Canterbury. *Yes, he's sitting in the library, reading the morning paper. No, at this hour, he'd be reading the evening paper. Still, as lonely as he might be feeling, at least poor Georgie would never have to cope with rejection. Yes, the sorrow, the denial, the rage.* Rupert paced awhile. *What do I do about poor Anastasia? How do I gain her forgiveness?*

The cribbage game continued, and the dealer turned up the jack. 'That's three for my heels!' he cried out.

Rupert crawled over to the corner, where someone had affixed a photograph of the provost marshal's patrol vessel to the tarp. *Maybe there's nothing to do but sail home.* He wondered if he might determine something meaningful to do to announce to himself a new beginning before he went. *Why not make a pilgrimage to Jerusalem? Palestine, the Promised Land. Why not climb the Mount of Olives? Yes, I'll locate some simple sacred token to bring home to poor little Georgie.*

Inside Rupert's eyeball, the evil spirit seemed to kick. Afterward, the ancient presence recommenced with its Oceanic chant.

Rupert revisited the dream, the revelation, the memory of Father's business contact—the crimes he had committed against Rupert. *No, I can't go home. Not until I've conquered the dæmon.* For the first time in years, he recalled a girl from his schooldays—a poem she had written about the old man who often abused her and 'beat her clean.' Rupert sensed the colour drain from his face. *I can't go home until I've beaten myself clean.* Miraculously, the peal of the gleeful goat bells resumed—or so he wanted to believe. Bent on freeing himself that day, Rupert removed a bottle of Greek *ouzo* from beneath his camp bed and slipped the bronze hairpin into his morning coat's right hip pocket. *That's the only hardware I'll require.* He lowered his head and waited for the hallucinatory goat bells to relent. *Enough of that God-awful noise.* When the bells ceased at last, he pushed himself up to his feet. His hands went limp. He felt the illusory falcon return to his shoulder, the creature's talons digging deep into his muscle and bone—deep enough to sever the whole of his right arm from the rest of his body. As he winced in pain, he realised the two cribbage players were staring at him.

'What's wrong with you, then?' one of them asked. 'You come off like you're bloody shellshocked. Either that or you've just seen the ghost of Semiramide.

Rupert could not think of any response, so he strode from the sick tent without saying a word. *Into the wild*. He plodded along for hours. Never once did he even pause to consider either the exceeding grandeur of the crimson-coloured mountains to the north or the austerity of the horizon stretching out to the east. *Where do I go? Where to gouge out that eye?* In time, he hallucinated various avatars of Oceanic gods and ancient Babylonian court astronomers peering at him from behind a jumble of large, black basalt rocks. Given the sun's power, along with his growing apprehensions and the effects of the warm potent *ouzo*, there could be no avoiding the descent into delirium. After a while, he scanned the wispy orchid-shaped clouds and could swear he espied a whole array of sounding balloons.

When he looked down from the sky, an explosion shattered the silence. At least, he believed he had heard the disturbance. The ghostly falcon roosting atop his shoulder dug its left hind toe deeper into his flesh then—almost as if the maniacal creature intended to scrape some symbol onto his collarbone. 'Do you want to know what made that blast?' the illusory creature asked in a strained whisper. 'It must've been a sounding balloon bursting into flames somewhere along the limits of the Earth's atmosphere.'

Whatever the source of the commotion, Rupert sank to his knees. He nursed his splitting head, and by the time he had collected himself, the sky had grown quiet. Deep inside his eyeball, the dæmon had ceased with all its chanting. Rupert pressed his lips into a fine line. *Three cheers*. He sprawled himself out across the earth and examined his hot, aching, sweaty feet. Already, several vexatious blisters had formed.

The illusory falcon chortled, exposed its foreneck, and caressed Rupert's right temple. 'So, just what'll you do now?' the apparition asked him. 'Do you suppose you'll find yourself a tin of heel cream out here in the countryside? If not, don't panic. Why not ring the duchess? Or post her a letter.' Once more, the spectral bird of prey snickered.

'Do you want me to die out here?' Rupert asked the imaginary creature. 'Well, I'm not ready to die,' he continued. 'Not by a long shot. Whatever fumes and fungus have sickened me, that don't matter at all. I mean to survive the malady.'

From high above the clouds, another explosion splintered the peace and quiet—and the aural hallucination seemed so real his eardrums ached. He struggled to his feet but fell right back onto his knees. 'No more of them bloody sounding balloons. Just one more of them horrid explosions, and I'll be as deaf as the mainmast.' He gathered his strength and marched onward, shading his eyes from the sun's oppressive glare. And the day turned to night, and the night passed by.

The wilderness of Sinai. 23 June 1920.

He awoke late in the morning in a Bedouin encampment. Someone must have found him lying in the desert. *And he brought me here.* Rupert shook his head and studied the rooftop of the large black goat-hair tent. Feeling both thankful and embarrassed, he crawled over to the side and threw open the cloth curtain. 'Who the devil found me and brought me here?' he asked the children. They did not answer, but one of the girls tugged on yet another cloth curtain—and an old man lifted it from the other side. '*Shuqran,*' Rupert said, bowing his head in thanks.

I'm a fool, he thought, as he trudged out of the camp. *I've got to gather my nerve and gouge out my eyeball.* He marched onward. *I've got to let the gods of the desert help me find the right spot to perform the rite. The gods of the desert—they won't let me down.*

When he came on a heap of partridge bones lying beneath the blazing sun, he stopped to study the desolation all around him. *Where am I?* He took refuge in a memory of his schooldays and recited a bit of verse:

'And yonder all before us lye

Desarts of vast eternity.'

A shadow streaked across the shifting sands: a solitary bird of prey. How long before a whole wake of honey buzzards descended on him? With no better alternative, he forced himself to keep going. *Onward to the field of battle.* Rupert licked his cracked lips and sucked his cheeks—anything to alleviate his parched throat. As he made his way forward, he detected a trace of methane such as might emanate from a bed of coal. Dizzy, he hallucinated a vivid avatar of Anastasia. 'You're not real, are you?' he asked the apparition. 'Tell me you're not real. Please.' When the beautiful young lady remained silent, he advanced. 'Take me back into your confidence,' he pleaded. When Anastasia remained as silent as before, he lowered his gaze to his feet and wept. 'Let's be friends again. Yes, let's be the best of friends.'

'No,' she told him. 'Why should I wish to be friends with *you*? Remember, whether it's some kind of fungus or natural gas that's killing you, you're *dying.*

'Why you giving me the beans?.

'I'm not. Why would I wish to deceive you?'

Almost hysterical, he reached out his hand to take her by

the wrist—and the apparition faded away to nothing.

In tears, he faltered along. Coming at dusk, he paused before an array of basalt boulders. They did not belong here in the wilderness of Sinai. Unlike all the earth-yellow granite and sun-washed limestone, each basalt boulder shone almost the same colour as the ancient volcanic-ash statues standing sentinel all across the windswept fields of Easter Island.

Deep inside his right eyeball, the dæmon grunted out the Oceanic chant—three beats per measure, like a solemn overture.

Rupert snapped his head back, sneered, and placed his hands on his hips. 'Damn you to hell, you bloody bagpipe.' Loudly and spitefully, the goat bells returned, menacing him—and he tipped his bottle of *ouzo* to his parched lips. When he had downed every last drop, he smashed the bottle against the rocks and threw himself down. He lay on his back in the hot sand, and squinting in the sunlight, raised the bronze hairpin to his right eye. *Let's do this here and now.*

The goat bells died down, and the Oceanic chant fell silent, until no sound remained save the whistle of the desert breeze.

'Why can't Rupert crouch to the fore?' an illusory voice asked.

'I'd say he's crocked up,' a second voice announced.

'Yes, the young man must be playing silly buggers,' a third voice spoke up. 'Behold that length of wire in his hand. I'd say the mad Kiwi means to poke his own eyeball out!'

Rupert pushed himself up. Each one of the basalt boulders had assumed the shape of a living, breathing, talking Easter Island statue. 'Ye gods!' He jerked, nearly dropping the hairpin. Calming himself, he paused to think. Had some kind of Christian magic conjured the whole illusion? *Perhaps the woman in the black* burqa *has engineered the hoax.* He checked for any sign of her. 'Are you here? Who might be responsible for all this? Speak up! Let's hear it.'

Up ahead, an undressed Veronika appeared. But for a muslin apron draped over her shoulder, she had nothing to shield her body. Whether it was her, whether it was an apparition, she whistled and clapped her hands three times over. 'Just where in the name of Jesus do you think you're going?' she asked him. 'Janey Mack! Are you going down the spout?'

He rubbed his eye and glanced over at his side—where a perfect, illusory lady slipper orchid drooped, its yellow-green stem much too weak to hold the blossom. *I've got to come to my bloody senses.*

The apparition drew close to him and shook her head. 'Poor Mr Rupert, your woes would bring a tear to a glass eye, so they would. Ha! A tear to a glass eye!' The dreamlike figure knelt before the lady slipper orchid. 'You've got no idea how priceless a bud like this ought to be,' she continued. 'Bring this to market, and you should make enough of a profit to purchase the whole of Orchid Isle, and just think of what an honour that'd be. You'd be king of the finest realm.'

Another apparition appeared now: Mr Dalrymple. With a self-satisfied smile, he took Veronika's hand and guided her off into the shadows.

Rupert curled up into a ball, and by the time he peeked, the starry night had already arrived. He shivered, for the desert had grown just cold enough to be discomfiting. Once he had bundled himself up in the warmth of his robe, he stumbled up onto his feet. No matter how many points of light in the sky, he fixed his gaze on the star Betelgeuse. *Hello.* He felt hopelessly lost. When he looked down, he scanned the desert—the endless desolation. Given the darkness, how to espy any sign of life? Once more, he lifted his gaze. As he examined the stars, he gasped for breath. More than anything, he yearned to witness something miraculous—a meteor shower flashing through the northern sky. *Anything to disturb this solitude. Anything.* Off to the east, a doomed shooting star broke apart over the horizon—and the disheartening omen incensed him so much he clenched and unclenched his hands until his nails bit into his flesh.

From somewhere amid the stars, one last explosion rumbled. Might it have been a sounding balloon conducting atmospheric measurements, and if so, who had released the gasbag in the first place? What if the responsible party happened to be an astronomical society from antiquity, a team of futuristic, pioneering meteorologists commissioned by someone from the House of Ptolemy? Rupert nodded his head rapidly. *If so, that last exploding weather balloon would have been thousands of years old.*

He settled himself beside a purple rock—a meteorite, perhaps. Beguiled, he soon thought he heard music. As he strained to hear, he wondered if it might be an Irish pipe band performing the tune of an American song, perhaps 'Finnegan's Wake'. For five measures, Rupert hummed along with the air—until he finally fell asleep and lost himself in a dream.

His expression blank, Mr Impérial appears at the foot of young Rupert's bed. 'Why don't you curse my name?' Mr Impérial asks him. 'If you say anything, I'll claim it's slander, libel, yet another attempt at a frivolous lawsuit. I'll plead my innocence, don't you know?'

The dream concluded, and Rupert awoke. Though he remembered the dream, the shock of it all preserved him from too much torment. *I suppose I ought to be grateful for that.* He shot a glance off to his right. *Did I hear something stirring in the darkness? I think so.* Shivering, he tottered to his feet and scanned the shadows.

The moonglow illuminated something lying over to one side. He peered at it. The object seemed to be an empty dromedary bag.

Has someone come around? At that hour, the intruder could be anyone: a highwayman, perhaps. *What if he works for a larger syndicate that helps him to fence whatever goods he manages to secure out here in the wild?* Rupert climbed atop the purple meteorite and studied the shadows. *Back in Cairo, what if the intruder has a whole network to help him launder his ill-gotten gains?* Rupert clenched his fists. Despite the lack of any evidence, he felt quite certain a murderous thief drew near—beneath the cloak of night. Rupert searched for a weapon of some kind. *What does the intruder intend to do to me? Scalp me? Behead me? Maybe he aims to consume my heart.* Rupert shivered. The atrocious idea of cannibalism made him think back to his schooldays—those lessons regarding the ancients' habit of devouring this or that prisoner of war— the victim's life force becoming one with the victor. *That's what happened to that chap from Captain Cook's expedition. I remember.*

He rubbed his arms as the night grew colder. How sublime the desert seemed at that hour, too—as if nothing separated this world from Outer Space. *How long before I float off into the stars?* He studied the shadows of the night until he felt homesick. The landscape reminded him of the stark beauty and grandeur that was New Zealand—the North Island's volcanic plateau, all the fine crater lakes dotting the otherwise barren fields.

The weight of the illusory falcon returned to his shoulder,

and the spectral creature's mantle seemed to brush up against his ear. Before long, the uncanny being seemed to reach down and trace its downy crest across his neck. 'What do you suppose the highwayman should do to you when he finds you here?' the falcon asked. 'Maybe the highwayman should toy with you like a little child tormenting an insect. Or maybe the highwayman should dismember you and arrange your entrails in some strange psychotic pattern of symmetrical shapes, everything aglow here and there beneath the stars.'

Rupert resented the illusory creature's presence, for it reminded him of how the children back home once piled on poor Georgie. The more Rupert thought about it, the more he blamed his father. *Why did he leave London?* Back in England, the Royal Trust might have felt dutybound to find a charity ward willing to tend to Georgie's needs. *And the bloody physicians would've posted the bill to the Lord Treasurer himself. No, we never should've left London.*

The nighttime breeze whistled through the empty dromedary bag. What a sinister tune the current made, too. The soft, eerie music sounded like the chirps of those songbirds back home—the laughing magpies that lived out among the lava plateaus.

The breeze died down, and the bones of Rupert's shoulder rattled beneath the weight of the illusory falcon roosting there. 'What do you suppose makes the highwayman so wicked?' the creature asked. 'Do you think maybe his mother neglected him? Might that explain why a thieving fingersmith only ever feels *self*-pity?'

A cloud shifted, and the moonlit dromedary bag cast a peculiar elongated shadow—the tip pointing toward a rock shaped like a pig's bladder. As the shadow faded, Rupert scrutinised the night sky. He espied an almost-imperceptible constellation to the north, Berenice's Hair, and pointed at it. *Yes, I'm sure that's what it'd be.* Then, as he lowered his hand, he wondered just how many galaxies a vast star cluster like that might include within its confines. If he were home now, he would come around to one of the private stargazing society's observatories one balmy night and ask some beautiful young lady. She might check charts showing various constellation declinations. *And then she'd give me a grin. And she'd furnish the answer.*

The wind grew stronger, tousling Rupert's hair, the strands stinging his eyes. His musings turned to Anastasia. *What might she do if she lay here beside me?* He held himself close and pictured Anastasia tenderly running her fingers through his hair, which he'd allowed to grow a touch too long. 'Do you recall the story of Berenice's Hair?' she asked. 'The loyal, dependable queen feared her husband would not survive the war in Syria, so what did she do? She sacrificed her long, beautiful hair as a votive offering. And the Gods of Olympus descended to the altar, collected the gift, and placed it in the heavens. Hence the constellation shining down on us, a constellation as bright as the peacock.'

Rupert imagined the light of the peacock constellation shining down onto the nape of his neck. Georgie had always loved the myth of the peacock's tail—the story of that goddess who had placed her faithful watchman's eyes within the creature's glorious fan. Rupert ran his hand along his scalp and pulled his hair—until he could not bear the pain any longer. If he had a pair of shears, he would have sliced away a clump. *Why not dedicate a lock to some maniacal god?* Once more, the wind seethed—and his eyeball felt so dry that even though he blinked five times over, it did nothing to counteract the unpleasant sensation.

'Perhaps you ought to reach up and pluck out your eyeball and sacrifice the damn thing already,' Anastasia might have told him, if she were to materialise at his side just now.

And so the night passed by, and he could not help but sob. *Anastasia.*

The wilderness of Sinai. 27 June 1920.

When the light of dawn arrived, Rupert had never felt so thirsty, so hungry, so bloodless. Still, as the sun rose higher and the morning light grew hotter, the illusory falcon seemed to depart. *Right, then, no more delays.* He left the latest Bedouin camp where he had taken refuge, blundered back into the wild, and soon came to a split rock boasting a series of esoteric Bedouin symbols etched into the sandstone. He continued forward three steps, stopped in his tracks, and raised the hairpin to his face. A charcoal-black Egyptian vulture crowned with a long, spiked feather mane descended from the sky. 'Go on!' Rupert shouted at the creature. 'If I have to gouge out my eyeball, I'll not feed it to the likes of *you.* So, go on then. Go piss up a window shutter.'

The vulture wailed, as if it intended to conjure some ignoble vulture god to come help it with its demands for sustenance. When nothing happened, the winged creature soared off—its shadow gliding across the desert sand. In time, as many as three of the vulture's sombre feathers fluttered to the earth—so Rupert crawled over, collected one of them, and stroked his sun-scorched nose with the vane. How soothing the little barbs were. But the morning breeze billowed strongly enough that the feather escaped his grasp and drifted off. While the desert sun seared the back of his neck, he contemplated the hairpin.

A vivid apparition of Anastasia approached. 'Why must you play for time?' the bright-coloured hallucinatory figure asked him. 'Go on and place the tip of the hairpin against the corner of your eye, whereon you've only got to apply increasing pressure, until …'

He tried to spit but could not manage. Then he sought to swallow the saliva but could not do that either. From the east, myriad true-to-life goat bells pealed, like a stampede of a thousand or more true-to-life goats racing westward. *Goodnight, McGuiness. End of story. Nothing more.* The earth rattled with the approach of the stampede. Rupert drew a deep breath and compelled the hairpin into his flesh and ever deeper toward the optic nerve.

The dæmon belted out the chant for a moment. Then the entity rattled about. 'We ask that you go no further!' The dæmon transmitted its appeal in the majestic plural, its disdainful voice reverberating all throughout Rupert's being like the sound of fifty or more lordly ghouls whispering in concert.

The dæmon's pride only inspirited Rupert to push the hairpin further in. *It's now or never.*

Anastasia shook her finger at him then. 'You just wish to impress me. Wouldn't that be right? You hope to compensate for some deep-seated insecurity by showing me how valiant you could be. How terribly prideful.

As the apparition boarded an illusory army truck, Rupert studied her. 'Where are you going?' he asked her. 'Might there be a citadel nearby? Do the soldiers mean to kill all the revolutionaries?' The apparition did not answer, and the illusory army truck drove off and dissolved simultaneously. 'Please come back!' Rupert cried out.

The dæmon whispered the chant for a moment. When it

stopped, it adopted a loving tone. 'We plead with you, and we ask that you let us live!'

Clenching his teeth and crying out, Rupert worked the hairpin this way and that—until he had succeeded in severing what felt like every last nerve fibre. The agony offset by the deadness of shock, he plucked his right eyeball out of its socket. *I'm free.*

A moment later, the stampede passed by. Afterward, when the goatherd drew near, the old man studied the bloodied eyeball in Rupert's cupped hands. Rupert laughed hysterically. 'So, I did it, didn't I?' The old man trembled and muttered the most heartfelt invocation. With that, neither spoke a word—and then, as the awkward silence lingered, Rupert closed his one good eye and swooned.

When he awoke, he realised the goatherd must have dragged him back to his camp and placed him inside one of the spare tents. Rupert breathed in the odour lingering in the air and decided it must be the scent of some powerful medicinal herb, a Bedouin folk remedy for killing pain. Gently, he patted the bandage over his right eyeball socket. *I wonder what's become of my peeper? Yes, and what's become of the dæmon?*

Something stirred in the shadows: a gaunt Abyssinian cat with withered limbs crept into the tent. First, the creature paused to study him and to sneer. Before long, the cat darted away to examine a parcel of cotton fabric lying in the corner. Rupert sat up. *Might that be my lost eyeball bundled up there?* When the cat finally unravelled the length of cloth and removed the bloodied, fleshy item from within, there was no doubt. 'Yes, that's my eyeball you've got there.' He held out his hand and snapped his fingers. 'Bring it here. I mean to bury it, eh?.

The severed eyeball clenched fast in its jaws, the hungry animal flitted off through the tent's flap and vanished into the night.

'*Bon appétit*,' Rupert whispered, for lack of anything better to say. He lay back down and was soon lost in the same old dreams—visions of Father's business contact, that vile, condescending, self-satisfied businessman, Mr Impérial.

And he creeps into Rupert's bedchamber and shows him a handful of papers from the local state-owned retail bank. 'Listen here, Roo. Do you know what I aim to do? I've decided to invest in a factory in England. A factory for making weapons of war. Parliament has already made assurances they'll support the endeavour with subsidies. So, how could a deal like this go wrong? The munitions industry! That should get us thriving!' With that, the sinister old man slips into Rupert's bed and ...

Slowly, the dream died out. Rupert woke, but he could not move—something like a concertgoer who finds himself immobilised by the end of some stirring musical interpretation, the final devastating chord.

XVIII.

The wilderness of Sinai. 8 July 1920.

Late that morning, Anastasia slipped into a luxuriant patchwork Bedouin robe she had purchased from a local woman a few days before. The woman then shared a rumour of Rupert's death that day. Over the course of the following days, Anastasia had come to believe the hearsay. *Rupert has perished out in the wild. Let that be his punishment.* Anastasia closed her wardrobe trunk softly. *I've got to go. I've got to learn to live and to love again.* She felt her way outside.

Some of the Oxford scholars approached, and they alluded to some other site where the surveyors wanted to employ her.

'No,' she told them. 'I've resolved to depart. I think I'll go back to the seaside village nearby. Maybe I'll meet someone. A fine gentleman who never quite made it to Oxford.'

'Don't go,' one of the scholars told her. 'That place down by the sea is a hotbed of revolution and political intrigue. The locals have got everyone bewildered down there.'

'That's right,' the second Oxford man said. 'Not long ago,

231

some of the locals torched a cargo steamship bound for the Port of South Sinai. She never even reached her destination, that one.'

Anastasia feigned hunger and continued along. Down at the mess tent, she hired one of the Bedouin girls to take her out across the sand dunes and into the seaside village. Forty minutes later, when they reached the modest hostelry, Anastasia checked into the room in which she had stayed two years before. The Bedouin girl drew close and held Anastasia's wrist. 'No you speak to the revolutionaries,' she admonished Anastasia, the little girl's breath as sweet as fig jam. With that, the Bedouin girl departed.

The hostelry keeper's daughter guided Anastasia up to her room and sat her on the edge of her bed. 'The last tenant we had left behind some lovely Irish linen-and-lace gowns,' the little girl continued. 'You should wear them.' The little girl patted Anastasia's hand. 'You should tell everyone you come from Ireland. *Aiwa*. You tell the world you make some good investments in the production of ginger ale, and you tell everyone you are a Dubliner. *Aiwa*, because we know the Irish fight against the British Empire. Yes, we Egyptians, we admire the Irish because they riot up and down Eccles Street. Yes, yes. All the time, day after day, we read about the Irish in the papers. *Aiwa*.'.

Twenty minutes later, the hostelry keeper's daughter helped Anastasia find her way through the marketplace and back to the garden once owned by the mirror-making society. For a moment or two, Anastasia listened to the sounds of nature—the windswept fig trees, the swaying of their boughs. The fragrance of the Egyptian lotus made her happy, too, so much so she felt her eyes dance. Blinking, she reached out her hand to find the gate felt cold to the touch. When she pushed the gate open, she felt as if she had opened an ice-cabinet door and stood in the emanation of cool air—not unlike a loyal maidservant wondering which ice-packed fish to prepare for supper. Anastasia tapped the tip of her walking stick against her right heel. If only someone from the old days might have approached, the footfalls belonging to Ernesztina or someone else from the mirror-making society. 'I'm so glad you're here,' the old acquaintance might say, taking hold of her wrist.

The sweet aromas of the summer flowers guided Anastasia forward. With a little help from the hostelry keeper's daughter, Anastasia plopped herself down into the rocking chair that had always occupied the heart of the glade. Littered with an array of lotus petals, the rocking chair felt soft, but oh so *frigid*. Laughing, she imagined herself a staid Edwardian Englishwoman visiting the Chelsea Flower Exposition. And now Anastasia held out her hand and imagined she held in her palm a glorious orchid bud. *That's right, an orchid bud resembling a gentleman's ... eggs, the manly parts that dangle down. Oh God, how scandalous.*

The garden grew colder, and Anastasia breathed in the wintry air. She detected the erotic salty sea breeze whirling its way from the shore. A cold gust made her shiver, and she wondered if perhaps the peculiar sensation might portend something awful. *What if it is my fate to have some irate revolutionary kill me today?* She rocked back and forth, recalling some of the handsome Russian officers who had lived not far from her childhood home in Saint Petersburg. With a loving sigh, she pictured one of them sitting beside her on the seashore—the pair of them resting atop a length of tight-knotted driftwood. *What a lovely scene.* As the wild surf roared, she pictured the foam swirling all about the beach.

What a fool I was to believe I'd find someone to love here. She cursed her gullibility and loneliness and stood up to face the sea. Clenching her fists, she endeavoured to force herself to see again, so that she might behold the crest of a wave—any wave. *Yes, let me see again. Oh, let me see the wave crash down by the north breakwater.* Even with the indomitable blindness, she wondered how the waterfront might appear. *Beyond the crest of that wave, a fishing vessel will be sailing past the coal jetty. Perhaps no more than two nautical miles away, a coral island should be rising from the waters.* She pictured herself swimming all the way there, and holding her breath, she thought, *Why not dive into the water?* She pictured either a school of butterfly fish or perhaps even a school of Red Sea clownfish guiding her down to the narrow underwater passageway. Her lungs almost ready to burst, she would break the surface and find herself safe inside a warm womblike cavern filled with salty air. She imagined herself gasping for breath, pulling herself up onto the ledge, and curling up beside the uneven wall, the echoes of the sea breeze wheezing from the fissures above. *I'd close my eyes and sleep.* She knelt, feeling the small summer flowers. When she raised her head, she heard a pleasing peal—a string of pretty little bells from the Arab market.

The hostelry keeper's daughter muttered something unintelligible beneath her breath and exhaled loudly through her nose. 'We no stay out too long,' she whispered. 'If we do, maybe the rebels grow cross with you.'

'Do you think a revolutionary might've followed us out here? If so, I'll tell him I very much sympathise. And it won't be a fib.'

The hostelry keeper's daughter nudged Anastasia's ankle. 'Do you think the Moon should always appear in the sky?'

'Why do you ask something like that?'

'Please. Just tell me. Do you think the Moon should always appear in the sky when we look up at night?'

'Yes, after all, doesn't the Moon orbit the Earth? So, the Moon must be something like a slave. A weary, woebegone slave with no hope of ever going free. Who knows? Maybe the Moon envies the stars, the constellations. Most of all, the Moon envies those stars and constellations so far away from here no student of astronomy should ever learn anything about them. Anyway, what a miserable slave, that silvery rock that orbits us. The Moon will never go free.'

'No, maybe the Moon should be pulling away a little bit every year,' the little girl countered. 'And maybe in another eight hundred and eighty-eight years, the Moon should be nothing more than a soft little point of light.'

The precocious little girl's words took Anastasia by surprise. 'Who taught you all that business about the Moon breaking its orbit?.

In measured terms, the hostelry keeper's daughter explained all. Evidently, she had heard the idea two weeks earlier from a Jew who had rented a room for a couple of nights. She remembered only he'd been a Dardanelles muleteer. 'The Zion Mule Corps out of Palestine,' the little girl said.

The more Anastasia sought to envision the curious fellow, the more she thought about Rupert—and the more she contemplated *him*, the worse and worse the snakebite on her ankle smarted.

The girl sobbed. 'Maybe I take you back now. My father could find someone to tend to you. Good?'

Anastasia could not manage an answer. The snakebite smarted more and more—until she trembled all over. *If some irate revolutionary doesn't kill me, perhaps the venom inside me should.* She braced herself for a second serpent attack. *Yes, soon the creature ought to come along and bare its fangs.* She listened for any sign of a serpent. *How about the clatter of a large viper's scales?* She heard nothing. Other than the wild sea breeze blowing through the treetops, the whole world seemed lifeless—so much so the silence affrighted her and her heart twittered. *I've got to come to my senses.*

The summer breeze wafted through the garden, shaking the boughs of the fig trees. 'Take me back to the garden gate.' Anastasia felt for the girl's hand and kept pace with her as she continued. *What an ordeal.* The earth beneath the soles of her walking shoes felt as cold as the tundra. Even worse, a jumble of cold fig-tree boughs swaying in the wind scraped against her arms and face. Worst of all, an icy strand, perhaps the remnant of a spider's web, passed across the base of her neck. The uncanny cold sensation played on her mind. *It's got to be a portent.* She shook her head. *All that venom inside my body—it's too much for me to bear.* Little by little, her body temperature dropped. *Yes, I feel it … I'm dying.* She sank to the earth, sprawling in an array of lotus seeds.

The hostelry keeper's daughter yelped and called out for help.

As disoriented as some poor soul suffering from cold exposure, Anastasia touched one of the lotus seeds with the tip of her finger. 'Are you a hailstone?' she asked. As her befuddlement intensified, she squeezed the seed as hard as she could—until she had succeeded in crushing the kernel into a sticky smudge. Growing more and more erratic, she arranged the disagreeable mess on the tip of her tongue and imagined how good and how savoury and how buttery the crushed treat might taste—if only it did not suggest the bitterness of freshly fallen Russian snow.

The little girl nudged her. 'My friend, he's coming. *Aiwa.* Let's ask him to take us back to the hostelry.'

Anastasia tried to say no, but could not. Her lips felt numb from the cold, and when she attempted to talk, she sounded like an ecstatic preacher speaking in tongues.

The village of Al-Hubu, the wilderness of Sinai. 18 July 1920.

Back at the hostelry, on the other side of Anastasia's room, the clock's little brass bells pealed and proceeded to count out the afternoon hour: four o'clock. She woke. *Shall I get out of bed?* She stretched her arms. *Am I feeling stronger? Yes, I'm feeling as strong as I ever felt. Ready for anything, ready for love.* Despite trying to convince herself, she wondered if she felt too weak and too unhealthy to rise from bed. As the quiet persisted, she attempted to will herself to fall back to sleep. Against the nape of her neck, though, the bed felt cold. As she tossed and turned, she soon decided it was a sensation like the agony of frostbite.

Little by little, the scent of summer flowers drifted through the window—until she could no longer resist the allure. *Let's do something.* She hauled herself out of bed and struggled to her feet, feeling as if she held a pair of icicles in the palms of her hands. *Or a couple of hailstones.* She hobbled off to the side and bumped into the wall—or rather she bumped into what felt like one of those tin-bronze mirrors the mirror-making society once produced. How cold the frame was, too, but even so, she reached out and passed both hands along its smooth surface. *What if this tin bronze here still had a little bit of life in it and possessed great magic? Perhaps I could slip through the surface and escape. Like one of those souls*

237

who survived the fall of Troy, only to sail off to wherever it was. Rome, perhaps?

From somewhere down in the marketplace, a local busker strumming a proper Egyptian lute sang a song of protest popular with the revolutionaries of the day. As she wondered if he was playing a little bit out of tune, she placed the palms of her hands flush against the tin bronze. *Oh God.* The surface of the mirror felt like an impenetrable frozen pond. Unable to bear the cold, she withdrew her hands, felt her pendant dove, and pictured her mother standing at her side. *Yes, she's here.* Anastasia raised her hand. 'Hello.

'What are you doing here?' Mother asked. 'Do you think you've forsaken the king back there in the cult pyramid? Do you fear you've turned your back on God Almighty? Yes, that's right, in siding with all those falcons, you fear you might've proclaimed a willingness to worship nature. Don't be deceived, though. Come back to gentle Jesus. If you do, He'll forgive all your sins.'

From the direction of the kitchen, the innkeeper shouted to his daughter, asking whether they ought to prepare a supper of lamb with pine nuts for Anastasia. As hospitable as the two sounded, Anastasia did not feel hungry. Her throat was swollen—*an effect of the venom*, she thought. *Oh, that awful serpent.*

The hostelry grew quiet. *Did a company of soldiers tell the minstrel to cease the music?* Alone, she found her way downstairs to the lobby and continued out into the marketplace. Guided by the unmistakable, intoxicating scent of spices lingering in the air, she made her way forward. Soon, she paused to gauge her precise location. *Am I standing near the millinery shop? No.* She wondered if she had reached the narrow alleyway pointing toward that desolate colonnaded courtyard. *Yes, I remember this place.*

From up above, perhaps in a flat facing the courtyard, someone played on a viola. At the same time, a second busker on the street quavered a tune on a traditional Egyptian shawm.

A patter of rapid little footsteps approached. *A pounce of Abyssinian cats*, Anastasia thought. As they hurried by, one of the curious creatures permitted the cold tip of its tail to brush past Anastasia's shin. She pictured the cat stopping in the courtyard up ahead and studying her with its chocolate-brown eyes. 'Don't you fret,' she told the cat, if it was even there. 'Summer's slipping by quickly enough. Soon, very soon, your village should be good and idyllic again. And once the glorious revolution runs its course, there will be no more summer-holiday crowds, no more endless processions of fussy English ladies wandering about, no more vestiges of Western civilization.'

From up inside that same second-floor flat, the viola broke into a series of slow augmented études. Anastasia wondered if the tune might be a fragment from that celebrated Von Weber opera, *Oberon*. Guided by memory and intuition, she marched forward. *Keep going. Yes, yes.* Once she had exited the marketplace, the sound of the fountain itself ushered her along the dusty road—and guided by the rush of the water flowing from the jets, she groped her way into the heart of the roundabout. There, she positioned herself so she faced where the opera house had once stood. Breathing in, she discerned the odour of burnt ash. *The wondrous opera house is really gone.* She pictured the building as it appeared in the days and weeks before she had gone blind: a fine Byzantine-revival structure standing atop the wind-swept hill. *But the revolutionaries have burned it all down. No more opera.* Feeling lonely, she allowed her thoughts to drift to the demented, limp-wristed youth who had once lived in one of the opera house's dressing rooms. As the summer breeze ruffled her robe, she set her hand on her bosom. The thought of him pining for her should have repulsed and infuriated her. *And it very much does.* Still, she closed her eyes and imagined the opera house where it ought to be—and the demented youth asleep in the dressing room, the heat and humidity having caused a dozen or more little sky-blue mushrooms to sprout up along the skirting board. 'Do you enjoy sleeping there?' she longed to ask him, if she only could. She imagined him answering: 'Yes,' he said. 'It's better than sleeping on a clothesline.' At last, she pictured the troubled youth taking her downstairs and performing a piece on his glass harmonica. *And where might he be now?* She imagined him working as a busker back in London, perhaps Paddington Station or maybe Petticoat Lane Market. *I wonder if he even remembers me.* She became lost in deep reverie.

The youth approached. 'I'm sorry for all me mischief back in the day,' he whispered into her ear. 'I weren't trying to affright you any. Something came over me, that's all. You've no idea how sorry I am.'

The daydream concluded, and as the sky grew quiet, cold, and impossibly still, she felt for the fountain that had always occupied the heart of the roundabout. When she touched the basin, how cold the marble felt—like a block of ice. She lifted her eyes to the sky. If only a sign of life might resound, a cast of angry falcons, perhaps. When she finally turned back to the hill, she pictured a glorious new structure looming over her—a mosque as grand as any fine Roman basilica, a building fit to represent an entire people emancipated from slavery.

She heard the crunch of boots on the sandy road. *A company of soldiers*, she thought, as they marched by, belting

240

out a familiar parlour song.

> *'And our roads may be far apart*
> *But there's one rose that dies not in Picardy*
> *'Tis the rose I keep in my heart.'*

She waited until they had passed before removing an incomprehensibly cold silver sixpence from her breast pocket. After a moment, she dropped the coin into the marble basin. As the coin sank, the grating noise of an electric die grinder started up behind her. *The mirror works.* She pictured the building—the humble structure standing there shining the colour of fresh plums. *The way it always did before.*

The door creaked open. 'Come you here,' a voice as of an elderly Egyptian woman told her.

Step by step, Anastasia faltered her way over and continued inside. When she breathed in, she gagged. A good earthy desert scent had once pervaded the air, but at present, the entire place smelled like rotting fish. A violent shudder ran through her body, and she nearly lost her balance.

The Egyptian woman sat her down at the worktable. 'You shouldn't be out and about on a day like this,' the woman said. 'These days, the people have grown cross with foreigners, infidels. We've grown weary of British domination.'

Anastasia nodded. 'Yes, I know all about that. And I do pity the people. We're all of us born free, no?'

The Egyptian woman laughed wistfully. 'Yes, *free.* Through and through.' Tears trickled down the woman's wrinkled cheeks.

Had the soldiers killed someone she once knew? Yes, I think so.

Feeling nostalgic, Anastasia felt her way to the back. When she located the shearing wheel, she placed her palm flush against the cheek of the blade. Oddly, it felt as cold as a train track reaching through the tundra. Outside, from the direction of the market, an earsplitting explosion shattered the air. *Another bomb … dynamite?* She felt a cold mist enshrouding her, so she withdrew her hand and shifted—at which point her elbow touched the cheek of the shearing wheel's icy blade. From the direction of the marketplace, a dozen or more shots rang out. *It's got to be the soldiers and revolutionaries firing on one another.* She knew she should lie low, but she stumbled outside into the roundabout and felt her way back to the fountain. There, she imagined some irate Egyptian rioter approaching her, kneeling, and wrapping his hand around the throat of her shoe.

'Why do you intrude on our home?' he asked.

'I've got nothing to do with the British Empire's occupation,' she said.

'Are you blind? Did you lose your walking stick? I'd think that a fine Christian woman like you should have a walking stick of pure maple. With a derby handle and a brass collar.'

'That's the type of walking stick an *aristocrat* might use,' she told the sullen imaginary revolutionary. 'I'd never carry something like that. I'm no colonist. I'm no intruder.'

A serpent of some kind slithered by, the icy tip of its tail tapping her ankle. Or had she only imagined the animal? Her nose running, she knelt and felt the long cold track the viper had left in the dust. '*Quelle horreur.*'.

From the direction of the marketplace, the hostelry keeper's daughter called out to Anastasia. When the little girl drew close, she tugged on Anastasia's sleeve. 'Today a bad day. Let's go back to the hostelry before someone makes trouble for you.'

Anastasia refused to comply. Instead, she breathed in the

odour of the burnt ash wafting through the dusty roundabout. The fountain's jets roaring triumphally, she groped her way over toward the hill. For a moment or two, she paused to kneel amid the trodden weeds growing wild along the incline. *Am I truly here in the place where that opulent opera house once stood?* She felt the shrubs. *Yes, I'm here.* She heard ghostly footsteps and pictured the dreamlike visitant as a beautiful brunette wearing a long, immaculate gown. The illusory woman exhaled gently, her breath the scent of the noblest aged leather. Breathing in through her nose, Anastasia returned to her feet. She understood her unconscious mind had conjured the figure, and she just knew her unconscious mind preferred she believe the figure to be a great sibyl, perhaps even the one who greeted the fugitive Trojan prince who fled to Rome. What a tale: each time the sibyl offered to sell her oracles, the foolish refugee declined the offer. With that, she cast the scroll onto a fire. Then the sibyl increased the price for the balance left until the Trojan prince came to covet the last one and agreed to pay the now-extravagant price.

From the direction of the shore, the sea breeze scattered a storm of honey-scented flower petals, which rained down over Anastasia's shoulders. Each petal felt cold. *Like a snowflake.* She dragged herself up the hill until the odour of burnt ash grew overwhelming. *Oh, that's awful.* Despite her repulsion, she stumbled forward into that vast field of soot and fiery cinders, the remains of the once glorious opera house. 'I suppose this would be the best place for me to expire.'

'But don't you fear the solitude?' an illusory voice belonging to the sibyl asked. 'You shouldn't perish in a lonely place. Where you stand at present is a place of godlessness. I'd say your death scene ought to be something spectacular. After all, the venom has been building up inside you for quite some time. Yet now you content yourself to visit the ruins of some opera house?' The sibyl rent the yoke of her gown.

Anastasia ignored the aural hallucination and lay down in the warm, malodourous embers. And when she placed her hand on her belly, she wondered if even the deepest recesses of her womb felt terribly cold. Another storm of flower petals raining down, Anastasia stuck out her tongue in the hope she might catch one—just the way a little girl hopes to catch a snowflake. And after a minute, she succeeded in catching one of the petals—but it made her gag. Her breathing grew laboured. Twice, she grunted. At last, she turned on her side. *No more childish indulgences. No more.* Her breath grew shallow as the venom surged through her weak frame. And then she was dead and gone, her passing simple and natural and effortless and graceful.

XIX.

The wilderness of Sinai. 29 August 1920.
In the darkness before dawn.

A shapeshifting cloud of little red carrion flies buzzing about his head, Rupert collapsed at the gates of the English Army's citadel and cried out to the sentry. Almost immediately, the soldier opened the gate and knelt beside him. 'Where the bloody hell did *you* come from?'

Rupert took hold of the sentry's arm. 'I've been living out in the desert with a goatherd, and it's bloody hot out there, and I've lost an eye, and I think it's infected, and I've got the faints. Bloody hell, I'm as beached as ....'

The sentry turned toward a tall bespectacled lieutenant. 'What about this poor bastard here? I don't think he's quite the full quid.

A third soldier drew close. 'Aye, ring up the body snatchers. This one here is ready to take bread and salt.

Rupert grew hysterical. 'Get me to the pier and put me aboard the provost marshal's patrol vessel and take me home!' he shouted, his voice breaking. 'Take me back to God's

Own Country.

The lieutenant dug his hands into his pockets and studied Rupert a while. 'Govern your temper, I say. You got no reason to kick it off with us, mate.

The sentry nodded. 'That's right,' he added, pointing at the third soldier before turning back to Rupert. 'You don't want to touch off a row with this fine chap here. He served up in the Bosporus Strait. And I'm not talking about no reserve trench neither.

The three soldiers laughed in unison, like a gang of cruel little children. Then they assumed an immovable pose, as if not one of them wished to help.

Rupert swooned—and he did not regain consciousness until late that night. *Where the bloody hell am I?* He studied the darkness. *It's probably the citadel's hospital ward.* From out of the shadows, the hospital matron approached—the soles of her shoes silent against the tiles. She checked the cupboard standing to the side of Rupert's bed and removed a jar of aloe, a water bottle, and a tin of olive-oil soap. *Yes, I'm in the military hospital.*

When the hospital matron darted off, Rupert felt his face. Someone had wrapped a proper eyepatch around his head. He felt better, too—but even so, he detected the strong odour of rubbing alcohol lingering in the air. The foul smell commingled with a sickly sweet stench emanating from the far side of the dimly lit hall, and Rupert climbed out of bed and lurched over to the window to get some fresh air. Outside, the moonlit clock tower shone a blinding silvery white—as did the field gun lying in pieces off to the right. He heard footfalls, so he shot a glance over his shoulder: an Abyssinian cat appeared, some unfortunate creature clenched tightly in its jaws. The cat advanced into a section of the floor illuminated by a Turkish lantern dangling from the vault. At first, Rupert mistook the cat's prey for a mouse. As he drew closer though, he realised the cat held within its jaws a reef heron—its plumage as blue as Anastasia's eyes. Heartbroken, he gazed out the window once more. *Anastasia.*

A staff car drove by, its headlamps lighting up the room. A team of motor mechanics passed by from the opposite direction. Again, he glanced over his shoulder—just in time to watch the cat drop the lifeless songbird's body to the floor. Its eyes flashing like stars, the cat ripped the winged creature to pieces and consumed the remains. Rupert stumbled back to his bed, lay down, and endeavoured to collect his thoughts. *Am I dying, or have I prevailed over the effects of that mad fungus?* He propped himself up. Ever since he had extracted his right eyeball, he *had* felt better. *Wrong as I was to betray Anastasia, maybe God has forgiven all. It's possible.* An elegant fez clenched in its jaws, the cat drew close to the hospital bed and peered deep into Rupert's remaining eye. He frowned. For a moment, he doubted the cat even existed. After all, the nurses would have pumped his body full of elixirs—and perhaps some of them had wrought a strong hallucinogenic effect on him. Without warning, the cat leapt onto the bed. The creature positioned itself on his groin and stared at his chest, as if reading the evening newspaper. He wondered what the imaginary article might be—perhaps a detailed *exposé* on modern-day Jerusalem. There, the streets teemed with beggars and transients, prodigal sons and defrocked priests, migrants and tramps, drifters and pauper lunatics, and any number of thieves and vagrants and addicts, too. *People like me. Failures, all.*

The illusory cat yawned, and the illusory fez fell from the creature's mouth. A moment later, as the cat sauntered off, the fez dematerialised.

The damn thing was never even there. Having mustered his strength, he pushed himself onto his feet and followed the dreamlike cat outside. Down by the citadel's moonlit chapel, he crashed into a display of *terracotta* flower pots. As he reeled about in the broken earthenware, his left eye rolled back. 'I've gone blind!' he cried out, his voice laboured and wheezy. Had anyone even heard? He crawled through the broken pottery, but soon stopped. Had Anastasia called out? Perhaps she yearned for him to take her to Jerusalem. He did have every intention of making a pilgrimage someday soon, but would he even want to take someone as bitter as Anastasia? Slowly, he stumbled back inside—where the illusory fez reappeared atop his pillow. When the hallucination wore off, he lay in bed again. *I got to get to sleep.* He hummed the tune to a song—'Ballad of a Cat on Testy Dodge', a piece that Georgie had written years earlier about a lady beggar he had befriended. *His only playmate. Georgie!*

Later that day.

As infirm as he was, he became lost in a tormenting dream of Jerusalem.

He finds himself lying in a filthy, fogbound street, a spice merchant's shop looming over him. The ghost of a biblical scribe emerges from a dark alleyway. He has sallow skin, a long Levantine nose, and a long grey beard. 'What're you doing here?' the scribe asks. Rupert sits up. 'I've come to find something lovely and sacred and meaningful to take home to my little brother, Georgie. Perhaps I should take him a lady slipper orchid, or maybe a crate of grapes.' The scribe barks out a gruff laugh, as old men do. 'Here's a piece of wisdom to take him,' the scribe says. 'Tell him democracy ain't nothing but a swindle. It's always better to go with an old-fashioned monarchy. Yes, indeed, even the pretender-king variety. Tell your kin a proper government shouldn't ever concern itself with anything but the maintenance of a prosperous society. Absolute social cohesion, that's the top priority. No, never believe in some big lie anymore than you'd think to believe in the subtlest innuendo.'

At last, Rupert awoke—and an illusory fez appeared on the floor in a shaft of hazy light streaming in through the window.

Eventually, he spoke with one of the other patients and learned the most intriguing rumour: tonight, a long-distance truck driver intended to depart for Palestine. *I'm going.* As he lay in bed, he imagined how modern Jerusalem might appear. Would the Old City marketplace still boast signs written in the Turkish tongue, or would everything be in English? He breathed in. *What's that?* The sea breeze danced through the hospital ward, the wild current tinged with something sweet. *Glory Hallelujah.* His mouth watered. He closed his one remaining eye. By degrees, a sense of dread took hold. He pictured himself as a penniless beggar in Jerusalem. *If I have nothing to my name, I'll be no better than the pickpockets wandering all about.* He imagined himself a broken old man crying out 'alms for the poor!' to the various Armenian women passing by.

After a while, he climbed out of bed. When he found a cracked pocket mirror in the cupboard, he studied his reflection. At first, he did not even recognise himself. By now, he had a long, uneven beard and sun-scorched skin. Given the eyepatch, too, he bore a passing resemblance to a desert marauder. Even worse, his one good eye was bloodshot— like that of a drug fiend, the kind that sometimes wanders the business district of South Auckland. No matter his questionable appearance, he dressed himself in a fresh hospital gown and lumbered outside. A cool summer breeze awoke, and as it gathered strength, the scent of Crimean wine drifted through the dry, dusty air. He thought of Anastasia. *So, what's become of her?* Perhaps she had sailed far away. As the scent of the bouquet grew stronger, he imagined her disembarking in a place like Yalta. In no time, she would find her way to a cliff overlooking the Black Sea. *What might Anastasia think to do?* Forlorn, she would leap to her death. The very notion made him stagger back into the wall. Filled with guilt, he longed to run off—back into the endless wilderness. *What right have I to go on living?*

The stronger the scent of the wine grew, the more he believed his right eyeball had regenerated. Even if it had, it still felt terribly dry—as if some of the nerves had not grown back strong enough to communicate with his psyche to tell it to produce enough tears to keep the eyeball damp. *Am I healed?* After some hesitation, he drew a deep breath. His hand trembling, he felt at the dome of his eyepatch and reached up beneath the Egyptian silk. The tender, bloodied socket remained hopelessly empty. He withdrew his hand and decided he felt much better—for he considered himself undeserving of ever being whole again. Three times over, he patted the dome of the eyepatch. *Thank God.* A swift desert breeze blowing in his face, Rupert approached the clock tower. Oddly, the gears lost power—as if the clock would never peal again, nor count out the hour. *What's gone wrong?* Standing as tall as he could on the tips of his toes, he squeezed his eyes shut in concentration and willed the mechanism to live again—but to no avail.

From one of the windows overlooking the courtyard,

a gramophone recording crackled to life: the overture to *Semiramide*. He closed his good eye and imagined he had reached the vast courtyard of a brightly painted Babylonian palace. In time, he pictured a greedy courtier coming to teach him all there was to know—the art of tax evasion and the best way to choose an offshore investment, perhaps even something pertaining to the pros and cons of tax havens.

'What do I do once I get to Jerusalem?' Rupert asked the Babylonian, as if he stood at his back. 'How the devil should I ever raise enough funds to survive there, and how will I ever make enough money to afford to book passage home to New Zealand?'

The courtier calls for the court astronomer to come along, and the court astronomer taps Rupert's shoulder. 'I know what you'll do,' the fellow says, stroking his beard. 'You'll establish a proper insurance company. Tell everyone you're the finest of actuaries. Verily, you know all the dividends and statistics such as they relate to mortgages and automobiles, too.'

'Are you quite sure?' Rupert asked.

'Yes,' the court astronomer answered. 'You'll tell the people of Jerusalem you alone possess the power to assess risks, and you alone fathom just what constitutes the most favourable premiums and deductibles. Soon enough, you'll have the greatest riches. No, not for *you* the pettiness of penny stocks.'

The overture to *Semiramide* concluded, and when the gramophone remained silent, Rupert opened his one good eye.

A homely nurse approached him. 'So, who said you've got the right to knock around whenever you wish?.

He followed her back to his bed. There, he grabbed the cracked pocket mirror and studied his reflection as he had before. In the present light, his face looked dry and weathered and much too old. Even worse, he realised the hair at his crown had grown thin. Most displeasing of all, several flakes of dead grey scarfskin littered his shoulders.

The homely nurse tugged at Rupert's hospital gown. 'What happened to you out there in the wilderness?'

'What do you think?'

'I'd guess one of them Egyptian revolutionaries shot your eye out with one of them newfangled exploding bullets.'

'Yes, that's what happened.'

'Oh? Well, maybe you ought to get some rest.' Without another word, the nurse returned the mirror to the cupboard and sauntered off into the shock ward.

Nightfall.

Rupert lay in bed and did his best to act nonchalant and to bide his time. *By dawn, I'll be in Jerusalem. When tomorrow comes around, I'll be there.* His jaw set, he stared at the ceiling fan up above—until the sound of footfalls approached the bed beside his own. *Anastasia?* In that moment, he sincerely believed she stood there—the beautiful young lady dressed in a simple flutter blouse and harem skirt, her eyes gazing off into space, and her long golden hair tumbling past her left shoulder.

When he finally gathered up enough nerve to peek, the presence proved to be a portly, raven-haired nurse. She had come to change the linens, as if preparing the bed for the arrival of some new patient. Sure enough, a party of medics brought in a soldier—his face burnt beyond recognition. The nurse dashed off. In her place, the light of the Moon shone through the window and crept into the cool, sombre hospital ward.

Rupert arose from his bed. His plan was simple. *I'll pilfer the new patient's freshly pressed regimentals. And I'll approach the truck as it's pulling out. And I'll leap into the back.*

The new arrival arose from his bed and gently collapsed on the wooden chair standing to the side of the window. 'You going somewhere?' the disfigured soldier asked him.

'No,' Rupert lied, his voice a whisper. 'Go back to sleep, mate.' When the soldier refused to do so, Rupert stumbled over to the cupboard and fussed with the cracked pocket mirror.

'Are you a Kiwi?' the wounded soldier asked in a wheeze. 'I recognise your accent,' he continued, panting and grimacing. 'My uncle once worked the foreign-affairs desk at the *New Zealand Herald*,' the soldier finally managed to say, holding up his gashed fingers.

Outside, a truck's engine stirred to life, and Rupert heard voices. He caught a reference to a Royal Navy ship berthed at Haifa and stiffened. There could be no doubt the truck outside was the one heading for Palestine.

The disfigured soldier pointed at Rupert. 'Let me tell you something. I admire what all ye Kiwis have done down there in New Zealand. Ye tend to your wee gardens and make them grow in ways they never did before. I suppose ye mean to conquer nature itself and bring order and sustenance in all directions.'

Outside, while the truck continued to idle, a door opened and slammed shut with seeming finality. *God, no.* Rupert's heart pounded so forcefully he felt an ache in his left arm. He tapped his foot against the tile, but it did not calm him. Trembling all over, he dropped the cracked pocket mirror.

The disfigured soldier must have noticed Rupert's discomposure. 'What's wrong with you, then? I always supposed the typical Kiwi must be as strong as a miller's mare.

But you don't look good at all, if you don't mind my telling you. Maybe I ought to make you a cup of herbal tea.'

Outside, the driver gunned the engine. Rupert gestured toward the new arrival and nodded. 'Yes, go into the kitchen and make me a cup of tea. Please, mate. I think the nurses have got themselves a whole proper tea cart in there. Right, and don't forget to get me a spoonful of peppermint oil. I can't have tea without it.'

The other fellow picked himself up and lumbered off, only to return. 'You ought to know something,' he said slowly. Then he paused, as if for dramatic effect. The moonlit hospital ward filled with the faint trace of exhaust from the truck outside. 'I'll tell you what's gone wrong with the world,' the disfigured soldier continued, his voice wavering. 'There's nothing out there in this repulsive world but *defilement and fetish burglary and ethnorape*. Psychosexual fears. That's what informs everyone's sense of political persecution.'

A raggedy Abyssinian cat emerged from out of the shadows. Slowly, the curious creature approached the dirty dishes stacked up at the foot of Rupert's bed. The animal could not have been the stuff of illusion either because the disfigured soldier espied it, too. He even chased the cat down the hall some way. Afterward, he made his way to the window, where he stood still and listened to the truck's engine.

The inscrutable cat sniffed at one of the dishes and lapped up the remnant of the soup the nurses had served at suppertime.

'Please, how about that tea?' Rupert asked.

'In a minute,' the other fellow answered. 'I got something more to say, if the knot in my insides permits it.' He placed his hand over his right eye, as if to check whether he himself had an eyepatch covering it. At last, he breathed in and out.

'Whatever you do, you must not detect yourself in things. Not in history. Not in pictures in the newspapers. You mustn't be so vain as all that. Too much vanity confounds a chap's mind. Just like a fib, a falsehood. Aye, and once you've gone puzzled, you're lost forever, because you got nothing more to think on but imbecilic comparisons.' With that, the disfigured soldier finally lurched off.

As quickly as he could, Rupert grabbed the other fellow's British regimentals and faltered outside. With no time to check whether anyone had even espied his presence, he climbed into the transport's darkened bed and crouched behind a large wooden crate. How long was it before the truck finally pulled out? To Rupert, it felt like an hour or more. As the truck passed through the citadel gates, he trembled like a child. *Will I make it to Palestine?* He slipped out of his hospital gown and into the Royal Army uniform. In time, he imagined Anastasia crouching there beside him. 'Have I got you desperately mashed?' he asked her. If she were there, she would not have even answered. Even if he attempted to take her hand, she would have said nothing to him. And in the end, he would have had no choice but to let go of her hand.

The truck exited the village, and he watched the citadel lights fade from view. *Anastasia.* The more he thought about her, the more discomfited he felt—until the palms of his hands burned so badly his flesh soon came to betray faint crimson welts sure to last the rest of his life. *What if Anastasia were here?* They would sit awhile, and he'd look into her eyes. 'You ought to let go,' he would say, trying to appear stern. *Hopefully, she'd ignore me.*

Hours passed by before the truck stopped to idle. Had the driver paused to check his map? Rupert wondered where they might be. As the breeze swirled about the truck bed, he preferred to believe they had reached some sandstone valley—perhaps even White Canyon. What a fine, magnificent world: a moonlit landscape as irreal as it might appear in an excitable child's watercolour. Rupert pictured a whole covey of Barbary partridges fluttering down out of the sky, the winged creatures longing to take shelter in the crown of some nearby purple tamarisk tree. *Yes, that seems right.* He twitched his moustache and thought of Georgie and the watercolours he had painted back in the summer of 1909. Had he not made a rather ambitious portrait of Father's business contact? Rupert trembled all over. *Mr Impérial. Yes, indeed.* The awful memories returned, and Rupert brooded over his uncertain future. *Back home, I've got to lay bare the crimes that happened all those years ago. No, I've got no choice but to seek a measure of abiding justice. Redemption, that's what I must have. No, not mere revenge.*

The truck slipped into gear. Soon, the driver veered out onto an open desert road and put on speed.

Rupert felt giddy. *Perhaps as early as tomorrow evening, I'll be haunting the fabled streets of Jerusalem.* Once more, he pictured Anastasia sitting beside him. 'If you let me come with you, I'll serve you neck and heels,' she said. 'Just think of how much I could make as a beggar maid. And I'll bring you everything. Hundreds of guineas, maybe more, yes, a whole week's wages.'

'Yes, how lovely.' he said. 'And just think of that moment we climb aboard some ship down there in Aqaba. A vessel fitted out for deep water and bound for New Zealand. Back home, they'll stare with wonder when we tell them how we raised the funds for the voyage.'.

A terrific odour arose, as if the army truck must be driving past a vast Egyptian compost bin. Rupert gagged, and with thumb and first finger, wrapped his hand all around his nose—the way Georgie had always done before downing his breakfast porridge. Once more, Rupert thought of his brother. *What might be the perfect gift to take him?* Whatever it was, the offering had to be sacred. Poor Georgie required something like that. His whole life long, the children had always been so cruel. There had always seemed to be someone kicking him when he was already down and had already suffered the worst kind of debasement, the worst kind of defeat. One after the next, the sadistic little children had always taunted him and had always piled it on—one cheap shot after another.

Rupert became lost in a round of nervous laughter, for the closer the truck came to the Promised Land, the more excited he felt. All through history, many pilgrims had felt similarly. For a moment, Rupert paused to consider the perils of religious fervour. He wondered if, during some processions, a band of pilgrims might become so excited a stampede might ensue with countless souls trampled to death in the melee. He sighed. How could anyone permit something as profane as desire to turn a pilgrimage into a human tragedy? He blamed the whole notion on ritual and pageantry and such. *To hell with ceremony. That kind of thing could never take the place of spirituality. To attempt to live by too many rules, only that could ever constitute heresy.* At last, Rupert curled up, fell asleep and became lost in a dream.

And as he wanders Jerusalem, Mr Impérial stops him before the Damascus Gate. 'I've got a scheme,' Mr Impérial explains. 'When the war for the Promised Land begins, we'll sell just the right amount to each side. That way, no one should ever win. And the warfare should never end, which means endless profits for us. Untold riches and the trappings of power.'

Rupert awoke and remembered every single thing Father's

business contact had ever done to him. *Yes, Mr Impérial.* Rupert laughed like a petulant little boy who has only just come to accept his mother's wisdom—and only because the exceedingly clever woman had chosen to call his bluff and to leave him to his own devices.

END

A Note from the

Author.

If you enjoyed this book, I would be very grateful if you could write a review and publish it at your point of purchase. Your review, even a brief one, will help other readers to decide whether they'll enjoy my work.

If you want to be notified of new releases from myself and other Alkira Publishing authors, please sign up to the Alkira Publishing email list. In return you'll get a free ebook by an Alkira Publishing author. You'll find the sign-up button on the right-hand side under the photo at www.alkirapublishing.com. Of course, your information will never be shared, and the publisher won't inundate you with emails, just let you know of new releases.

Acknowledgements

Thank you to everyone at Alkira Publishing. Thank you to everyone at Literallypr. And a very special thank you to Barbara Scott Emmett.

www.ingramcontent.com/pod-product-compliance
Ingram Content Group UK Ltd.
Pitfield, Milton Keynes, MK11 3LW, UK
UKHW041916261025
464365UK00001B/24